Forever Home

Aimee Martin

A Lake Shores Series Novel

by Mercy Books,
a division of Mercy Pictures

ISBN – 13: 978-0-9963063-1-7

FOREVER HOME

Published in the United States by Mercy Books,
a division of Mercy Pictures

Dedicated to my husband and children… without them I never would have had the courage to embark on this journey. Jeff, Braeden, Ella and Laura… I love you all forever.

Acknowledgments

Wow! If anyone would have told me two years ago that I'd be writing this page for my first published book, I'd have said that they're crazy! What an amazing journey this has been.

First and foremost, I have to thank God for putting me in a place where I was able to make this fantasy become a reality.

To my wonderful husband, thank you for being my very own Jaxson. Thank you for putting up with my mood swings when I was in the writing zone. Your never ending faith in me helped me more than words will ever be able to express. You give me butterflies every day. I love you forever, mo grádh.

To my three awesome children, thank you for understanding when Momma couldn't always play Candyland or go for a hike because I was nose-deep in my book. I love you my babies.

To my parents and mother-in-law, thank you for your undying support during this venture. I will always appreciate the encouraging words you all gave me. Especially to my mother who gave me the push to start writing again.

To my amazing editor Dixie, with Mercy Books, I truly believe we were brought together by divine intervention. I never could have asked for a better person to help me on this journey. Your time, effort, criticism and encouragement helped me get here today and you will forever be in my debt. Thank you isn’t nearly enough.

To all of my friends–you know who you are–that took the time to listen to a scene, give me input on specifics and just be there to listen and read my drafts, thank you to the moon and back.

And finally to you reading this now. Without the support of readers and fans, this would never be possible. I truly hope you enjoy Jaxson and Brinley’s story. Theirs was an emotional one for me to write in every possible way. But incredibly fulfilling all the same. Be prepared for Alex and Melanie’s story… next in the Lake Shores Series.

Thank You All and Happy Reading!

Note from the Author

Depression is never something that should be taken lightly or handled on your own. If you or someone you know might be suffering from depression here are some sites that may help.

http://www.depression-understood.org for access to chat rooms, forums, emergency numbers and more.

http://www.health.com and search for 'Coping with Depression'.

Struggling with your faith is probably one of the most taxing situations a person can experience. Please, seek help with your clergy. If you're not comfortable bringing it out into the open, these sites offer great anonymous support.

http://www.christian-faith.com

http://www.christian-counseling-online.com

And as always, study your bible. There are more answers available in those pages than you'll find anywhere else. All scriptures in this book came from the King James Version.

http://www.kingjamesbibleonline.org

Forever Home

PROLOGUE

"Lo, children are an heritage of the Lord: and the fruit of the womb is his reward." Psalms 127:3

May 31, 1996

"Shh!!!" I whispered. "Annie, stop giggling. You're going to wake up my parents."

Annie Cross was my best friend. We met in kindergarten on the first day of school. We couldn't have been more opposite. She was an outgoing, tender hearted child. I was quiet and kept to myself.

At recess, I noticed her watching me with a sweet little smile on her face. Then she ran across the play yard, took my hands in hers and pulled me to my feet. She coaxed me onto the playground and, in time, out of my shell.

After a single game of hopscotch, we became inseparable.

Annie inhaled sharply to stifle her laughter. "I'm sorry, Brin." she said. "I've just never snuck out of a house before. This is going to be fun!"

"We're just going outside." I whispered. "Don't get all excited." I wanted her to think I was calm and collected, but I was as giddy as she was.

Sneaking out of the house, even to the backyard, was daring for a couple of eleven year olds. That day had been the last day of the school year. We were out for the summer and anxious for an adventure, and this was the best we could come up with.

We made it down the hall and into the living room without getting caught, then tip-toed to the back door. I stretched my arm out to stop her and she cocked her head to the side, her expression questioning.

"Wait!" I said a little louder than I'd meant to. "The back door squeaks really bad." Chewing my bottom lip, I was thinking hard and looking around the room at all our options. "Got it! We're going out the doggy door. I'll go first if you'll keep a lookout for Schotzie." Her lips were pinched tightly together and I knew she was trying very hard not to laugh.

So, she gave a nod and kept her eyes out for our big German shepherd. Slowly, I slid the dog door open, gritting my teeth so hard my jaw started to hurt. It looked like a tight squeeze, but we both wiggled through with ease because it was built to accommodate our oversized pooch.

Annie and I scrambled away from the house and ran through the yard. By the time we got to the playhouse my Daddy built, we were both out of breath. We stretched out on the roof side by side for a long time before we stopped giggling.

We were still for a while, looking up at the twinkling night sky. Watching for shooting stars was one of our favorite things to do and that night was perfect for it. Especially since clouds were nonexistent, the air around us wasn't as sticky as it usually is this time of year and the warm breeze felt nice on our faces.

After a few minutes, Annie asked me, "Brin, what do you want to be when you grow up? And I don't mean the stuff we tell our parents and teachers, like a doctor or a lawyer. I mean what to you really want to be?" I didn't even hesitate because I'd always known.

"I am going to be a famous actress. Star in movies, have people come to see me in them at the theaters. Go to big parties all the time and dance till the sun comes up. Maybe even make a film with that really cute guy from Blossom (one of our favorite television shows)."

"Oh, you mean Joey, the brother!" Annie almost squealed. "He is so cute. It would be so cool if you got to make a movie with him."

We were just kids. We didn't care about talent. It was more than enough that Joey Lawrence was indeed cute and I had such a crush on him.

"What about you, Annie? What is your dream?" She was quiet for a while, gazing so intensely at the sky I thought she was waiting for it to help her answer. Just when it seemed she wasn't going to tell me, she closed her eyes, took a deep breath and poured her heart out.

"I want to be a singer. I want to make the kind of music that people can feel in their hearts. When they listen to me, I want them to feel like the words were written just for them. My songs have to touch them really deep. They need to hear me and not just the lyrics." She opened her eyes and looked at me, a faint smile curled her lips and she said, "Music can help people, you know? I want to make them feel love and even sadness when they listen to my songs because that's what people go through. I want to be like King David with his psalms. God loves music, Brin."

Then she turned back and watched the stars with a sheen of tears in her eyes.

I lay there in awe, thinking about everything she'd said and how grown up she'd sounded. There was no one in the whole world like Annie Cross. She was smart and incredibly talented and I never doubted that her dreams would come true. She had the voice of an angel.

Annie was destined for great things and I would have followed her anywhere.

Even then, though we were just kids, I knew that the little girl with the big voice and even bigger heart would always be more to me than just a friend.

"Hey Ann," I sat up so fast I had to shift my weight around to keep my balance. But I just couldn't keep still any longer.

Not when a glimpse of a future of fame and fortune had just flashed through my mind.

"Be careful silly, you'll fall and break your neck." Annie turned toward me and levered her upper body up with an elbow. I was grinning from ear to ear. "Okay Brinley, let me guess, you've got another one of your nutty ideas."

"Let's do it!" I was so excited my voice was squeaking.

She looked at me with her brows drawn. Curiosity and a hint of caution ghosted over her features.

"Let's do what?"

"Let's go to California. Just you and me, as soon as we get out of high school. You'll be a singer. I'll be an actress. We'll both be really famous. And live in a beach house and have lots and lots of money and go shopping everyday and___"

"You better take a breath before you pass out Brin." Her mouth curved into a smile and then she burst out laughing. "Okay, you and me!" She promised. "When we graduate we'll leave Lake Shores in the dust and move out to California!"

"We can do it, Annie. Cause you're a great singer and I can be an actor. I know I can."

"I know; you were so good in the school play. You were the best Mary Lincoln ever." I started giggling.

"Did I tell you we are doing Peter Pan for the fall play? I'm trying out for Wendy."

"I know you're going to get the part." She squeezed my arm with her free hand. "You're going to be amazing! We're really going to California, right? No changing our minds?" I thought for a few seconds. Could we really leave this place, leave our parents? Then I grinned and gave one sharp nod.

"Pinky swear?" Annie held her right fist out with her little finger pointed toward me, waiting. I linked my own with hers.

"Pinky swear." I said.

Annie shook our linked fingers up and down once to seal the pact. We dropped our hands, I laid back down and we turned our faces back to the sky that was beginning to fill up with big fluffy clouds turned gray by the night.

We were still for a long time, comfortable and silent. My mind was wandering, envisioning the great futures we were determined to carve out for ourselves. Annie was no doubt thinking the same thing.

When we finally started to get sleepy, we made our way back into the house through the doggy door. I gave Schotzie a pat on her head to keep her from barking and we went back to my room and climbed into bed.

I fell into a deep sleep filled with dreams of the day that Annie and I would be grown up enough to start our ambitious lives.

CHAPTER 1

"Except the Lord build the house, they labour in vain that build it: except the Lord keep the city, the watchman waketh but in vain." Psalms 127:1

September 6, 2013

I woke up screaming again, sheets soaked, drenched with sweat, and gasping for air like I had just been hit in the chest with a wrecking ball.

I sat up against the headboard, trembling and trying to determine whether I was actually awake or still lost in a never ending nightmare.

But this was not a dream. I was awake and Annie was still dead. And I still felt so empty and worse, so guilty. All we really had was each other; no husbands, no serious relationships, just each other. At that time in our lives, it was enough. Now, I felt as if half of my identity was missing and

I had a cavern in my heart that had swallowed up the person I once thought I was. I could not imagine ever being whole again.

Human life is as fragile as the wings of a butterfly. How is it that we thought ourselves so invincible?

Annie and I were in our mid-twenties, strong, independent and successful. Full of ourselves. At that time, life meant the next rung on the career ladder and the next good time. We thought that no matter where the future took us, we'd get there together.

We couldn't have been more wrong.

. . . . .

October 17, 2012

"Hey Brinley," Annie called from the other room. "Are we going tonight or what?"

Annie stood in front of the bathroom mirror putting the last touches on her make-up, something she never really needed. She was naturally beautiful, tall and graceful with long blonde hair and guileless blue eyes. Annie truly didn't know how stunning she was. And it was that innocent humility and her incredible energy that drew people to her like a magnet. She had an amazing way of making everyone around her feel better about themselves. Hollywood is practically devoid of genuinely selfless people but Annie was the real thing. She coddled the insecure and lonely that flocked to her like chicks to a mother hen.

And everybody loved her.

"Brin, you have to come with me. Tonight is going to be a blast." She was all pumped up about an A-list movie premiere downtown. Theater tickets and invites to the cast parties afterwards were hard to snag. But Annie had no trouble getting them for us. She could charm the candy shell off of an M&M.

In the summer of 2004, right after our high school graduation, Annie and I kissed our families goodbye, packed up the bed of my 1989 Ford pickup and headed for Los Angeles. We left behind a small town in southeast Texas and everyone and everything we had ever known. There were times growing up when I wondered if either of us could really leave Lake Shores.

But Annie and I had plans and pinky swear promises were never meant to be broken.

We were both raised in close knit, Christian homes. We loved our families and that little country town, but the lure of the bright lights and the big city was just too strong. Success for a woman in Lake Shores, Texas was marrying your high school sweetheart and having your first kid shortly thereafter.

Or, if marriage wasn't in your stars, you could always work your way up to manager down at the general store. No, we had no interest in growing old in small town America.

The first few years on our own were so hard. Instead of breezing into L.A. and being handed the town on a silver platter, we were just two more unknowns lost in a sea of wannabes.

But when things got really tough, we'd share a pizza and talk about our dreams. Then we were those two adolescent girls again, stretched out on the playhouse roof instead of sharing the futon in our living room. An hour or two of junk food and reminiscing kept our childhood pact alive and our dreams still attainable.

We lived in a shoddy basement apartment with bars on the windows, waited tables and saved every dime. Annie and I both enrolled in acting classes and joined little theater groups. We showed up at every open casting call. It took more than living in a rat infested building and subsisting on cold cuts and day old bread to dampen our enthusiasm.

The city fascinated us. We loved taking the bus downtown on Friday nights. We'd stand in front of clubs for hours, dressed in cheap imitations of the hottest designer styles and mingle with the crowd. Sometimes a few girls would catch the bouncer's eye and he'd unhook a thick, velvet covered cable and wave them inside.

Eventually, patience and parading paid off and we were the ones singled out from among the other hopefuls. Before long, we'd found our niche in the L.A. club scene. We were on a first name basis with a dozen B list actors and budding directors. Each introduction seemed to propel us closer to our goals.

We went to every party, concert and premiere we could, trying to keep our faces out there, always hoping to get a glimpse of the glamour.

It was no secret that the vast majority of young actors spent most of their 'careers' struggling as waitresses or bus boys. The lucky ones got call backs as extras or stand-ins. The truly talented landed bit parts or even lead roles in commercials.

But most of them eventually gave up and left the city to pick up their lives and start over in whatever place they'd called home. Los Angeles was teeming with beautiful people, every one of them hoping for their big break. It just wasn't enough to have a pretty face, and we were no longer star struck eleven year olds.

We studied hard and Annie worked to develop her already beautiful voice. I was surprised but learning the craft, beyond high school drama, actually came easy to me. True, we racked up our fair share of disappointing rejections.

But in time, we started to earn more working in the entertainment industry than we did from slinging hamburgers.

In early 2007 something so fantastic happened that it still has me scratching my head in amazement; we hit the jackpot.

As a rule, we followed our instructors' advice to the letter. *Don't over reach. Wait until you've earned your marks before you try out for A List roles. That type of rejection can stop a career before it even gets started.*

But one afternoon, on a hunch, we grabbed our portfolios and answered an open casting call. The movie was set during World War II and was already attached to some of the biggest names in the business. Whoever watches over the City of Angels must have been smiling down on us that day, because we were *both* called back, and not as extras or stand-ins.

I was shocked to be cast in a speaking role in three scenes opposite the leading actor, and Annie was finally able to showcase her voice. It was ironic how art imitated life. She played the role of an ambitious country girl who moved to the big city hoping to be a star, but instead, ended up singing for her supper in a smoky Nineteen-forty's nightclub. Annie was absolutely brilliant. The movie was nominated for an Oscar for best picture. It didn't win, but the recognition we earned from our roles in that film changed everything for us. Instead of standing in line and waiting for auditions, we signed with top agencies. Less than a year later, I could pick and choose my jobs and Annie's first album was climbing the charts.

In the beginning we both reveled in our hectic, Hollywood lifestyles. But in time that awkward, reclusive part of me I thought I'd left behind in Texas started niggling. I began to long for things I never even knew I wanted. A home. Not like the house Annie and I bought in Malibu, but the kind that came with a husband and maybe kids. Anonymity. I daydreamed about walking down the street without a single person recognizing me.

I didn't tell Annie what was troubling me, I didn't have to. She knew me that well. But it seemed the more I tried to pull away from the lime light, the more determined Annie was to draw me deeper into it. She started dragging me out with her more often, talking up the lifestyle.

That night, she was practically begging me to go with her to that red carpet premiere.

"Are you sure you don't want to just stay in and watch the T.V. coverage, Ann?" I asked her as I walked into her bedroom.

That suggestion earned me a pointed glare and a scowl. And then she started pushing my buttons.

"Brin, what do you think you'll find sitting in front of the television? I don't even have to ask what's been eating at you lately. I already know." I rolled my eyes, turned away from her and stilled myself to ignore the lecture I knew was coming. She just couldn't let it go.

"I know you think you want to settle down," she said in her most understanding tone of voice. But regardless, it still sounded like an accusation. "I can understand that Brinley, I really can. You're thinking your biological clock is running out of time. But even if that was true, which it isn't, you will never find that perfect guy if all you ever do is work and hide."

"Annie, seriously, biological clock! That's so ridiculous it doesn't even deserve a response. But let's say you're right, which you aren't, even if I was looking for my soul mate, I'm not going to find him in L.A. And definitely not at a movie premiere. When I do settle down I want an old fashioned relationship with a normal man. And, my friend, I hate to tell you this, but there are no normal people in this town." I was almost shouting at her and I truly didn't mean to sound so harsh.

She stared at me, the corners of her mouth turned down. Her eyes were glistening and I could hear a tremor in her voice.

"You don't know that Brin," she said, almost in a whisper. "We're here. We're both normal."

I never could handle her tears and as always, Annie got her way. I shuddered and slowly exhaled a breath I didn't even realize I was holding and gave her a tight, resigned smile.

"I'll be ready in twenty."

It was a typical blockbuster premiere. Paparazzi and reporters all over the place. Everybody dressed to the nines. After the movie we went to the cast party and I shook my head in disgust at all the white and black limos lined up and down the street, glistening under the street lights like they owned the block.

Not unlike the patrons inside the party. Everyone who was anyone was there.

They were drinking, dancing, talking over each other at ninety miles an hour. People were nodding and smiling at me, but I avoided making eye contact and drifted off by myself. I glanced up and saw a group of them crowded on the second floor landing snorting coke, smoking pot. Some were paired off in dimly lit corners; I didn't even want to know what they were doing. I was so sick of the total absence of any kind of mortality.

Oh, we made it big alright. But at what cost? I glanced around at the crowd and thought to myself, *This is not who I am.* I didn't belong there. And at that moment, I knew I never would. The louder the music, the noisier the chatter, the more I felt the walls closing in on me.

All I wanted to do was hit the door running and never look back. And I would have, if not for Annie.

She was born for this life. Flying around the dance floor in her emerald green gown, her hair whipping around her bare shoulders. Giggling and laughing, a dozen pairs of eyes glued to her.

Always the life of the party, I thought, shaking my head. Just watching her was exhausting.

I backed farther away from the crush and leaned against a marble pillar, yawned loudly and stared at the floor. Just when I'd managed to zone out most of the craziness, Annie called my name. I looked up and our gazes locked. She looked like a charging bull in a green evening gown and I laughed at the imagery.

But Annie wasn't laughing. She flew across the room and stabbed her finger in my chest before I could have counted to ten. I growled at her and pushed her hand away.

"You are dead on your feet," she scolded. "Give me the valet ticket, I'm driving you home." I glared at her.

"I'm tired, Annie and I'm bored to tears and sick of this kind of crap." I waved my hand around, cocked my thumb at the coke heads on the landing. I gestured to two women dancing in their underwear. "Yes, I'm leaving but I'm driving my own car," I said. "And frankly, I don't like your tone. I'm not trying to spoil your evening." Her eyes softened and I felt a twinge of regret. Maybe, subconsciously, I wanted her to feel as out of place as I did. "Look, just stay here with your friends. Get a ride with one of them or call for a limo. You don't have to leave with me."

"Did I say you were trying to spoil anything?" Annie snapped at me. "I just said you were falling asleep. There is no way I'm letting you drive." She was shouting now and didn't notice the throng of onlookers that started gathering around us. "You were two seconds away from curling up on the floor."

"Explain to me again why that would be such a problem? With all the crap going on in here who would even notice?" I asked, my voice dripping with sarcasm. Her eyes darted around unconsciously and I started to laugh. "Annie Cross, do you really care what these people think?"

"Back off." She turned in a sweeping circle, barking at our growing audience. "Go on. Everything is fine here." As the crowd thinned she turned her attention back to me. "Give me that damn ticket, Brinley."

I stared at her through narrowed eyes.

"You can leave with me if want to," I said. "But it's my car and I'm driving."

The valet brought my B.M.W. around and five minutes later we were heading down the highway.

The top was down. Our hair was blowing behind us. Damp sea air was stinging our lungs. I thought the wind would be enough to keep me awake, but it wasn't helping.

"Ann," God, how I hated to admit this. "I really am very tired. You need to talk to me. You can even yell at me. I don't care, just help me stay awake."

I had to stay alert. We had a good forty-five minute drive ahead of us.

The route down the Pacific Coast Highway was beautiful but treacherous, even in daylight. At night, the sea is a vast expanse of black ink. It's difficult to tell where the sky meets the water. And soon, the road began to blend into the dark monotonous scenery.

Somewhere along the way, I guess she quit talking to me. I must have dozed off, because the next thing I remember was the shrill blare of sirens.

"Miss, miss can you hear me?" A deep soothing voice was breaking through the haze. "My name is Ben, I'm a paramedic. You've been in a bad accident. Miss, can you open your eyes for me?"

I was floating. Then I felt myself moving toward the sound. Soon, the fog receded and pain ripped through my head like a chain saw.

I heard screaming.

Annie, I thought, *that must be Annie.*

Seconds later, when I managed to open my eyes, I realized that the screams I heard were my own.

"That's it. Good girl," the deep voice praised. I blinked and squinted as the bright light he shone into my eyes caused a knife-like pain. I sensed someone kneel beside me.

"How's this one?" a second man asked. His voice was higher pitched, more urgent.

"Alive, Max," Ben answered and I heard him sigh. "This one's alive."

"She was belted in. Airbag must have taken most of the impact," Max said while he pulled a strap across my chest. He tugged hard. I sucked in a breath and moaned. "Sorry honey." he smoothed the hair back from my forehead and spoke softly. "I know it hurts, but it's got to be tight. We have to get you up that incline to the bus. Can't have you falling off."

I tried to focus on his face, but saw only his broad chest and a shirt pocket with a medical staff patch. There was a name above it that I couldn't make out. I don't even know why I was trying to read it.

A third man called from somewhere above us, "You ready down there?"

I don't remember much of being hauled up to the road except that every inch of the way was excruciating. I could comprehend that I was flat on my back, in pain and restrained.

But it wasn't until we were on level ground and I saw the flashing lights of the ambulances that it struck me.

Oh my God, we were in a wreck!

While the gurney was sliding into the back of the vehicle, I managed to find my voice. It was so scratchy and parched that I hardly recognized it as mine.

"Where's Annie?" I asked them. They didn't answer. But I saw them share a pained expression and I knew something was terribly wrong.

"My best friend was in the car with me," I started struggling and was screaming again. "What happened to Annie? Where is she?!"

Everything seemed to come to a halt as a burning sensation pricked at the backs of my eyes. Strong hands held me down at the shoulders, until I was finally still. Then the one named Ben answered me. His deep voice was practiced and professional.

"Calm down. The medics in the other bus are loading up your friend right now." He paused, and then he qualified, "But she wasn't wearing her seat belt. She was thrown at least fifty feet from the car."

"Don't," I pleaded with him, locking my fingers around his wrist. "Please, just don't say it."

"Sweetheart," he sighed deeply and cupped the side of my face with his palm, "I'm so sorry, but your friend didn't make it." I swallowed hard, trying to dislodge the lump in my throat, but said nothing.

Then I turned my head away from him and shut my eyes while the reality of what had happened gradually sank in. I felt something wet and warm trickling down my face and a gentle, gloved finger wiped it away. The tears that would be a part of my life for so many months to come had started to fall. And nothing, save Annie being called forth from her grave like Lazarus, could stop them.

Thinking back, I know that I was in complete shock. For those first few moments my mind kept trying to make some sense of something so senseless. How could this be? We were just at a party. She was just talking to me. How could someone be so incredibly alive one minute and dead the next? For the love of God, why didn't I notice she wasn't wearing her seatbelt? What made me think I was alert enough to drive?

Dear Jesus, why did you take Annie and leave me?

CHAPTER 2

"All his days also he eateth in darkness, and he hath much sorrow and wrath with his sickness."
Ecclesiastes 5:17

Journal Entry One - Sept. 8, 2013

"Dear Annie, I finally went to a counselor. My mom was driving me crazy about it, so I didn't tell her but I made the appointment and just went.

What a creepy little guy.

Anyway, he said 'Brinley, it's been almost a year since the accident, you should be farther along in the grieving process.'

He was kidding, right? I paid that moron three hundred bucks an hour to tell me something my dad's been saying for months___for free? But I did decide that he was right about one thing.

He said I should keep a journal, express myself to you. Just write down whatever I didn't get a chance to say to you. I won't waste another penny on him but I bought a half dozen of these notebooks. In a way, it does almost feel like you're going to read this stuff. I don't know, maybe you already know everything I need to say.

I'm so angry Annie. I haven't been happy for a second since the wreck. Oh yeah, everyone keeps telling me how lucky I am that I wasn't killed too. But I'm not so sure about that. Part of me did not survive that accident.

Then there was the court thing. I told the cops I thought I fell asleep at the wheel. That should have been negligence or something, right? I mean for God's sake I killed you! But no. The guy driving the Big Mac truck who called nine-one-one said he thinks his headlights caused me to think his truck was wider than it was and that I must have tried to pull closer to the edge to avoid him. What a crock. I never even saw the guy's headlights.

Then the man who was in the car behind us said I couldn't have fallen sleep because my speed stayed the same and the car was making all the turns just fine until the Big Mac came around the curve.

I tried to tell the judge that they were wrong, but he said I'd had a concussion and was just expressing 'survivor's guilt.' It's true that celebrities are treated differently by the legal system. And I'm not even that big of a celebrity. But hey, one more reason I'm so damn lucky, right?

You died so now you're a bigger star than ever.

It's been almost a year and your CDs are still flying off the shelves. Your recording company put up a **R.I.P. Annie** billboard on the interstate close to LAX. It's beautiful but I started taking cabs when I have to go that direction and I close my eyes cause I can't stand to look at it.

And the house, you should see the house. There is Annie Cross memorabilia all over the place. Everybody sent me complimentary items, like Annie Cross throw pillows and rugs. Annie dishes and a doll. The doll looks like a Barbie doll with a hand mike.

I can't decide if it's creepy or cute.

Every budding artist in the whole fricking world painted your 'memorial' portrait. Some of them are pretty good. I sent the really beautiful ones to your mom. I kept the not so good ones and the disgustingly obscene ones and boxed them up. I put one I liked on the wall in your room.

People sent hundreds of stuffed animals. I gave most of them to the Children's Hospital.

But I kept this one big stuffed dog. I don't know why. He just looked sad and lonely, kind of like me.

Annie, I'm so angry at myself. How could I have been so stubborn? Annie, how could you have left me here, alone? I'm so mad at God. He snatched you away and just left me here. I just stand in our front room and scream until I'm hoarse.

What is fair about this?

So I have spent almost a year isolating myself. From friends, family. I am always afraid I will end up hurting someone else. No one deserves to be hurt by me again. I got into a rhythm. I wake up, go to work, go to sleep. I never go out anymore. I will never allow myself to get emotionally attached to anyone ever again. I know what it feels like to lose someone close to you; so close that it feels like you've lost a big chunk of yourself. I will not let that happen again. I'm tired, Annie. I'll talk to you soon, love you."

CHAPTER 3

"And I will pray the Father, and he shall give you another Comforter, that he may abide with you for ever." John 14:16

For the first three months after Annie died, I was seriously depressed. It's normal, right? I know that's why my parents called all the time. They were worried and they wanted me to come home for a while. 'Just until you get back on your feet', they said.

But I just couldn't do that. In some strange way, Annie was still in our house with me. I sensed her all around me and I needed to hang on to whatever was left of her.

I kept myself busy making movies. As soon as one would wrap I would immediately start another project. But eventually the decent jobs seemed to dry up; I just couldn't develop an interest in a script anymore. It was the first time since the accident that I didn't have something to do.

Naturally, the lull in my schedule quickly became filled up with family obligations.

September 8, 2013

It was early evening and I was walking along the private beach in front of the house, wool gathering. The sun was reaching out to hand over its last rays of warmth before the moon took over.

My cell rang and startled me back to reality. It was my mother, of course.

"Hi Mom." I answered, trying to inject a semblance of cheer into my voice.

"Hello sweetheart. How are you? I haven't been able to get a hold of you in a week, I was beginning to worry," she said.

My mother was using her 'gentle' voice. Of course she was.

Don't say anything to upset Brinley, she's still so fragile.

"I'm okay Mom. In fact, I'm outside taking a walk." I didn't tell her I was less than twenty feet from my own back door. "We just finished shooting a couple days ago so I haven't really had time to return calls. Anyway, what's up?"

"I just wanted to check to see if you'd booked your flight for the wedding. Your Dad and I are going to pick you up from the airport so I need your flight information."

She sounded calm enough. But I could hear in her voice that she half expected me to have an excuse not to go. But, no excuses.

"Yes, I booked it. I'm flying in on South West on Thursday the twelfth at ten thirty in the morning. But Mom, I don't mind renting a car. I know you two will be busy with the wedding." I said.

"Don't be silly, honey. That's why it's great being the groom's parents. We don't have that much to do until Friday. I can't wait to see you and I want to be there when you get off the plane. It's no trouble at all."

I thought by now my mother could read my mind. Stupid of me, but we become accustomed to our parents being all knowing.

I hesitated for a minute and decided I might as well level with her.

"Okay but could you come alone? No offense against Daddy but he isn't exactly an unemotional conversationalist. He means well, but to be honest I just can't be cornered in a car with him. He upsets me with all that *my poor baby* and *Daddy's here for you* crap."

I inhaled sharply and put my free hand up to my mouth. "I'm sorry Momma. That really came out wrong. I know he's just being a dad."

"I understand honey. Daddy doesn't know that some things are best left unsaid. Truthfully, all men are like that. I know he's looking forward to seeing you too but don't worry, he can wait until we get back to the house. How is everything else going? Have you started getting out more?"

She was nosing, it was her way of asking if I'd forgiven myself yet.

My parents are the most wonderful, loving people in the world, but their constant worrying was driving me insane.

"Mom, when would I have a chance to socialize? By the time I leave the set, all I want is a bath and my bed. I've been really busy with work until just recently. Maybe after I get back from the wedding I'll take some time off and get back into the social groove." I heard a relieved sigh on the other end of the line. Maybe she actually believed me.

Then again, maybe not. But at least she dropped the subject.

"Listen, I'm almost back to the house now so I'm going to let you go. I need to grab some dinner and hit the shower. See you Thursday?" I asked.

"Sure Hun. Call me if anything changes. Otherwise I'll be there to pick you up." She added 'alone' for emphasis and then said, "I love you."

"Love you too, Mom. Bye." I hung up and walked silently back up the porch steps.

It's funny how you notice obscure things, like the paint on the door frame was fading and the small crack in the ceiling from the foundation shifting. Annie wanted the house from the minute she walked through that door. I thought it was great, but I wasn't as picky as she was. I was just ready to get out of our apartment. It's still a great place, but I quit thinking about it as my home. To me it wasn't mine anymore. It was always going to be Annie's.

It really was a beautiful place. Twenty-five hundred square feet, mid-century modern and right on the beach. The entire back of the house was made of glass so we could watch the ocean. It was our favorite part of the house and the main reason we bought it. Everyone thought I should sell it and move after her death. I knew where they were coming from.

New house, new start and all that.

But I couldn't bring myself to do that. It was all I had left of her and I couldn't lose it too.

I walked into her old room. Everything was just as she'd left it. Like she'd just gone to the other room instead of to her grave. I had no intention of ever putting her things away. I didn't care that it would supposedly help with the 'healing process.' Every time I even thought about boxing up her things it made me nauseous.

She'd left out a couple of evening gowns that she'd tried on before settling on the green one. They were still laid out on the bed with matching shoes in their open boxes beside them. I stared at them for a moment then plopped down in the glider that sat next to her bed and slowly rocked.

One wall was covered with publicity shots, hung in a kind of collage. I let my eyes wander from one photo to the next.

Everything about her room made me sad, but I didn't cry very much anymore. It still hurt like my heart had been torn from my chest, but I think I was all cried out. I just sat there rocking and daydreaming, and thinking to myself that this was all that was left of my life. I wondered if I'd ever get used to it.

In the morning, I woke with a jerk to find myself soaked with sweat and still sitting in Annie's glider. The nightmares were more vivid when I stayed in her room. Maybe that's why I slept in there sometimes. Reliving the night Annie died revived my sense of self-loathing. I never wanted to forget what a waste my life had become. I dragged myself from the chair and went to take a shower; mulling over how everything had changed since that horrible night last October.

The first six months after Annie's death seemed to pass in a blur and honestly, I don't remember much of those days. I do recall flying back to Lake Shores for the funeral. It was the last trip we would ever take together. But instead of sharing a row in first class, I rode in coach close to the bathroom because I threw up all the way home.

And Annie? She was in a bronze coffin in the cargo hold. Her parents and I had kept our distance from each other that trip. They didn't seem upset at me, per se, just handling their grief in their own way. Not that I would have blamed them if they'd have screamed and told me to yell. It would have been just another type of injury.

I had checked myself out of the hospital against my doctors' advice in order to make the flight back with her. I had a severe concussion, a broken arm and a broken heart. My head and arm would heal with time. But once a human heart is shattered, I doubt that all the king's horses and all the king's men can ever put it back together again.

When I came back to L.A. and the haze cleared, time seemed to slow to a crawl. The last six months took an even greater toll and not because I symbolically buried myself in scripts.

Depression is exhausting, and I have no idea how I managed to get through each successive job when in truth, I was operating on auto pilot. Slowly, the crush of constant, debilitating sadness began to ease. I could think clearer and it was not such a struggle just to get through the day. I don't know, maybe I'd finally moved into the acceptance stage of grief. Acceptance does nothing to ease the throbbing ache in your chest nor does it fill the chasm in your soul. All it does is move you from a place in life where the loss defies reality to the place where you grasp that your loved one is really and truly lost to you forever. Acceptance is an open wound that does not heal.

I didn't want to heal, not fully anyway.

Talking to my mother yesterday brought back the lump in my throat. I stood under the shower head and as the hot water ran in streams over my face and I found myself rehashing the 'what ifs' yet again…

What if I hadn't caved in and let her pressure me into going to the premier?

What if I had let her drive?

What if... What if... What if...

I know that everything is supposed to happen for a reason and that with God, all things work together for the good of those who love Him. I know all of the flowery rhetoric by heart, but what good can come from the death of a vibrant young woman?

Before the accident, I saw the hand of God in everything. When things worked out so that we really did move to L.A., that was God. When we got grants for acting school, well that just had to be God. When we actually accomplished what we'd set out to do, no doubt about it, we were living in the F.O.G. 'Favor of God.' We use to laugh about that whenever anyone mentioned the perpetual haze that floated over Los Angeles. Annie would say, "Oh, that's just F.O.G."

Yes, she and I both saw His influence everywhere. But I don't now, not anymore. I have come to the conclusion that God really is a deadbeat dad. If He were around and paying attention, I'd be dead and Annie would be going on with her life. After all, I was the one driving. What kind of father punishes the innocent?

Everyone regurgitates the same tired clichés, and I'm sick to death of them. *It's alright to be angry. Blaming God is a perfectly normal response.*

But what I felt about the Almighty was worse than anything covered by those familiar platitudes. I wasn't just mad, I hated Him. And faith? Yes of course, if I just had a little faith, in time everything would be fine.

But, in my case, faith is not the essence of things unseen; it's the remains of something that no longer exists. I've got nothing but doubt left. I doubt God. I doubt I'll ever have faith again. I don't even think there's a Mr. Right somewhere out there anymore. Even if he did exist, even if I found my dream man, I'd turn around and run in the other direction. I drove Annie's future, along with any happiness I deserved, off a hundred foot cliff. If Annie had to go alone through the valley of the shadow of death, then that is how I intended to go through life.

Alone.

September 12, 2013

I hate to fall asleep on airplanes now. I never know when I'm going to wake up screaming and scare the heck out of other passengers. So, I downloaded a book I've been trying to find time to read on my tablet. A really juicy page turner, one I just couldn't put down. Nothing keeps me awake like a good mystery.

I was flying home to Lake Shores, Texas. My older brother, Aaron, was getting married and my future sister-in-law, Jessica, had asked me to be a bridesmaid. Jessica is great girl, I guess. What I think doesn't matter anyway. My brother is crazy about her.

When Aaron first introduced us, she was a little bit star struck. Before the accident she couldn't talk to me without asking something like; '*What's it like to be a movie star?*' or '*Is George Clooney really that good looking?*'

Afterwards, everybody's attitude changed. Even Jessica's. I hadn't seen anyone since Annie's funeral. But she made a point of calling at least once a week. She was not alone in wondering if a wedding so soon after a funeral would be too much for me.

I don't know, maybe it was something about her tone. I got the distinct impression she was more worried that I'd wig out and ruin her wedding than she was about my emotional health. Had it not been for Aaron, I might have
told her what she could do with her ugly purple bridesmaid's dress.

But my big brother was getting married and I owed him.

Going home was going to be painful. It was a combination of things, really. Childhood memories were strongest at my folk's house. The playhouse still stood in the backyard. People walked on egg shells around me. But hardest of all was that there was only one road leading to the house, and to get there, we had to drive past the cemetery.

Annie's grave was in a new section near the front. Her body was buried beneath a cement slab and a huge monument stood at the head. I really don't know what the slab was for. Did anyone really think someone was going to dig her up? This was Texas; people don't desecrate graves here. I'd read some idiotic article in a trash rag, something like "Satanic Cult Vows to Steal Body of Annie Cross for Use in Summer Solstice Ritual."

But if there is one place on earth devoid of satanists, it's Lake Shores, Texas. I guess a big hulking slab of cement might deter such a thing, though. Grave view not withstanding, I had obligations so I'd put on a smile and do what I did best. Act.

My mother, Tina, was waiting to pick me up from the airport alone. She still looked great. Just over five feet with dark blond hair and blue eyes crinkled with laugh lines. She had a smile that was infectious. It was a crying shame that in the past six months deep worry lines had etched themselves in her forehead, competing with the tiny lines near her mouth that I'd always associated with her amazing laugh.

"Did you have a nice flight?" she asked as I hopped into her car. When I didn't answer and just shrugged my shoulders, she continued. "Are you still having a hard time sleeping? Maybe you should talk to a doctor." she stopped as soon as she'd finished that sentence when I scowled.

I hadn't told her about the creepy therapist, so as far as my mom knew, counseling was still not an option. And, since I had no intention of ever going back, therapy was still not open for discussion.

So Mom tried another tactic.

"You have to forgive yourself and trust that God has His plan." She droned on and on, but I had already closed my mind.

I didn't want to hear a word about God.

The rest of the drive home was pretty quiet. Soft country tunes were playing on the radio. Open fields passed by the windows as we drove south on Highway 288. Cows were laying in the shade on both sides of the highway, trying to escape the muggy Texas heat. I admit I did miss the country. Everything and everyone was always so peaceful and serene. I was glad that my mother didn't push the need for conversation. This is why I wanted her to pick me up alone. She would be concentrating on driving and not be able to quiz me.

As we pulled into the town of Lake Shores, I knew I was home again. In L.A. cars are either zipping around or hung up in bumper to bumper traffic. Pedestrians are in constant motion. Everyone is always in a hurry.

Here though, there are more pick-up trucks than cars and I loved to pick out the different shades of rust on the old farm trucks. The ones with the brown rust had weathered the worst for the longest while the bright red rusted trucks were just showing their age.

And the people just sit around visiting outside the stores on Main Street, never in a rush to get to school or work. That rush from the city though, it helped me stay busy so I didn't have to sit around and reflect.

"We're here," my mother said.

I must have daydreamed the whole way because I didn't notice we had pulled into the driveway of my childhood home. It still looked the same; various shades of gray brick with a bright red wooden door.

I slowly climbed out of the car and made my way up the drive, trying to ignore the balmy air surrounding my body like a cocoon and making me feel suffocated.

I walked inside and was immediately greeted, more than generously, from the dogs. There were three of them vying for my attention as my Dad, Mitch, met me in the hallway.

He hugged me tightly into his six foot one frame and told me it was so good to have me home. I smiled hesitantly, not wanting to give away my anxiety.

That clawing panic was trying to make an appearance, pushing me to turn and leave as soon as possible. This place had too many memories.

My Dad was usually a man of few words when it came to women so he, like my mother thankfully had been on the way here, kept quiet and let me go to get settled in. My parents were high school sweethearts and they walked off together holding hands. I watched them for a minute before turning and heading down the hall.

My old room hadn't changed despite the fact that I'd been gone over ten years. Pale blue and yellow paint covered the walls. Those old glow-in-the-dark stars were still all over the ceiling and made me smile sadly. I can't even remember how many times Annie and I had laid here at night, looking at those stars, talking about how someday we'd make it to the Big City.

The nightmares came again that night. Only, instead of me crashing the car on the PCH, I crashed it on Main Street in town and took out the old Miller brothers' checkers board in front of the hardware store.

When I woke up panting, I was confused at first and the darkness outside didn't help clear my head any. I decided my location must have something to do with my dreams. But it didn't matter because the end result was still the same.

I still killed her.

September 13, 2013

I woke up again several hours later feeling exhausted from not sleeping and really wanted to crawl back under the covers.

But today was my brother's wedding rehearsal. I had to at least attempt to be social and encouraging even though enthusiasm was the last thing on my mind. I wanted to hide out in the closet until Tuesday when I could fly back to LA. *Why didn't I pick a sooner flight?*

Riding to the church with my parents gave me time to go over what I remembered of the others who would be there. I knew most of the people in the wedding party; my brother Alex–who's two years younger than me–and a high school friend of my older brother, Chris, were the groomsmen. The other bridesmaid and maid of honor, Haley and Sarah, were old friends of Jessica's. I had met them both a few times and they seemed like really nice women. If you didn't pay attention to the clique attitude they seemed to thrive on.

Whatever, they're not my friends so it's not like entertaining them is my job anyways.

The only one I didn't know was Aaron's best man. My Mom had told me that Aaron met him after I moved to Los Angeles and, since I didn't come home much, our paths had never crossed. All of these thoughts rambled around in my head during the five minutes it took to make it to the church.

Everyone arrived at around the same time since we were expected there by five-thirty. While walking up the steps to the entrance, memories bombarded me. We had been members of St. Timothy's Episcopal Church since the day I was born. And, while I loved our church and the entire congregation involved with it, coming here proved to be harder than I expected.

I was filled with so much regret and shame as I walked into the chapel. Not to mention the disgust. For God, looking down as if He loved me.

Looking at the cross standing tall behind the alter, the only thing I could see was the disappointed look on Annie's face. The one that stayed in place as she walked over to leave the premiere party that night. The one that remained even as we fought in front of hundreds of people.

I shook off that thought with a shudder that ran down my spine. I tried to focus on the joy that was this occasion and caught Alex looking at me from across the aisle with a question in his eyes. I smiled to put off an inquisition and made my way over to him.

We hadn't seen each other in over three years. Alex wasn't able to come back for Annie's funeral. He was out on deployment when she died and the Navy only grants leaves for the death of an immediate family member. He caught me in a huge hug and held tightly, whispering nonsense about how sorry he was at not being here last year.

"It's so good to see you, Alex! When did you get in?" I leaned back but held tightly to his forearms. When did he get so muscular?

"I came straight here from the airport. Flying from Florida with two layovers takes a while." He gazed at me with that unspoken question in his eyes.

I took the quiet minute to really look at him. He looked so grown up in a suit and tie. Tall at just over six feet with light brown hair and eyes, he had the solid build of a member of the armed forces with the proud posture to go with it. He was a force to be reckoned with.

"You look great."

I hugged him again, grateful he didn't bring up the elephant in the room. He and I had always been so close growing up. It was nice to have someone around me who just knew to let things alone. He promised to give me a ride back to our parents' later since he was staying there too and we took our places at opposite ends of the alter.

I focused on Aaron and Jessica who were still standing in the middle aisle among all the members of the bridal party.

Well, all except one because Aaron had said his best man was running a little late.

Leaning up against the railing, I took a minute to study the happy couple and their obvious love for one another. You couldn't help but notice how perfect my brother and his bride-to-be were for each other. They were both blond and blue eyed. They were both fit with runner's bodies. Jess only came up to Aaron's shoulders but it seemed perfect because his arm was always around her.

Time was passed by talking to the minister about how we, the bridesmaids, maid of honor and bride, would be processing in. I listened with as much attentiveness as I could, but was actually imagining a different scenario. Wondering what it would have been like if Annie or I were the one getting married. What music we would have chosen. What our dresses would look like.

When Aaron yelled my head snapped up as my thoughts slowly came back to the present.

"Finally! Dude, I was beginning to wonder if I needed to find a new best man!"

I turned from the alter to finally set eyes on the mysterious best man and was immediately taken aback. My feet were literally rooted to the floor, frozen like David coming face to face with Goliath for the first time.

Maybe it was the way the cathedral lights hit his face. Maybe it was my lack of sleep from the previous night. Then again, maybe he was actually the most gorgeous person I had ever laid eyes on. Whatever the reason, I couldn't take my eyes off him.

He strolled to the front of the church, respectfully removing his silver belly Stetson cowboy hat as he walked. There was such a sense of strength, poise and masculinity about him that I couldn't help staring. He went around saying hello to everyone and apologizing for being late. I couldn't determine the tone of his voice over the chatter of everyone else.

But it didn't matter because all the while I was just watching, admiring.

He was incredibly tall, enough so that with me being five foot eight inches and wearing four inch heels I still had to look up at him. Even though he was fully clothed I could tell he was built like a blue collar man. Could see the hard muscles on his chest and shoulders screaming to get out of the blue and white plaid pearl snap shirt he was wearing. His long legs, snugly encased in a pair of starched Wranglers, flexed with power in his stride. He was surefooted and confident without being over bearing. I was in a complete daze and didn't realize I had been staring for so long until Aaron walked him over to finally meet me.

"Brinley," my brother lightly tapped my arm, bringing me out of my stupor. "This is Jaxson Mathews, my best man."

"Pleased to meet you," he paused, "Miss Brinley Lambert." Jaxson's voice was so deep and smooth it sounded like an echo in a canyon.

I held out my trembling hand to shake his that was already extended and waiting. As I stared into his eyes, a dark chocolate color with small flecks of gold and green, I couldn't help but feel like I had seen him before. Like I had known him for years. My mind knew that wasn't possible; he moved here after I left.

But my heart was battling for control. When his gaze caught mine it felt like he was looking straight through all the pain I held inside. To a place where happiness still lingered.

Pull yourself together, Brin! I told myself. *You're acting like a lost little school girl!*

When my voice came out a tad scratchy I cleared my throat and tried again.

"Very nice to meet you too, Jaxson." My voice still felt weak, a little shaky and breathy, like it did on my first audition when I was so full of nerves.

I finally shook his hand and that's when I experienced a feeling that made an uncontrollable tremble work its way up my body. Despite the roughness and calluses his palms had, his hand felt so supple and safe, strong. And it sent a hot, electric sensation that passed from my fingertips, up my arm and straight into my heart.

I knew in that moment, with that feeling that I would be in trouble. I needed to distance myself from this man so as not be tempted by fate, like Adam and Eve and the tree of knowledge, or whatever it was that had been out there.

My mind was racing with questions. Is God trying to play some kind of trick on me or is this His cruelty taking root in my life? Taking my best friend wasn't enough. Now He has to make me meet someone like this, knowing that I can never act on the feelings I'm experiencing. The feelings that I have forced myself to suppress so I wouldn't have to deal with them. If there was any doubt as to how brutal He can be, I now had my answer.

I mean seriously, how was I supposed to be suffering for killing my best friend when this man has just walked into my life? The one I had a feeling was who I dreamt about for so long, which is why he must look so familiar to me. As a matter of fact, I don't believe I would be suffering. Not judging by the vibe I got from this guy standing in front of me.

Needing to get some fresh air, I extracted my hand from his, probably more forceful than was necessary. I excused myself from the congregation and made my way to the entry doors of the church. Once I rounded the corner I ran to the courtyard, desperate for distance. I began taking in deep breaths over and over again as my heart beat erratically. Two words had snuck into my mind and were haunting me, keeping my train of thought on one subject…

Jaxson Mathews.....

Aimee Martin

Chapter 4

"Ever learning, and never able to come to the knowledge of the truth." II Timothy 3:7

Standing in the courtyard, trying to quiet my racing heart, I desperately pondered at what had just happened. There was an undeniable urge to run back to my parents' home and forget about ever meeting Jaxson Mathews. Of course I knew it wasn't possible but that didn't make the feeling any less demanding.

Suck it up, Brinley I said to myself.

I focused on the chirping of the mockingbirds singing on a magnolia branch above me. On the wind whistling to a tune of its own making as it drifted between the building walls.

After several minutes I felt more sure of myself and walked back into the church, keeping my distance from *him.* I kept my head down so I didn't chance making eye contact.

There wasn't much to keep my attention focused on the rest of the rehearsal. Or dinner and drinks afterwards for that matter. I had been trying so hard to be as inconspicuous as possible while I watched him. Jaxson. Just because I didn't want him approaching me didn't mean that I couldn't study him. And that's exactly what was happening. I was studying.

Not in the 'I want to learn more' way but in the 'Why does this matter' way.

Making sure that I never had to chance the risk of being alone with him proved harder as the evening wore on. Everyone kept leaving, making the possibility more likely. For some reason the thought gave me incredible tension.

Soon–finally–the night came to an end and after saying my goodbyes, Alex and I made our way back to my parents'. Pleading exhaustion and a headache so there would be no late night conversation I shut myself in my room and went straight to bed.

That night, for the first time since the accident, my nightmare changed drastically. Before when these variations happened it was a change of place or maybe a different car. But always it was Annie whose life I took.

Always.

Tonight though, I saw the entire crash happen, back in LA again. It was like I was a bystander watching in horror. Rooted to the pavement, I was standing at the top of the cliff between the beach and the highway. The stars twinkled above, shining their beacon of warning to the oncoming traffic. The car went over the edge, rolled and rolled.

Once the car finished flipping, instead of seeing Annie lying there, dying on the asphalt, it was him–Jaxson! Screams stuck in my throat as I tried to reach out to him.

September 14, 2013

I woke still sweating with that dull ache I always had, like a two ton weight had planted itself inside my chest. Gasping for air made me feel like I was on the verge of hyperventilation. Only now my mind was filled with so many questions and uncertainties.

Why would he have been there? Why would Jaxson cause me to feel the heartache? That gut wrenching hollow pain from losing someone I loved?

I closed my eyes but visions of him lying there, dying, danced around relentlessly. Of course I couldn't go back to sleep. My brain was reeling with thoughts that didn't make any sense.

Why him? What did it mean; this lightning strike grasp he already had on me? How was that even possible? And most of all, why now when I'm too damaged to do anything about this odd turn of events?

I knew one thing, my questions deserved answers but I didn't have the slightest idea of how to go about finding them.

Dragging myself out of bed and walking into the kitchen, I made some coffee and waited impatiently for the brew to finish. With steaming cup in hand, I sat at the table and pulled my laptop out from its case sitting on the floor, deciding that the World Wide Web was a good place to start. I was prepared to search for the key to my nightmare and Jaxson's presence in it. At least that's what I told myself I was after.

I booted it up and went to work, thinking it was time I found out more about Aaron's best man. I hated the internet and social media was a bane on my very existence, but it sure does come in handy. As much as I despised people looking into my personal life, I bargained that looking into his was necessary as a means to an end.

Through Google alone I found that Jaxson had graduated from a small high school outside of Charlotte, North Carolina in 1996. *Which would make him eight years older than me,* I calculated.

He never went to college because apparently his Dad, whose name was Landon Mathews, owned and operated one of the biggest cattle ranches in North Carolina. The article, dated 7 years ago, stated that Landon ran it with the help of his wife, Beth, his daughter, Rachel and his three sons; Thomas, Brent and Jaxson.

I went to another website and found, in addition to his North Carolina roots, that he was connected to the sale of a ranch here in Lake Shores, Texas. I read that he had bought it at a real estate auction just over four years ago and has been raising cattle there ever since.

I thought back to my childhood and the only cattle ranch I remember being in this area was ole' Mr. McIntyre's place. So I assumed this was the same one.

Two and a half cups of coffee later there was nothing more interesting to be found on the web, and zilch that would help to tie Jaxson to California, Annie or myself. It was frustrating.

I realized that I was secretly hoping there would be something, anything, putting him in our paths. That at least would have given me an excuse for recognizing him. I didn't want my fears to be true. The fear that he *was* the one from my dreams long ago. My dreams of a happy ever after. Those dreams needed to stay buried, like Annie.

With nothing left to do, I shut down my computer and decided to start getting ready for the wedding. The women were meeting at a local beauty parlor to get all dolled up for the ceremony and I was due there in an hour. I showered, dressed and walked out the door forty-five minutes later feeling like I was about to be thrown into a pack of wedding-day wolves.

Once I got to the beauty shop I went around and gave the normal wholehearted hugs that were expected. I overheard the maid of honor telling Jessica, "You are so blessed by God to have found Aaron. This is a true sign that God is always looking after us and our happiness."

I fought the urge to snort at her, knowing that God does not respond to our lives for only happiness. Anyone who thought that should take a look at the life of Job. And even if He did, then Annie would still be here, instead of at the cemetery five miles away.

Listening to them gave me that sick feeling again. The one that sent nauseous pains though my gut at the very mention of God and His blessings and Annie. Of course I still doubted all of it. How could I not?

Let it go, I thought. Let them have their misguided beliefs for today.

It's not my place to interfere.

I sat in my assigned chair while the beautician went to work on my hair and dutifully kept my mouth shut. Besides, watching the other women at all the different work stations kept me plenty focused.

The clique girls were seated next to each other under the row of hair dryers, the ones with the big bowl that folds over, talking loudly over the noise. My mother was chatting with the lady giving her a manicure.

Two other women, I assumed they were Jessica's mom and grandma, were in stylists chairs getting their locks rolled up into neat chignons. I was seated across from them and was able to watch in the mirror as they turned to greet Jess when she came back out front from getting her pedicure. The look of maternal love on their faces reinforced my suspicions.

When Jessica and I were finally alone for a few minutes, I decided to ask some questions. See what more I could find out about Jaxson. As nonchalantly as possible, I took a deep breath and said, "So Jess, tell me about this Jaxson guy. What's his story? It's not like Aaron to get so close to someone so soon. How'd that happen?" There, that didn't sound too implicating on me. Just a curious sister.

Jessica proceeded to tell me a lot of what I had already read this morning. His birthplace, his father, his ranch here in town, blah, blah, blah. But then she added a few details I hadn't seen in all those web articles, something they obviously didn't have access to.

Score one for personal privacy, I thought.

She started talking more about why he moved here in the first place and my interest in what she was saying definitely elevated.

"And after his Dad died, I guess he couldn't stand to be up there anymore. Which is how he ended up buying Mr. McIntyre's ranch. Aaron told me that Jaxson found out about the auction from an old high school buddy that he's stayed in touch with. The friend, Blake Thompson is his name. We've hung out a few times and he's really nice. And good looking in a hard working way. Anyway, he moved down here to work with Mr. M at the request of his parents. They went to college with Kathy McIntyre, Mr. M's daughter, who introduced them one night at a frat party. The Thompsons, Bill and Sarah, were inseparable after that and told Kathy that if she ever needed anything from them, she had only to ask.

"So, when Mr. M took sick with pneumonia, Kathy called Sarah and asked her if her son was still looking for work. I guess Kathy never had any kids of her own and wanted someone she could trust to run the place temporarily. Anyway, Blake came down and has been here ever since."

I couldn't help thinking that the cliché about gossip and beauty parlors was never more true than it was right now. Refraining from shaking Jessica to stop with all the extra little details, I focused on the end result and kept listening.

"Blake called Jaxson first thing when Mr. M. died and talk got out about an auction. I guess he knew that Jaxson was looking for a ranch to own by himself. And a reason to get out of North Carolina. Jax came down for the auction, got the bid and the rest is history, I guess you could say. He paid cash for the place with some of his inheritance, packed up and moved to Texas. He and Aaron met at The Bar–" named that because it was the only bar in our little town "–one night during college football season and they immediately hit it off. They've been best buddies ever since." She smiled and chuckled to herself as she continued, "I was beginning to wonder if Aaron was ever going to ask me to marry him or if he was going to settle for eternal bachelortude with Jaxson."

I laughed with her at her remark about my brother, who is known for being a major procrastinator as well as someone who runs from responsibility. I could definitely see her fighting for a place in Aaron's life next to Jaxson. *I would fight for the place next to Jaxson.*

I started as the thought came unbidden to my mind but at the same time felt so natural. I began to drift away from the conversation after that, hearing Jessica talk in the background but not really listening. I was too busy wondering what happened to his Dad and where the rest of his family was. And, oddly, if his pain made him feel as trapped as mine did. Was that why he came here? To get away from the memories held in Charlotte by his deceased father?

Lake Shores isn't exactly the kind of place people come looking for. Our residents are typically third and fourth generations. Which means you're either born into this town or marry into this town. And yet, he was here, calling this place his home now.

I pondered over these reasons until the entire bridal party was finished at the salon and we headed out in to the bright sun, shining down on us like a spotlight for Jessica's Big Day. Three hours after my conversation with Jess had finished, we were at the church for the ceremony. The women were all getting dressed in the Guild Room and 'oohhing and aahhing' over the wedding gown. Too many hands on the dress allowed me the chance to sit back and just watch. When six o'clock came around, we made our way to the chapel.

The wedding was beautiful, as was Jessica.

I watched my brother as he watched her walking down the aisle. I couldn't help but to feel happy for him, even if he had prolonged the inevitable. To feel happy that he had found her and that my torture was designated to me only, which allowed me to enjoy the ceremony more than I thought possible. I would despise myself even more if my family had to suffer because of my ludicrous mistake.

I kept my gaze forward while the words were spoken by the minister. But during the vows I looked over again to study the couple and *he* caught my eye.

Jaxson was staring at me with those deep set eyes, a slight mar to his brow, like he was trying to figure something out about me.

And then he smiled so sweetly and quickly that I might have missed it had I not been looking at him. I felt a flutter in my stomach and as it sped up, I turned back toward the front. I tried not to make eye contact with him again, though I know it was obvious there was a lot of fidgeting on my end. I did not want to face these confusing feelings I had when I looked at him. I wanted to go home to LA and not have to deal with any of it.

After the wedding and all the pictures with the bridal party, parents and grandparents (which seemed to drag on and on), we were finally off to the reception.

Ironically enough, it was being held at Jaxson's ranch. I couldn't wait to get there and help myself to some champagne, thinking it would help to keep my mind from over-thinking whatever *this* was. Or just put me in a frame of mind in which I didn't care. Either option would work.

They had the entire barn–which was large enough to put about five full sized tour buses inside it–decorated with white twinkle lights and flowers everywhere.

Calla lilies of red and white, red and white daisies, red, white and dark pink roses on all the tables as centerpieces let off their mingled scents to make the room almost glow in perfume. All the colors were perfectly planned to tie into the other flowers.

White crepe myrtle trees, also covered with white lights, were at every corner of the barn and dance floor. The place was stunning and the smell was lovely without being overwhelming.

I briefly wondered where the horses were as there were six empty stalls along the left wall.

But once I spotted the table holding the wine, champagne and beer I headed that direction and forgot all about it.

After a dinner of barbequed chicken and grilled vegetables I found myself standing at the entrance to the barn. Staring out past the expansive door, rolling my empty champagne glass between my hands while looking into the pasture.

The sun was beginning to set and the horizon was filled with dark pink and orange blankets, lying over the land as if to keep it warm for the night. The small rolling hills, dark green with the setting sun, seemed to go on forever with their yellow wildflowers dotting their open ground.

And there, on those hills, were the horses I wondered about earlier. There were two blacks, two appaloosas, one blue roan and one buckskin. They were beautiful to watch as they roamed, gracefully bending their necks to nibble on the lush grass.

It was peaceful and helped to occupy my mind from all the joy spreading around the party. I was all joyed out and tried to ignore the laughter, music and toasts going on behind me.

So I kept my focus on the horses and the red tractor to the right of them with its loading rails attached to the front. For some reason, that old song 'She thinks my Tractor's Sexy' popped into my head and I couldn't help but to picture Jaxson sitting atop that tractor, skin glistening with sweat as he worked under the blazing sun plowing the….

"They'd like for all the wedding party to join them on the dance floor."

I was startled out of my daydreaming by the sound of a deep voiced angel. His voice sounded as smooth as butter, maybe silk.

I turned hastily to see Jaxson standing there holding out his arm to escort me back inside. I put the glass in his hand and quickly put my hands in a tight lock behind my back. I didn't want to risk the feel of that undeniable current his touch had sent through me. Like yesterday when we shook hands.

"Oh… sure." I said quietly. "I'm coming."

His face couldn't hide the disappointment as his brow furrowed and he let his arm fall slowly to his side. He didn't push the issue and instead set the glass on a nearby table. We walked side by side to the dance floor in silence.

Fortunately, they had already started the bridal party dance by the time we made it back to the floor. Which meant I didn't have to stay there for long.

Unfortunately, everyone else had already partnered up which left Jaxson and I standing there alone.

He casually and yet sternly took my right hand in his left and placed his other hand on the small of my back; my body quivered.

"Shall we?" his look could be termed triumphant as he pulled me close. It wasn't really a question.

Before I could think of an excuse to get out of it, he had me twirling around the dance floor to the strands of Van Morrison's *Into the Mystic*.

My bridesmaid gown was flowing out like purple flower petals around us, twining around our lower legs. He was so sure of himself on the dance floor but very gentle at the same time, leading me around and around to something between a waltz and a Texas two step. Keeping my hand firmly in his grasp and his left secure on my lower back, we moved amongst the others effortlessly.

Well, he's a good dancer... I'll give him that... When I looked up it was to meet his gaze, watching me closely and attentively. When he spoke, in this close of proximity, I almost melted in his strong hold at hearing his satiny voice.

"Your eyes are so green. I don't think I have ever seen anything quite like it before. Like summer moss with hints of amber." I quickly looked at our feet again, trying to hide the heat rushing to my face.

I guess I'd have to add sweet talker to his list, too.

When he spoke again, I couldn't help myself but to look up and watch his full lips move as he apologized.

"I'm sorry if I embarrassed you. That wasn't my intention. I've just been trying to find the right time to tell you that since I noticed yesterday. I figured this was as good a time as any but I guess maybe I was wrong." He sounded sincerely remorseful.

"No, no it's ok." I reassured him. "I just haven't really had a compliment like that in a long time. It caught me a little off guard."

"How you could *not* get compliments all the time is beyond me. I've been watching your movies for a long time now, since before I met your brother. You've always been beautiful. I have a hard time believing no one else has told you the same." His voice was so deep and smooth.

There was a part of me that wished he hadn't seen my movies. Then instead of feeling like celebrity and fan, we'd be on more even ground.

"You have to remember that all of my company in LA is known for their acting skills. So, I tend to take everything with a grain of salt." I smirked at him, trying to lighten this intense moment.

It was then that I noticed that the music had stopped. Everyone was already headed back to their tables filled with drinks and desserts to be eaten. How long had we still been swaying around the dance floor? Had he noticed and just not cared?

I stopped and dropped my hands but he held my left at his side firmly, not letting it go despite my effort to coolly do so.

"Would you like to take a walk with me?" he asked with such an apprehensive boyish charm that I froze.

Everything in my head was telling me to say no. To not risk getting drawn into whatever web he was weaving around my shaky emotions. To tell him I didn't deserve to be happy. To run away back to Los Angeles to the comfort of my home and to all the people who, in a sense, lied to me for a living.

But I simply couldn't bring myself to leave. I couldn't bring myself to jerk my hand from his because I didn't want to risk losing that heady sensation he gave me. Honestly, I couldn't even speak, much less voice any concerns or excuses.

So I just slowly nodded yes. He visibly relaxed and kept his eyes locked on mine as he pulled me off the dance floor, out of the barn and into the now moonlit meadow where it was only us.

Chapter 5

"Blessed is the man that walketh not in the counsel of the ungodly, nor standeth in the way of sinners, nor sitteth in the seat of the scornful." Psalm 1:1

We walked for a while without saying a word, making our way towards the pasture where the horses grazed. The silence would have been deafening had it not been for the crickets chirping and the frogs croaking in an attempt to wake up for the night. To come out to meet the silver moon that now hung from the sky like a mobile over a baby's bed.

He never did let go of my hand and I couldn't decide if that was a good thing or a bad thing. What's worse was that I had no desire to remove my own from his hold and that had me confused.

I guess I left it in his simply because it felt nice and it had been so long since anything felt nice to me. I didn't want that feeling to end.

I tried to look anywhere other than at him but my gaze kept coming back. His sculpted jaw, his broad shoulders, his powerful chest. They drew my eyes to him like a moth to a flame. I shouldn't watch him and yet I was lost in his beauty.

Don't get caught up in looks, Brin. Lord knows you've seen enough to last a lifetime in your line of work.

My personal pep talk gave me the kick in the pants I needed.

Forcing my eyes away, I looked out over the hill at the crescent moon resting above the horizon. After what seemed like several miles of walking but was really only about a hundred yards, we made it to the fence surrounding the pasture. Jaxson propped one foot up on the lowest rung and stared at me for several long moments. I got the feeling he was contemplating how to begin a conversation. Then he spoke again in that deep yet tender, electrifying voice that I was quickly becoming addicted to.

"Can you give me one good explanation as to why I feel so comfortable with you? Why, even though we just met yesterday, it feels like you have been a part of my life for years? Because I have never felt this secure with someone before, especially someone I just met, and I am completely baffled by it." The look in his eyes said he was serious.

To say I was shocked would be an understatement. And yet, I couldn't bring myself to tell him that I was feeling the same way. That his face was the one I used to see in my dreams all those months ago. Before the nightmares had taken over.

That his face had been the one in my nightmare last night.

I knew that if I did, my soul would be giving in to something, a feeling or a chance maybe, that I didn't deserve. If not giving in, then at least acknowledging it. And I might not be able to stop whatever takes place after my admission. So, one solution came to mind.

Deny. Deny. Deny.

"No. There is no explanation because there is no truth to that."

I gently but purposefully removed my hand from his and crossed my arms over my chest so he couldn't take it back. I felt more secure like this. Maybe I was just subconsciously trying to guard my heart. I should just walk away now.

"Then tell me why it is–" he pressed on even though I was trying to head back to the reception, "–that I feel so drawn to you. To your spirit. To your character. To everything about you."

I paused in turning, taken back by his words. If he only knew the truth then this wouldn't be an issue. He would understand my view of love and all that goes with it, including character and spirit. I swallowed hard and tried to be as confident as possible without showing my vulnerability. Because that was something he would not have access to.

"I don't know why anyone would feel that way toward me. My spirit was broken almost a year ago. I have nothing to give. Maybe you're just caught up in the moment of all the wedding bliss around you or something. I don't know. I'm sorry." I shook my head, turned on my heel and tried to walk back to the barn.

But he cut me off.

He was very careful not to touch me. I guess from pulling away earlier. Or maybe because he wanted me to know his intentions were not harmful.

But he did hold his hands out in front of him to stop me. He had to be able to tell how reluctant I was to be out here with him. Even less now with what he was saying. Surely he wasn't so ignorant as to not see my edginess. Still, he stood there waiting for me to stop and, what, listen? Acknowledge? Agree?

I stopped. It was either that or run into him, which required touching, and was completely out of the question. In the moonlight, I looked up and took notice of his eyes again. Those intense and mysterious eyes. They looked to be pleading with me to stay. I searched them for anything that might give me an excuse to take off running. I found nothing but fascination. *Damn!*

So against my better judgment, I waved my hand in front of me, indicating he should continue. Again the silence came and we stood there looking intently at each other. I was perfectly content with not saying anything; afraid the wrong words would come out if I did. And, again, he was the one that spoke first.

"You know, it's all right if you don't feel the same way I do. For now. I'd be pleased just being your friend and getting to know you better."

Why did his voice have to be so hypnotizing to me? And why does he have to sound so logical and accommodating? "But I don't believe that's how you really see me, as just a friend. I saw it in your glowing green eyes when we met. That glimmer of recognition. I know you feel this too. Whatever this is."

I butt in then, not wanting to chance him saying something that might send me over the edge of my self-control.

"It's not what you think it was. It was just that I didn't know who you were, having never met you before, and was trying to figure you out. I can be a little protective of my brothers." Scowling for good measure, and ignoring the fact that I was rambling, I went on. "Besides, I have too much on my plate to be analyzing what you *think* is going on here. I'm like that tractor out there." I waved my hand toward the machine of my discussion. "Big enough to do the work but never enough time in the day to get it done."

I was glad the darkness acted like a shield to my face. Otherwise he might see through what even I felt was an extremely weak response. He might see how hard I was fighting against all the urges to run into his arms and tell him

I knew exactly what he meant. I didn't deserve this kind of connection and couldn't let it go any further.

"Have you always been so cynical?" If not for the hint of laughter in his voice, I would have thought he was insulting me. I could tell he was trying to lighten the mood and was thankful for that.

Even though I did shoot him a harsh glance. I am not a cynical person; at least, I didn't used to be. *Maybe I am now… huh. Annie would be pissed.*

He interrupted my musing.

"Well, I can wait. In the meantime, what do you say we give that whole friend thing a try? Do you at least have enough time for that? You can never have enough friends and I think we would be good for each other."

He waited patiently for me to answer. I got the feeling that he would have waited all night for me. "I'll see what I can work out." I sighed, smiling for the first time since we had been alone.

He returned my smile and chuckled which made me deem we were on safe territory but I reminded myself to keep my defenses up. Which I could already tell was going to be a full time job around Jaxson. The first time I let it down, I was afraid he would pounce on the opportunity to see what else could become of us. *Us…Hmm… sounds promising… NO, Brinley!*

We started walking again, slowly heading back toward to barn, not necessarily in any hurry to get back to the crowd.

Making casual conversation seemed to be a lot easier than I had expected it to be now that the tension had eased.

I told him what I was like growing up and how I had always wanted to act. About puppy love crushes in junior high and high school. My favorite teachers, Coaches Beckers and Binkman. And subjects which were English and Drama. I talked about playing all kinds of sports every chance I got. Everything from soccer to tag football with my brothers. And of course what it was like growing up in Lake Shores where, with a population of 3000, everyone knew your business.

"It wasn't always a bad thing, having our news known around town. Luckily, being raised in a Christian home, I didn't get into much trouble so there was never a lot of gossip about me. Plus, it was always nice to know I could rely on the community when something dreadful came up. Not that I ever took any of the towns people up on their offers for support."

He looked genuinely concerned and asked me, "What is it that came up?"

I took my eyes off of him for the first time since we started talking in an effort to shy away from answering that. Like the cloud passing quickly over the moon just now, my mood clouded over to switch gears. That was information that didn't need to be divulged yet.

He must have taken my silence and change in demeanor as a clue that I didn't want to discuss it. He didn't press for an answer and gratefulness swelled in my chest. I took the opening to shift the conversation to him, itching to know more about the man who had captured my interest.

"Tell me about your childhood. What was it like growing up in North Carolina?" He didn't hesitate in responding and went right on into his own story, our conversation never having a gap in it.

Obviously, I didn't tell him that I already knew some of what he was telling me. I was sure he would think of me as a stalker, at best, and that was not the impression I wanted to give him.

"It wasn't too different from here, I suppose. Except that I was home-schooled until I was a teenager. My family was always so busy with the ranch that it was kinda necessary. I hated it when I was kid because I never had the 'normal' childhood that most of the other kids had. If anyone can say they had a normal childhood." We both laughed. God that felt good.

"I guess, looking back now, it was kind of a helpful thing. I didn't have to go through all the embarrassing puberty stuff around other kids, mainly girls. I liked to play football a lot but never really took it seriously. The coaches were mad when I wouldn't play in high school. Having a six foot five defensive end would have helped them get to state but what can I say? I'm more content with just watching it on T.V. Especially college, that's where the players really have heart.

"Let's see, I had a pretty serious girlfriend in high school; Bonnie Sadler was her name. But, by the time we were seniors, she started having more fun with the baseball team than me so I ended it."

"The team???"

I stopped walking and tried not to sound too immature by the declaration. I couldn't help my gaping mouth or the stunned expression on my face that was full of shock.

"Yes." he laughed at my disbelief, "The team. Better to have found out then rather than later in life, I guess. Anyways, after high school I went to work with my father full time until I moved here five years ago. And now met you." His eyes met mine again, probing right through me.

I fought for something else to say so I wouldn't be hypnotized by those brilliant brown orbs. Then I remembered wanting to ask him about the name of the ranch because it was so different.

"Where did you come up with the name *Burnt Aggie Ranch*?"

"You're probably going to think I'm crazy."

"No I won't. It's just so unusual. I wondered how you came up with it." I tried to encourage him. When he still looked doubtful I help up my middle three fingers on my right hand, "Scouts honor."

"Well, I've always been a fan of Texas football teams. So when I moved here, I knew I wanted to incorporate that somehow. I always thought that someday when I got married and had kids of my own, it would be cool to have one that went to A&M and another that went to UT. So, I merged the two for the ranch name. Burnt for the color of UT and Aggie for the A&M mascot." He shrugged a shoulder like it was no big deal. It was really quite ingenious, though. I liked it.

We were getting much closer to the barn and fell into a comfortable silence for the remainder of our walk. The chandeliers that had been strung up on the ceiling and the candles on the tables burned low and spilled their glow to the surrounding grass. I could see inside the open doors that the party was dying down, some guests starting to leave and others preparing the 'human tunnel' that Aaron and Jessica would walk through.

I realized, to my amazement, that I was eager to find out more about him. And genuinely sad that we were back at the barn now because that meant our walk was over and I wasn't sure I wanted it to be. But, we had to go send off Aaron and Jessica.

I quickly shook off the thoughts of maintaining our chat, realizing I needed to stop fooling myself. We were only going to be friends and that didn't mean long talks on a regular basis. Sharing intimate and personal details of our lives. Surely my happiness would not be improved by simply making a new friend.

As long as I could keep it at a friendship. And that was my infinite goal, right? To remain unhappy. I just had to ensure that it stayed that way. Fight off all the impulses telling me to stay with him.

We nodded to each other and went separate ways when we walked into the barn; he with the groomsmen and I with my parents.

Everyone gathered around with their bottles of bubbles to blow, cheering loudly as Aaron and Jessica made their way down our makeshift tunnel. They both stopped to hug their parents and then switched to hug their new in-laws. I was smiling, waving and cheering them on as they climbed into their waiting transportation which was covered in the typical cans and condoms.

Once they were in the limousine, driving away to their future, I noticed Jaxson striding over to me, so sure of himself again. I caught my breath just watching him, knowing at any moment my wall could come crashing down. I pulled myself together and stood up tall, refusing to let that happen.

We're just friends, that's it!

He stopped a few feet from me, standing with his shoulders straight and his head tilted a little to the side. He studied me for a few seconds then asked simply, "Would you have dinner with me before you leave for LA?"

Everything around me seemed to slow down to a blur the way a video camera does when it blurs out of one scene and into the next. All activity blocked out except for the man in front of me. All sounds became nonexistent, as if hit with the mute button, except for the words coming out of his mouth.

I needed to tell him no so I didn't risk losing the battle with my fragile barricade. I needed to tuck tale and get the heck out of Lake Shores before I did something really stupid. But once more, like the other times he's approached me, I felt my voice defy me and I could not answer. Swallowing so hard I could hear my throat working, and against my better judgment, I nodded my head.

Yes, I was telling him yes.

Chapter 6

"We are troubled on every side, yet not distressed; we are perplexed, but not in despair." II Corinthians 4:8

Journal Entry Four – Sept. 15, 2013

"Dear Annie, I've really screwed things up now.

I'm sure you already know but I'll tell you what's going on anyways. I met my brother's best friend, Jaxson Mathews. Jaxson… who has a name like that? It sounds more like one of the character names in a book rather than in real life.

Anyway, I met him a few days ago and he has totally tipped me off my rocker.

First of all, it should be illegal to be that good looking. He has this face that is rugged, I suspect from ranch work all his life, but still beautiful at the same time. And his body.

God, it's the type that all the Hollywood guys go to the gym for but his is all au' naturel. Strong, dominant, mesmerizing.

But it's not just the looks. His whole attitude is full of compassion, understanding. And funny! Oh, he made me laugh. But that's all beside the point. The point of this letter to you was about the mistake. He asked me to have dinner with him.

And I said yes!

Granted, I didn't really say yes, just nodded it. But it's the same thing. What the hell was I thinking? It's like I get all tongue tied around him and forget my place in this world. My resolve to stay single. For you. For what you can't have.

What am I going to do, Annie? I really can't go through with this dinner. Just the thought of seeing Jaxson again has my insides all twisted up in confusion. There's this draw to him that I'm afraid I can't fight.

I need to go home. At least there I can wallow alone without having to face the possibility of 'meeting someone.' What a joke that is! And there's also the added benefit of not having to worry about the town fretting over my well being.

I mean, it hasn't even been a year since you died. That's definitely not enough time for me to let the past lie and move on. Truthfully, I don't know if I ever will. If I release the past, I'm afraid I'll lose you. In more than just the physical sense. And just the thought of that makes my heart feel troubled.

I'm functioning, yes. I don't bawl like a baby all day anymore. I don't curl up on the couch from the physical pain that depression caused. But letting you go fully? I don't think that's even an option, much less one in the near future.

I wish you were here. You'd know exactly how to handle this situation with Jaxson. Heck, if you were here, you'd probably be searching through clothes for the perfect outfit for me to wear. Telling me to stop acting like a pre-pubescent kid and to put on my big girl panties. That it's just dinner and to stop over thinking things.

But you're not here. And even though I know what you'd say and do, I can't bring myself to calm down about the whole situation. It feels like a betrayal against you, the way Peter betrayed Jesus in his final hours. By not acknowledging you the way Peter didn't acknowledge Him, I'm forgetting my reasons for this loneliness my path has taken. It's not fair.

Obviously, my anger is still ever present. But honestly, I'll take anger over depression any day. At least with anger I actually feel something. But it's not just God, or you, that I'm angry with. Right now, I'm angry with myself. I should have had the strength to just tell him no. To walk away and not look back. You would have been that strong.

Too bad I can't channel some of your strength from the grave.

Speaking of graves, I hope you understand why I haven't gone to yours since I've been in Lake Shores. I want to. Really, I do.

But every time I've started to walk in the direction of the cemetery I get a little nauseous and end up plopping down on the sidewalk, struggling between my need to see you and my need for self-preservation.

I remember that wacky therapist telling me I needed to find a way to bring about closure. He said going to your resting place would be a start. But we both know what a crock he turned out to be so why would I take his advice? Self-preservation in the form of remaining single, with you by my side via a journal, is the only option for me. And damn anyone for telling me different. Until they can put themselves in my shoes, they don't get a vote.

Anyhow, back to the mistake I'm fussing over. I guess the only option is to go through with this dinner date and pray that I'll make it through with my wall intact.

Pray. What a fraud. If praying worked, you'd still be alive. At least I still have you here, in the pages of my journal. Wish me luck with this date. No, not date. That sounds too formal. Meeting, that sounds better. We'll go with that. Wish me luck with the meeting. I'll talk to you soon. I love you, Annie."

Chapter 7

"When I would comfort myself against sorrow, my heart is faint in me." Jeremiah 8:18

After laying my journal on the table beside my bed, I plopped my head back on my pillow and lay there with so much disbelief it was maddening. I was furious with myself for conceding in accepting the dinner invitation. Just like I had said to Annie, I couldn't seem to tell him no.

I felt like the stone wall that had been built up the last eleven months to protect my heart was slowly crumbling. Falling all around me like the collapse of the Berlin wall because of him. Except their circumstances were agreed upon by both sides while this entire situation was beneficial to only one. And it's not me and there was nothing I could do to stop it.

Well, that was just not good enough. Building up my resolve, I decided I would still go to dinner tomorrow. It would be rude and un-southern of me to cancel now and I am nothing if not a southerner at heart.

But I would be on the first flight back to California the day after. Maybe once home I could get back to the numbing everyday routine that kept my emotions in check so well. Kept them hard and unforgiving of my mistake.

And then maybe I would be able to forget all about Jaxson.

Unlikely.

My Mom quietly knocked, drawing my attention to the closed door. I guess she didn't want to wake me if I was still sleeping since it wasn't even eight in the morning yet. Maybe if I don't answer, she'll assume I'm asleep and not risk waking me.

"Brin?" her soft and comforting voice made me want to cringe and at the same time confess everything to her. "Are you awake, honey?"

I watched her from beneath my eyelashes. She walked in and eyed me lying in bed with my arm resting over my eyes.

But just as my Mom started to turn and walk out I decided I needed to talk to her. Plus, I just couldn't lie to her, even if only by omission. That old Shakespearean line came to mind, 'A rose by any other name is still as sweet.'

"Yes, I'm awake." I brought my arm down to rest on my belly. "Don't go, come sit with me. I'm just kicking myself in the butt for not getting an earlier flight."

She sat down on the edge of the bed and sweetly patted my leg.

"Are you that anxious to leave us? It looked like you were enjoying yourself last night"

And we both knew how much she and Daddy had been dying for me to enjoy life again.

I guessed that my mother was referring to the dancing. And the walking. And the talking. Or just the overall fact that I had ended up spending the better part of the night with Jaxson.

"It's not that, Mom. I've enjoyed coming home and seeing all the family. And I'm so happy for Aaron and Jessica. Six and a half years is far too long for her to have waited so I guess maybe I'm happier for my new sister-in-law than my 'commitment phobe' brother."

I was grinning at my own sarcasm and teasing aimed toward my brother. My Mom knew I was kidding; that's the way our family is. Always joking with each other which had allowed for a nice and fun childhood. But also always looking out for one another. Which is why there was no comment on my jibe.

I continued when she eyed me carefully, obviously ready to outlast me in a contest of wills.

"It's just that… uhh… I'm supposed to go to dinner with Aaron's friend, Jaxson, tomorrow night and I really wish there was a plane ticket to use as an excuse to get out of it. I just don't think it's a good idea."

My mother frowned at my resistance to the dinner date.

"Jaxson is a really nice young man, you know. We've gotten to know him pretty well over the last few years. I think it's a good thing for you to be seeing him outside of your brother's presence; as a man and woman instead of as a sister and best friend." She paused pensively, evidently debating on whether or not to go on. In the end, her determination won out. "God works in mysterious ways, honey. Maybe you should relax and trust Him with the date."

I moaned at the word *date.* And the mention of *God,* which I definitely intended to put a stop to. As I rolled over in bed to my left side, propping my head up on my elbow I took a minute to look into my mother's eyes. I could see concern there. And a little hopefulness.

Then again, maybe she was just tired from yesterday's excitement.

Regardless, I didn't want to fight with her on our differing views about faith, or the lack thereof, so I let it go.

"I know he's a nice man. At least from what I've heard. It's just that–" I trailed off not wanting to feel like the captain of a debate team, fighting for my opinion to be accepted. But her pleading eyes left me no choice. "–I need to get back to my routine life in LA. I need to work because it keeps me grounded. I can't stand trying to fight these feelings. They're trying to pull me into a happy place that I know I don't deserve to be in."

"Then stop fighting the feelings, Brinley. You do deserve to be happy. You do deserve to find someone that you can relate to on an emotional level. Like that of a husband. Annie would want that for you. She would be highly upset with you right now for trying to deny yourself a chance at happiness. Or at the very least, a chance to 'hang out', as you young people call it, with a very good looking man."

Why did she always feel the need to bring Annie into this? It's for Annie–*or is it because of Annie*–that I feel this way period.

And Jaxson's good looks should have nothing to do with it. Shaking my head slightly to get the image of a certain gorgeous cowboy out of my head, I continued my argument.

"It's not realistic for me to be happy when I took that from Ann. She can't find her happy ever after so I am going to make sure I don't find mine either. This is my punishment, and it only seems fair to her. I'm still going to dinner because you taught me better than to cancel last minute. But I'm leaving for LA first thing in two days. I just have to Momma. Please understand."

At the use of 'Momma', she knew I didn't want to talk anymore. It was my pleading name for her, used only when understanding was desperately needed or my affection showed through. I was fighting the tears prickling my eyes and didn't want to argue with my mother. We had different opinions on the matter and that wasn't going to change, point blank. I loved her in spite of her prying worries, because I knew they came from a good place, but only to a certain extent.

As of right now, her meddling had reached its limit on me.

She nodded her acquiescence and leaned over, with definite concern in her eyes this time. She kissed my forehead then got off the bed and retreated.

Before walking out the door, she turned and said with a wily grin, "By the way, just so you know what kind of effect I think Jaxson has on you… you didn't have any nightmares last night," and closed the door with a soft click.

I sat there trying to remember my nightmare just like I did every morning. They were usually so fresh that it didn't take much to bring them to mind. But, try as I might, I couldn't recall any screams lingering in my psyche.

Wondering what that meant for a few minutes, I took stock of what I knew about this entire situation. Everything in my life had become confusing since I met him and it'd only been three days.

My soul didn't feel so dark. My heart didn't feel so broken. My smile came easier. Those things I knew.

But why? Why would meeting him, spending the evening with him last night, have any effect on my night terrors? On everything that made up my murky life?

I needed to make myself busy so I didn't dwell on it. I'm sure it meant nothing but still, peace and quiet seemed the best option. Since we didn't have anything planned and my brother and new sister-in-law had left for their honeymoon, I opted to spend the rest of the day lying out in the backyard.

So I dragged myself out of bed, made my way to the bathroom to brush my teeth and changed into my swimsuit then gathered everything I needed to lay out. Making a point of not looking down at the dog door when I got to the back patio door, I drifted into the backyard.

Once I was settled on a big beach towel with a coat of sunscreen applied, sunglasses in place and the sun shining down on me, I was brought back to what my Mom had told me. Desperately trying to analyze it, but to no avail, I dropped it from thought again and vowed to leave it out of my mind.

Lying there with the rays soaking into my skin, I couldn't help but to think about one of the biggest differences between Los Angeles and Lake Shores… the heat.

LA is warm in mid-September with seventy degree weather. But in a bathing suit on the beach and with the wind blowing, sunbathing isn't exactly a welcome event.

Here, though, it's still hot in the upper eighties and the humidity hung around ninety percent, making it feel like it's really in the mid-nineties. The muggy air could suck the breath right out of someone if they aren't used to it. A lot of visitors would, and do, complain about the weather but to me it felt nice. Laying here in my swimsuit soaking up the vitamin D without a breeze or cloud to be found.

The heat relaxed me, taking the puzzling thoughts away, and by noon, I was asleep.

I was on the cliff again. I was watching the accident again. Only the accident seemed to be frozen in one moment, like someone had hit the pause button at the instant the car had stopped flipping. My B.M.W. laid there, a crumbled mess off the highway. Everything flashed before my eyes and the next thing I knew I was in the car again–instead of watching from the cliff–and *he* was there.

Jaxson was lifting me out of the crumbled metal and plastic that had been my car and holding me close to his chest. I could feel the movement in his incredibly powerful arms. I remembered seeing them bunch under his shirt the night we met. He smelled like sunshine.

"Where's Annie?" I asked him hoarsely. "She was with me in the car. You have to go back and save her too!" I was pleading with him and he was peacefully looking at me. No hurry or panic in his expression whatsoever.

"You are the only one I am meant to save." He said to me. His voice was so reassuring I felt its depth in my chest and felt my panic begin to dissipate too. "Just like you are the one who is meant to save me."

What? What does that mean? He leaned in, inches from my face. I could feel his breath–barely strained despite the fact that he was still carrying me–mixing with my own.

His lips had begun to slightly brush against my own. I closed my eyes and held my breath…

My parents' three barking dogs woke me. I was gasping for air and beyond confused. Nothing in that dream made sense. No paramedics. No sirens and flashing lights. No screams.

But the two scariest things were that one, there was no Annie and two, a lot of Jaxson.

Maybe the heat is getting to me. How long have I been sleeping? The sun was just beginning to move into the west so I assumed it was somewhere around five in the evening. *Why didn't my Mom wake me?*

I took a deep, refreshing breath and tried to remove the scowl marring my forehead, despite the fact that no one was around. I was desperate to shake off the dream that hadn't yet turned into my nightmare.

I knew that something destructive had been getting ready to happen in it. That's the way the nightmares worked. Just when I would think things were going to be okay, they always ended with the tragic. That's why I always woke up screaming, sweating. And I embraced those reactions because it helped remind me of the loss from my past and the loneliness of my future

I stood, pulled on my black wrap-around sarong and methodically drug myself inside, thinking I would head straight to the shower. A nice cool shower should help to clear my thoughts and chill down my body.

The smell coming from the kitchen, however, stopped me cold in my tracks. Mom was making her famous homemade fried chicken which was irresistible.

"Hey sweetie. Did you have a nice nap?"

"Mom, why didn't you wake me? I must have been out for close to five hours." I asked her. Shower forgotten, I walked in to help her turn the drumsticks and breasts browning in the grease.

"You looked so peaceful, content even. I thought you could use the rest so I let you be." I smiled at her, grateful that she didn't feel the need to push the exchange any more. After all, I did feel more rested.

Except for the dream.

"Well." I moved to flip the wings, "I guess it's a good thing I've got some Italian blood in me and don't burn. Maybe I can use this new sun exposure to get a movie part." I said, winking and doing a little turn. She laughed at my antics and I joined in with her.

It felt good to laugh. We finished making dinner together while talking about the wedding yesterday and reminiscing about my childhood. I took care of mashing the potatoes and stirring the green beans while she made the chicken gravy for the biscuits.

Just as Daddy got home Mom pulled the biscuits out of the oven. Placing them in a linen-lined basket and setting everything on the table, the three of us sat down to a very soothing and country home cooked meal. We ate and talked for over an hour as if no time had passed since I was last home, almost a year ago.

I filled them in on the latest Hollywood gossip and they filled me in on the latest Lake Shores gossip–not that there was much of it. It was surprisingly satisfying being here with my parents. I always felt safe when I was here, regardless of what I felt inside.

Conversation died down as our plates were emptied and Daddy made his way into the living room to watch the latest episode of NCIS. Momma helped me clear the table then I shooed her out of the kitchen. After I cleaned up all the pots and pans and placed the dishes in the dishwasher, I took that long shower I'd been waiting for since coming inside a couple of hours before.

I felt much better when I got out. Well, I felt cleaner anyway. I lay down in bed, wearing my cool and comfy cotton pajamas and opened one of my favorite books–The Wonderful Wizard of Oz–and read… and read… until I became so distracted and I couldn't concentrate on the words anymore.

My mind was wandering to the dinner date that was now less than twenty-four hours away. I was lost in reservation about it and contemplating the entire rendezvous.

I thought about Jaxson and the things he had said last night. I replayed what had happened in my sun-induced dream this afternoon. Maybe it was sun-induced delirium. That made more sense.

My mind was so filled with Jaxson that I never would have guessed, or believed, that it was his presence in my subconscious that allowed sleep to finally overtake me.

Chapter 8

"Him that is weak in the faith receive ye, but not to doubtful disputations." Romans 14:1

September 16, 2013

Why am I so nervous? Get over yourself, Brinley! It's just dinner.

As I continued to get ready for the evening my mind was wreaking havoc on my nerves.

Jaxson was probably just being cordial because I'm the sister of his best friend. Or maybe he thinks I can talk a producer into using his ranch for a set. It's not unheard of and Hollywood does pay a lot for that sort of thing after all.

I knew what I was doing to myself and my heavy sigh was proof positive of that.

I was literally trying to sabotage any hopeful feelings I might have about tonight. Keep my logical self-intact with my heart heavily guarded because it would make it easier to turn and walk away.

I finished slipping into my shoes and looked into the floor length mirror hanging inside my closet door. The same mirror Annie and I used to excitedly examine ourselves in before all those high school dances like Prom and Sadie Hawkins.

I wanted to look nice, sophisticated but not too sexy. No sense in bringing any unwanted attention. I had settled for a pair of white Capri slacks and a simple, black satin tank top. The spaghetti straps might be a little on the sexy side but it was hot out. I don't know, maybe in the back of my mind I wondered what my 'date' would think of me in something besides that ugly purple bridesmaid's dress.

With my customary black sequined flip flops that I never went anywhere without on my feet, red toenails shining, my outfit looked casual but stylish. My hair was loosely pulled up into a clip because it was too warm to wear long hair down. But I had pulled a few tendrils around my face to soften the look. I decided to play up my green eyes that he had commented on before and wear some deep purple eye shadow with just a hint of mascara. A little rose colored blush to liven up my cheeks, some light pink lip gloss and I was ready to go.

Making sure I had my phone, wallet and keys in my purse, I headed down the hall and said bye to my parents, ignoring the encouraging look on their faces.

On the way out the door I thought once again about where I was going and had to stop walking for a minute. Taking a few deep breaths of humid, salt-tinged air to calm myself, I unlocked my Dad's truck that he was letting me borrow for the night and sat in the driver's seat. A quick turn of the key to the dark silver four-door Ford started the rumbling engine. One more deep breath, then I put the truck in reverse and headed to Jaxson's.

He had asked me to meet him at his house at seven. I didn't know where we were going after but there were only two 'good quality' restaurants in town.

And I expected he would want to take me to a nice place rather than the Burger Stop on Main Street. One was an old mom and pop café owned by Mr. and Mrs. Wilkens. They have been a part of this town for over sixty years and everyone loved their food. It was everyday home cooking that made you leave with a full belly and a smile on your face.

The other place was a little more romantic, by small town standards anyways. It was a quaint Italian place called Giovanni's. I had a feeling we were going to be eating pasta for dinner but gave up guessing as I pulled through the gate at Jaxson's place and drove a quarter mile up the dirt drive to his front porch.

I parked behind another four door truck, this one more menacing looking with its brush guard in front and large trailer hitch on the back bumper, and turned off the ignition.

Hopping out of my Dad's truck, I headed toward the front door and fought to suppress the sudden sensation of a thousand butterflies fluttering for freedom in my belly. I ignored them as best as I could; telling myself I had no reason to be nervous about dinner.

In reality though I think I was nervous because I was cautiously hoping it would go well. And how stupid was that? Nothing good could come from having a nice time. Nothing except hurt feelings and more decisions to doubt.

I raised my hand and knocked on the big, beautiful, dark stained oak door. Waiting for it to open, I admired the craftsmanship that went into the makings of the front porch. It went the length of the house and had beautiful cedar posts every six feet. The wicker swing at one end looked like it would be inviting on a night when the air was cool and the lightening bugs lit up the yard with their mini-tail flashlights.

Not thirty seconds later, Jaxson answered with a huge smile already in place. His dark, chocolate colored eyes glowed inside a face that gave the impression he was thrilled to see me.

The butterflies came back with a vengeance.

"Hi there! Come on in and make yourself at home." He was very animated.

I walked in guardedly and stepped across the threshold, taking in all the surroundings. The décor was very rustic and I liked it. Animal skin rugs–cow, deer, sheep–were spread out all over the dark, hardwood floors. Lamps and wall hangings were all of the same wrought iron make up. The colors on the walls were beige but the trim was a dark brown. *Like his beautiful eyes,* I thought and then scolded myself for it.

"What do you think?" Jaxson asked, thankfully interrupting my train of thought. His expression was one of quiet timidity, like he was afraid I might not approve of what I saw.

"It's very cozy. Country with that homey feel. Did you decorate the place by yourself?"

He chuckled and shook his head with an emphatic no.

"Only the furs lying around are by my hands. My mother came down to visit shortly after I bought the place and helped me get it set up."

I realized that was the first time I had heard anything about his Mom.

"Is she still in North Carolina?" I watched as a sad but loving look crossed his face.

"Yeah. That's her home and she couldn't bear to leave it, no matter how much I tried to get her to come here with me. So she just visits once in a while."

His smile that had been shining so bright when I arrived softened a little more with the talk of his mother. I took it as a sign that this might be shaky waters and decided to leave the subject alone for now.

All I needed was to start this evening off with more awkward vibes than there already were.

"So, where are we going to eat?" I asked light heartedly, trying to ease the tension. That big and beautiful smile returned along with a wink when he answered.

"The back deck." He must have seen the confused look I was so desperately trying to hide so he went on, holding out his hand for me, "I asked you to have dinner with me. I never said we were going to go out to dinner."

I was overcome by a mixture of feelings–nervousness and guilt, excitement and hope–they were pulling at my insides in two different directions like a game of tug of war. One side claiming this situation was okay and to take his hand and walk with him.

While the other said no. To leave now and forget about anything brewing between us. I bargained with myself, again, that I had to stick to my good southern upbringing and wait around.

Tentatively, fully anticipating that shock I felt the first time we shook hands, I placed my hand in his. That current was definitely there but instead of jerking, like I was afraid of doing, I only trembled slightly. Maybe because I had been expecting it the effect wasn't as strong. But as he closed his fingers around mine, the jolt intensified and I held my breath as he led me through a doorway that opened into a spacious kitchen.

Pots and pans hung on a bronze rack above an eat-at bar that could easily sit five people. Stainless steel appliances shone to a quiet gleam under the flickering lights.

Brown and sapphire blue granite sparkled with the reflections of its countertop occupants. Once we got to the door leading to the deck he released my hand, to my relief, and said to go on out, that he'd be there in a minute.

I opened the door, walked outside and was utterly blown away. The deck was large and imposing in itself. It ran the length of the entire back of the house, just like in front, but was at least ten feet deep. The wood under my feet was stained in a dark mahogany color. But the view is what was so breathtaking.

About fifty yards out was a large, round lake. The evening was clear, dusk starting to fade with only the dark purple hues left on the horizon. I could see the reflection of the stars that were just starting to come out in the still lake.

Bordering the deck on all sides were gardens full of hydrangeas in every color imaginable. Blues, pinks, greens, whites and lavenders all mixed together to emulate the sense of a rainbow.

The lattice work connecting the railing to the ground was covered in white jasmine, putting off an amazing scent that seemed to swirl around me through the air, wrapping me in its embrace like that of a lover.

Don't think about lovers, Brinley!

In the right corner was a large stainless gas grill complete with a set of bar-b-que tools hanging from pegs in the front. Off to the left of the deck was a bistro set, again made of the same rustic wrought iron material that I saw in the house. On the table were two china place settings, two crystal wine glasses and a bottle of red wine.

All the surroundings mixed together made the atmosphere soothing and gentle. And very sweet.

I stood still and closed my eyes, breathing in all the wonderful smells. Listening to all the crickets chirping, just waking up

after a day-long sleep. And the birds singing their last songs before settling down for the night.

While I stood there trying to take it all in, I heard the scream followed by the sound of the car rolling and crashing onto the rocks.

I opened my eyes, gasping for air, praying Jaxson didn't come out and see my brief lapse of sanity. I told myself it was only a little daydream and that it was meant as my reminder. Don't get too close or comfortable; pain is just around the corner. Or over the edge of a very steep cliff. At least, that's the only reasoning that made sense in order to keep me in my own personal hell.

About the time I convinced myself that this might not be the best idea, Jaxson walked out carrying a platter of food. Lamb chops, roasted carrots and potatoes, French bread. The fair smelled wonderful and helped to ease my uncertainty a little.

He set the tray down on a side bar sitting catty-cornered to the bistro table and turned to face me as he pulled out my chair.

The look in his eyes was filled with a variety of emotions that made it hard to decipher. Curiosity, content, seduction.

And then he smiled that big gorgeous smile (I was beginning to look at it as my smile), waiting patiently, and I felt completely at ease. I walked over, never taking my eyes off of his, and sat down in the chair he was still holding out for me.

"Thank you. Not very often I come across a real gentleman these days." I smiled up at him with a look in my eyes that said I thought he was anything but.

He laughed and took his seat across from me, "Well, my parents taught me that respect and courtesy are two of the most important qualities a man can possess. I guess it just stuck with me."

I laughed along with him and asked, "So, what are the other qualities?"

"Ahh… plenty of time to talk about that later. First, we eat. May I?"

He was waiting to serve my food for me. I began to feel that maybe he actually was a gentleman, despite my somewhat misguided joke before, and not just trying to impress me.

"Yes, please." I told him, unable to help myself from grinning largely but still trying to remain cautious.

After I had a helping of everything on my plate I took a bite of the lamb and moaned a little; it was scrumptious. The potatoes and carrots were just as tasty, not too soft or too firm. Everything was cooked to perfection.

"So Jaxson, where did you learn to cook like this? Because this dinner, the lamb especially, is so delicious." As I watched, a small blush crept up his cheeks and I smiled at that. Not every day I get to make a man like Jaxson blush. Score one for Brinley!

"I guess I've always had a knack for it. When I was young, I loved to watch my Mother cook. It was a nice break from the ranching with my Dad. As I got older, my Mom and both of my grandmothers helped me expand my horizons." he paused, looking for the right words, "Further my culinary skills I guess you could say."

"Well, I'm sure it comes in handy whenever you are trying to amaze the ladies."

I said this hoping that I could get him to admit to some sort of ulterior motive, be it past or present. I would have an easier time denying myself the happiness he appeared to be bringing out in me if there was something, anything, to view as a flaw with this night.

His eyes, always so intense and scorching, seemed to glare through me forever before he finally spoke in response to my statement.

"I've actually never made dinner for a woman before. With the exception of the women in my family, of course. This isn't something I'm accustomed to, Brinley. I don't go around cooking dinner for just anyone. Or inviting anybody over to my home. I truly feel drawn to you. It's like you are the light I had been searching for to fill an ominous place in my life. Only I didn't even know I was in the dark."

I could feel all of those words he had just said wash over my body. I glanced down and saw goose bumps rising on my arms and instantly wrapped my arms around myself though I wasn't cold.

It was a knee-jerk reaction.

I sat there pondering what Jaxson had just told me. It sounded so significant and amazing but I knew deep down that I didn't deserve it. Not after what I did to Annie.

After what I considered an appropriate amount of time, I got the courage to look up and confront him. His face looked concerned, lips in a straight line, which meant his beautiful smile was gone for the time being. And his eyes were searching mine for a response. Unfortunately, I couldn't give him one. My burden was not his to bear so I decided to give him something other than the whole truth.

"Jaxson, I think you are an incredibly sweet man. You are nice, obviously a good cook, and seem to be so sure of yourself, which I really appreciate." His lips started to turn up at the corners of his mouth. My insides were jumping up and down because I got him to smile again.

"But, I'm not in a place in my life where this–" I waved my finger back and forth between the two of us, "–is something I have time for. I fly back to LA tomorrow. I have to get back to work. Surely you can understand that.

Especially since you run this place for a living. You know what it's like to have to do your job. And mine is in California."

We sat in quiet for several minutes. I carefully watched his face; searching for signs of anger, disappointment, anything!

But all he did, which I'm still not sure I understand, was widen his smile even more. His grin was so large that it went beyond the contour of his face. If I didn't know any better, I'd think he was happy, satisfied almost, even though I was shutting down his obvious invitation to something more between us. It all became so confusing to me.

Here I am, trying to let him down gently so that I can go on about my painful and ill-deserved life. And here he is, smiling at me, flashing that beautiful smile like he's just won the lottery.

I looked down at my plate and continued to pick at the delectable dinner he worked so hard to make, trying to appear cool and calm. Inside, I was a complete mixture of feelings fighting against each other. Part of me was dying to know what he was thinking while the other was hoping this night would end without any more revelations. I wanted to know if he had any response to what I had just told him, other than the condescending smile. Or if he was ready to call this whole experience quits.

I was beginning to think that the dinner would end in silence and that I would go home to my parents' house tonight feeling distraught and relieved at the same time. Distraught because deep down I knew I felt something for this man across the table from me. Relieved because I knew the solitude I was eternally destined for finally looked as if it was within reach. Always alone like the moon and the sun. Each the other's counterpart but never able to come together.

I looked out at the sky to the west to see the sun setting fully, taking its light away. Then I looked to the east and saw the moon coming up, bringing with it a softer light of its own but never able to shine as bright. Funny that I thought of the light and dark between the two just like Jaxson had with him and me.

I jumped when he finally spoke, bringing me out of my deliberations.

"I don't know what happened in your life to make your wall be so guarded." his deep voice was carefully spoken, causing my gaze to meet his, "But just so you know, I'm a really good listener. And I'm not going anywhere anytime soon. I have waited this long to find you. I don't mind biding my time until you figure our future on your own."

It took every bit of will power I had to not get up, throw my arms around that masculine body of his and kiss him until the sun came back up. His words were so sincere, so heartfelt, that I swore I could feel my meticulously placed barrier collapsing in the present tense.

I straightened in my chair, knowing I was not destined for this, whatever this was, but for solitude. With a touch of flippancy and false bravado, I countered, “My future is already set because of my past. And I’m sorry to inform you that it doesn’t include anything pleasant. I hate to feel like I’ve disappointed you…” I trailed off and realized that I was hoping to ease this conversation in a different direction. One that was less serious. Willing my tone to come across to him as more teasing, I gave him a roll of my eyes and shrug of my shoulders.

It didn’t work.

“I’ll wait… I’ll always wait…”

Chapter 9

"Wherefore seeing we also are compassed about with so great a cloud of witnesses, let us lay aside every weight, and the sin which doth so easily beset us, and let us run with patience the race that is set before us." Hebrews 12:1

September 21, 2013

After a very quick and sad goodbye to my parents at the airport in Houston, I boarded my flight and headed back to California Tuesday afternoon. It was late by the time I finally pulled my little powder blue Mercedes CLK into the drive but, oh, it had felt good to be back in my own home and in my own bed. To the place where my nightmares were free to run my life.

I have been trying desperately hard to keep him out of my mind for the last four days. To keep my thoughts focused on my work and my suffering, like they had been before I met Jaxson Mathews.

It wasn't working out so well.

I'll always wait... What was he thinking?!?

I spent all day Wednesday and Thursday immersed at various studios auditioning for three different movies, giving all the younger hopefuls an appreciative glance. Looking at the co-eds in their late teens and early twenties standing in a long line for hours only to steal a couple minutes of time with the directors brought back so many memories.

Annie and I would do that over and over only to be rejected just as much. God, it was brutal.

But they all looked carefree and happy. I envied them as I walked around the studio to different audition rooms, alone.

One of the auditions was a thriller, one was a drama and the third was a romantic comedy. I've done a few dramas before and felt comfortable in that department. The thriller was something still new to me but it just felt right being in that particular audition room. Rom-coms, though, had been my go to script in the past and I've been kicking myself for two days now for even contemplating that role. Romance was not something I needed to participate in.

Especially if I had any hope of keeping my mind occupied and free from wandering. Like to those chocolate eyes, that dazzling smile, those big arms, his broad chest.

Dammit, Brinley!!! Get a hold of yourself!

FOREVER HOME

Kicking myself in the butt again for going there, I decided I needed to do something, anything, to absorb my time. Since it was a Saturday I headed to the beach.

Loading up my oversized tote with all the normal necessities–blanket, sunscreen, sunglasses, phone, water and iPod–I made my way down the back steps. Walking about twenty yards down the beach so I wasn't right next to my home gave me a small sense of freedom. But it also kept that security blanket readily available if the anxiety chose to creep up on me.

I sprawled out belly down on my beach blanket, wearing a pair of black shorts and a dark green tank top. It was too windy and cool for a swimsuit and wearing more clothes made me miss the heat from Texas.

I watched the water glisten under the watchful eye of the sun, dancing and shimmering for the bright ball in the sky. A bank of puffy white clouds that looked like spread open cotton balls passed over, making the temperature drop about ten degrees and goose bumps rose on my arms.

Lost in my reverie about weather, I jumped at the sound of my phone ringing; I thought I had put in on vibrate.

I reached out to pick it up and the caller ID stopped my hand mid air. I was scared stiff at the idea of answering. Should I answer it? Or should I just let it go to voicemail? What is he calling for anyways?

Finally giving in to my curiosity, I sighed heavily and rolled onto my back. Using my arm to block the sun that was peeking out from behind the passing clouds, as if wanting in on the secret phone call, I hit the talk button.

"Hi, Jaxson. It's been ages. How have you been?" I hoped he took my sarcasm as playful and not callous. I wanted to tease him but not hurt him or worse, turn him away. Why that thought had my gut clenching I wasn't sure.

His booming laugh on the other end of the line put my mind at ease.

"I'm good Brinley. How are you?" His deep voice sent chills up my spine, even over the phone. It was obvious, even to me, that I missed that sound resonating in my ears. It hadn't yet been a week since I saw him. And, I barely knew the guy. I shouldn't be having these feelings of yearning for anyone, much less someone I hardly knew.

"I'm okay. Just soaking up some sun at the beach. What's going on?"

"Well–" his enthusiastic tone was infectious, "–I was just taking an early lunch and thought I'd give you a call. I missed your voice. And I wanted to see how your auditions went earlier this week."

"How did you__" I started to ask but he cut me off mid sentence.

"Your Mom told me about them."

I narrowed my eyes and made a mental note to scald my mother–the traitor–later.

"They went well I think. I'm hoping the thriller comes through. If there's a choice anyways. That was the one character that felt the most natural, so I would really enjoy the opportunity to play her part. But, if it doesn't work out then I'm hoping for the drama."

"You don't seem like the kind of woman who is scared easily. Why would you be so interested in a thriller?" he asked.

If only he knew, I thought to myself.

I put up a good front but have been terrified and fragile ever since the accident. It's that fear that has fueled me in these roles. It's what helped me to do well at them. Putting my own horrors to use in my work is a great coping mechanism.

It doesn't hurt any that I'm able to draw upon the visions from the accident and use them to feed my screams either.

Wait, Jaxson asked me about something. What was it again? Right, why I like thriller parts.

"Well, suffice it to say that I have some pretty suitable life experiences that help me in that department."

I started praying to myself that he wouldn't want any more details.

Pray? Again? That's twice now since I met him that praying has come to my mind. I've got to get control of my thoughts before I start believing God has my best interest at heart.

"Huh. I'd like to hear about them sometime. Maybe it will help to give me some insight on you."

"Maybe." I told him reluctantly, "I'll tell you the tales. Not today, but someday."

As I paused I was caught off guard by an image of us sitting here, with the California sand beneath our feet, baring my soul to Jaxson. It felt so real, like a premonition. Impossible. Taking a deep breath to shake it off, I went on.

"Is that all you needed? I'm still trying to recuperate from the trip last weekend and this sandy beach underneath me is calling my name for some zzz's."

He was quiet for a minute. So quiet that I thought he might have hung up which would have made things easier on me. But also made my heart shatter. Again. Then he finally broke the silence.

"Sorry, I was just picturing what you would look like on that beach. Your strawberry blond hair shining in the sun and your olive colored skin glistening next to the water. The sand hiding those pretty red toenails of yours. That's a sight I wouldn't mind taking in sometime."

I sucked in a breath at his words. I had no idea he had paid that much attention to what I looked like. The compliments he was so intent on giving me were making it exceedingly hard to push him away.

"Would you mind letting me know what happens with the casting?" He seemed oblivious to the fact that I was struggling with his words. "I'll be praying you get the part you want. Even if I don't understand it. Nevertheless, I'd just like to know how they turn out."

I hesitated at first, wondering why he was so interested in my work, but eventually answered yes.

"Sure. When I know, you'll know. Thanks for the thoughts and the call. And the prayers." *However undeserved they might be.* "It's very considerate of you and I really appreciate it."

"It was my pleasure, Brin. I look forward to hearing back from you." I could hear some yelling in the background followed by a loud crash and a lot of mooing cows. "Aw man!!! Can't you guys do anything right? Give me a sec. Yeah, I'll be right there!"

I had to set my phone away from my ear. I knew he wasn't talking to me but there was obviously something wrong.

"Umm… is everything okay over there?" Sheer awkwardness was evident in my tone but I asked because it felt like that was the proper thing to do.

"Yeah, it's fine. My ranch hands were herding some of the late season calves into a pen for branding. But the idiots forgot to open the gate so all the calves ran head first into the metal. Bent it up pretty bad. Listen, I've got to go take care of this. You'll call me though? When you get your results?" He was persistent, I'd give him that.

"Yes, Jax. I will call. Take care. I hope everything is okay there, with the calves and the gate I mean. I'll talk to you soon."

With that, we hung up.

The entire conversation was confusing. No, not just the conversation. My entire life since meeting Jaxson last weekend was exasperating to me. He was clearly interested in me enough to call about my auditions, and everything he had said to me was full of romantic meaning. Yet he wasn't pushing for anything to happen. What kind of man sweet talks a woman but doesn't try to get into her pants?

My mind went a million miles a minute trying to put together the puzzle that was Jaxson Mathews. I turned on my iPod to help drown out the sounds of my random thoughts. Nina Simone's *Exactly Like You* came on and it wasn't long before I was starting to drift off in the sand. Thinking to myself that this was exactly what I wanted and needed to relax.

Before I knew what was happening, I was dreaming again and I couldn't wake myself up to stop it.

I saw a car, flipped over and totaled–just like mine had been–only it wasn't *my* car, just some random person's sedan that I've never seen before. And then I saw Jaxson appear out of nowhere, on a buckskin horse no less. I yelled at him, begging for him to help Annie. He looked confused but rode to the passenger side, hopped off the horse and pulled her out of the car.

I breathed a sigh of relief as they started walking toward me. But then, when the two of them were about twenty yards from where I stood waiting, they stopped in the middle of the highway. They both looked past me, farther down the road with frightened expressions. I turned, followed their line of sight and gasped.

My car was heading straight for them. I saw myself in the driver's seat, eyes closed and head bobbing. I screamed at them to move, to get out of the way.

Except they just stood there, like their feet were nailed to the ground, waiting and watching my car head directly for them.

"Move!! Annie, Jaxson! Get out of the way!!"

I kept yelling and tried to run to them to push them out of the way or stop the car. Something. But my legs wouldn't budge. I was helpless. They were both going to die at my hands and there was nothing I could do to stop it. My car was just a few feet from them now.

"NO!!!"

I was still screaming when I sat up; sweating, gasping and embarrassed because I was on a public beach. There were a handful of teenagers off to my right who had stopped in the middle of their volleyball game, frowning at me like I was some sort of fanatical person. I glanced to my left and saw a mother with her hands on two small children, trying to get them to turn their heads and not gawk at me.

I quickly gathered my things and headed to my house, anxious to get out of eyesight from the alien stares I was getting. Rushing up the back steps, I breathed a sigh of relief when I went in and had shut the door behind me; safe and sound.

I rushed down the hall and cranked up the air conditioning to help ward off the heat emanating from my body. Both from the sun and the lingering effects of my nightmare.

I couldn't suppress the tears anymore. Sliding down the wall, I let my face fall into my hands as the sobs tore free. They came streaming down my face, without pause, like… well… like I had just seen my best friend die at my hands.

But not only that. This man who, up until a week ago, only existed in distant fairytales of mine. And he was being taken from me too.

I was so confused as I tried to wrap my head around what that all meant. Why would I be so hurt that he was gone? Why would he play such a vital role in my dream? I barely knew him. Here I thought I was succeeding at smothering my 'would-be' feelings for him by coming home. By staying away from him.

Apparently, my subconscious had other plans. At least that was all I could come up with for an explanation. When my tears had finally slowed down to a trickle, I stood up on shaky legs and made my way to the bathroom, stripping as I went. Hoping that a cold shower would numb the pain.

I was soaping up my hair with conditioner when I got the feeling that maybe I needed to tell Jaxson what happened. To clear my conscience. Maybe then he could understand my view on self punishment and why nothing could ever come between us. And I would be able to put this mess of lovely feelings I had for him behind me. I could go on with my lonely life and no longer feel bad about possibly disappointing someone. About disappointing him. Because really, that's what my whole problem amounted to.

I didn't want to disappoint Jaxson.

Knowing this conversation was not one meant for being held over the phone, I rinsed my hair and turned the shower off. All the while knowing that the real question was not *if* he wanted to see me, he had made it perfectly clear that he wanted to be a part of my life. But whether or not he would be willing to fly to LA to see me. I needed to do this on my turf or else I might lose my nerve.

I dried off, wrapped a towel around my head and a robe around my body. If it felt like I was adding barriers to make this phone call then so what. It's not like anyone was here to chew me out about it.

I sat down on the bed with my cell in hand and glanced at the clock. *Five o'clock... seven o'clock in Texas. He should be done working for the day.* I took a deep breath to try to gain some confidence and dialed his number.

"Hey!" He sounded so excited to hear from me even though we had just spoken earlier.

How was that even possible? To be so happy to hear from someone you were hardly acquainted with? It caught me a little off guard and I almost lost my courage right then, but pushed through.

"Two times in one day. I just might be the luckiest man alive."

"Hi Jaxson. Listen." I was trying not to sound too desperate and weak but my voice came out as a squeak. I cleared my throat, took another fortifying breath and tried again.

"I was thinking about our conversation earlier. I decided you were right, and that I do need to tell you about those life experiences I mentioned." Though they're really more like demons.

"Okay. I'd like to hear about them. I seem to have a weakness for wanting to find out more about you. I'm listening." I could hear a hint of delight in his voice as he waited for me to go on.

But there was also something else. Hesitancy, maybe. Or uncertainty, like he was afraid he might scare me from opening up.

"Actually, they aren't the type of stories I feel comfortable talking about over the phone. They're much more personal than that and really need to be explained in person. So you can fully grasp the importance of them. Why I feed off of them in my auditions, and why those feelings have taken over my life."

"Hmm. I see."

I swear I could hear his smug smile extend to the edge of his face. Because I had a feeling he knew where this conversation was going. And then I began to picture his smile, how it lights up his entire face like the sun peeking out from a sky of clouds.

I began to picture him in his home. What is he thinking right now? Is he sitting on a chair with his feet propped up and a beer in his hand? Or maybe he just got out of the shower and is only in a towel. His deep voice brought my wayward thoughts around before they could turn obscene.

"Are you thinking of coming to see me again? Because that just might make me not only the luckiest man, but the luckiest person alive. Having the chance to see you once more so soon." Damn. His excitement is going to make this harder than I thought.

"No, I'm… I'm not coming back to Texas just yet. So… um… instead, I was wondering… have you ever been to California?"

Chapter 10

"And in this confidence I was minded to come unto you before, that ye might have a second benefit." II Corinthians 1:15

September 28, 2013

I was disappointed when Jaxson told me he couldn't get to LA for a week. He said that coming out wouldn't be a problem but that he had to get some things lined out for his absence from the Burnt Aggie.

I understood that.

Still, sitting in the LAX pick up lane, I kept wondering about the disappointment I had felt.

Was it because I wanted to see him so badly and didn't want to wait that long? Or because that feeling was mixed with the fear of losing my determination to pour my heart out to him.

Questions rolled through my head as I waited and went over the time that had passed since our talk the weekend before.

The week had gone by fairly quickly since we last spoke, thank goodness.

I had gotten callbacks on two of the three auditions; the thriller and the romantic comedy. I turned down the second reading for the romantic comedy and went in for the last call on the thriller. The producers offered me the part after my reading and I graciously accepted. That alone has helped to keep my mind, and my heart, from going into Jaxson overdrive.

I'd spent the last two days reading the script and trying to get a feel for my new character. She wasn't too hard to simulate. A young woman in her twenties who watches her boyfriend get killed in front of her eyes. It was simply a matter of changing 'boyfriend' to 'best friend' and I was set. The tears and screams came easily in my practice reading. While I was about halfway through the script, Jaxson had called on Thursday night to give me his plane information.

I spent the whole day Friday getting my house cleaned and ready for his arrival.

A lot of celebrities like to hire a maid service to manage their house upkeep. And maybe a chef to handle all their meals. But I find cleaning to be an escape so I have always opted to do it myself. Add in the fact that I've never felt like a celebrity, and my Momma always taught me the joys of homemaking, and saying no to maid/chef service was a no-brainer.

Now here I sit, waiting somewhat patiently, for a man I've known for two weeks to show up. All so I can spend the next three days with him and spill my guts to him about my tainted past and now doomed future.

When I looked up and saw him walk out of the terminal, I was overcome by feelings of both apprehension and fulfillment. Seeing him again awakened an unfamiliar part of my heart, sending palpitations throughout my chest.

I hopped out of the driver's seat of my car and stood by the door, waiting for him to notice me. He looked a little out of place for a city like Los Angeles. Those snug wrangler jeans–that showed off his well shaped derriere–his typical plaid shirt with the pearl snaps, the cowboy hat that sat low on his face giving an aura of dangerous masculinity, his ostrich boots.

He looked like home to me.

When he glanced my way and caught sight of me, he gave a small wave and made a beeline for my parking spot.

"Hey you!"

His excitement was very clear as he folded his large frame into the passenger seat of my car after I sat back down. He looked like he was about to lean over to kiss me, maybe out of anticipation, but stopped short. I thanked God for that, though I'm not sure why. Not like God has done a whole lot for me lately. Regardless, I'm not sure I would have had the strength to stop Jaxson at just a kiss if he would have followed through.

"Hi. How was your flight?" I asked as I checked for traffic in my rearview mirror and pulled into the north bound lane.

"It was good. Coming in over all those high rises was pretty amazing. However, I think I could see the smog higher up than the clouds. It was so thick I thought there might have been a fire nearby or something. This older woman next to me on the plane said that was normal."

I glanced over at him and saw that he was smirking at me.

"I don't know how you breathe without some fresh southern air."

"You know," I told him sarcastically, "If you're just going to be dogging my town, you can hop right on another flight and head back to Lake Shores."

I hoped he recognized my kidding because I really didn't want him to leave. The thought of Jaxson actually hopping on another flight to head back to Texas was literally hurting my chest.

Do I really only have three days with him? Are three days going to be enough to let my skeletons out of the closet? I prayed it would be.

When he laughed, a big belly laugh that made his whole body shake, I knew that he understood I was only teasing.

Whew!

"So, hot head," he said to me with a hint of a mock smile playing on his lips, "What have you got planned for us this weekend?"

I loved the way he said *us*. It made me think about what it would be like if we were a package deal. But that was dangerous too. What if he didn't feel the same way about me after I laid my cards on the table? What if he believed Annie's death was my fault too? I mean, it was but I don't know how I'd handle it if he felt the same way.

"Well, tonight I'm taking you to dinner. Nothing fancy. Just a little bistro called Café Caprí. It's on the way back to my house and it has great pasta and wine. Tomorrow, I thought I would drive you up and down the fabulous California coast. I love Texas beaches, I grew up there. But the beaches here tend to have more sand than seaweed which is a plus on the West Coast side. And on Monday I was going to take you down to the studio, show you where I go to work. Unless there's something else you would rather do."

I immediately regretted my last statement. I was afraid he would take it the wrong way; take it the way most men would. Expecting me to 'put out' since I invited him all the way here. That's not what I had in mind.

Not that I haven't thought about it. I'm a typical, healthy red-blooded American woman and Jaxson was an incredibly good looking man.

But this was about clearing my conscience with him not getting busy in the bedroom.

"That all sounds great to me." He was so full of life and I never caught a sense of cynicism in his voice. Maybe he really was pleased to just be around me.

The thought gave me hope and I hung on to that as we made our way to dinner.

September 19, 2013

"Dinner was really great last night. I must admit that I was a little leery when you said you were taking me to eat at a patio restaurant. I thought it was just going to be a place with outdoor-only seating, not an actual patio built off a house. But I was pleasantly surprised. Especially since the weather was so nice. I'll give your town the point for lack of humidity."

We were driving down the PCH, the same road where I wrecked my car on that vital night. I was trying desperately to concentrate on what he was saying rather than a flipping car and dying woman.

"Hey Brin." Him saying my name in that shortened way, with his rich and sultry voice, broke my concentration.

"Are you okay? You seem to have your focus elsewhere and uh… I'm not sure how I feel about that while you're driving. You know, seeing as how there's a one hundred foot drop-off cliff to my immediate right." He smiled sheepishly, trying to lighten my mood I guessed but there was obvious nervousness in his eyes.

“Yeah I’m okay. It’s just that this is the road where my…. When my….” I couldn’t articulate the words and started hyperventilating.

I quickly pulled over to a park and ride and asked Jaxson if he would like to take a walk. I had to get out of the confined space. I’ve never been a victim of claustrophobia but that’s exactly what it felt like I was going through. Like the car was closing in around me and Jaxson was sitting on the outside looking in.

I knew it was now or never.

Please God, if you’re there, please don’t let me lose my nerve. I need to explain this to him; why I will be reprimanded for the rest of my life. Why we can never be more than friends, even if I do want more. Please let me get this out!

We had been driving all day so by the time we got out of my car and started walking along the seaside the sun was just beginning to set. The sky was beautiful. Not quite like a Texas sunset but still brilliant with shades of deep orange, like a tangerine with its peel spread out over the water, blanketing it for the evening.

The air was cool and the wind whipping in my face was like a slap to help me snap out of my panic. Watching the orange turn to a dull red and fade even further to a dark purple, I knew I had to simply start talking and pray that I would be able to get it all out. Time was wasting. With any luck, Jaxson would understand why our relationship can never be anything more than a friendship and not push for more.

I took a deep breath, in through the nose and out through the mouth. And another. And another, like a professional swimmer getting those last few precious stores of oxygen in before plunging into the watery depths of a pool.

"Do you remember last week when I told you about being more comfortable with thriller movie parts because of personal occurrences?" I asked him.

"I do. Then again, here you stand, living and breathing, so it must not be anything too frightening. Tell me, Brin. What is it that has you so scared?"

"Well, it all started about eleven months ago. My best friend, Annie, and I were at one of the more noteworthy movie premieres of the year. It wasn't one of mine but a lot of heavy hitters were there. Afterwards, we went to the cast party, the ones that are typical of Hollywood. I was really just not into the scene that night." *And hadn't been for a while,* I thought to myself.

"I was really exhausted before the night had even started. I should have stayed home. I know that. I just needed a break from all the going and blowing, you know? We, Annie and I, had both been doing really well in our careers and, because of that, I felt like it was time to start looking for something more than fame. I was waiting for God to bring around the one He wanted me to spend the rest of my life with.

"I probably could have avoided the entire night but Annie had a way of getting me, anyone for that matter, to do whatever she wanted. That was just Annie. No one could tell her 'no'. She mentioned my insistence at finding someone, which was my weakness. Gave me some crap line about how I'll never find someone if I don't go looking. So we went and stayed at the party for a while. Eventually, Annie saw how sleepy and sidetracked I was, so she came over to me and said we could go on home. I know she was only trying to be helpful but at the time I took it as her being obnoxious with this 'greater than thou' attitude and I lashed out at her for it.

"She had offered to drive because of my being so drained. I needed some time alone because I was mad at her. But it was obvious that she wasn't going to stay, even though I desperately wanted her to. I told her I was fine and we left in this stony silence. We were right up there." I pointed to the highway Jaxson and I had just been driving on.

It was full on dusk now, shadows creeping out from behind trees and rocks along the road like fingers grabbing on to the dark memories. The exact spot of the crash was illuminated by two street lights on either side of the pavement, flickering on for the night.

It was now I realized that we had stopped walking. Other beach patrons were gathering up their towels and ice chests, ready to head home for the night. Maybe for cook outs or to treat an unruly sunburn.

Jaxson was watching me very closely, those deep set eyes looking intently through me, hanging on my every word. I could feel tension coming from him because it was that tangible; like he wanted to reach out and hold me but he resisted so I resumed my story.

"I remember getting drowsy and telling Annie I needed her to help me stay awake. God, that sucked. I didn't want to ask her for anything but I had no choice.
After that there was a lot of blackness. When I woke up, I realized that someone was talking to me, trying to get my attention. It was a paramedic and he told me we had crashed. That we had flipped the car."

I was starting to get that all too familiar chest pain. I could feel myself fighting the tears that were stinging my eyes. My heart was beginning to race violently, fighting for a way out of my chest and I placed my hand over it as if that could keep it in.

Despite my erratic breathing, I had to go on; to finish the account.

"Annie died at the scene. She died at my hands because I was too stubborn to let her drive. Or maybe it was just because I went out at all. I don't know. The 'why' doesn't matter. What matters is that I killed my best friend!"

The tears no longer held themselves back. It was a free for all with them falling wildly like a rainforest waterfall. I was in full sob mode, shoulders shaking uncontrollably as I buried my face in my hands.

Jaxson didn't hold back any longer either.

I heard his booted feet in the sand as he walked toward me slowly, as if to not frighten me. When he wrapped his arms around my waist I leaned my face against his chest and held on to the front of his shirt for dear life. He didn't squeeze too tight yet he held me strong enough that I felt safe. It was like he was my own personal cage, protecting me from everything surrounding us. Including my terrible memories.

He reached up and stroked the back of my hair with his right hand while keeping his left on my lower back, slowly rubbing circles against my shirt covered skin. I could feel the power in his blue collar ranch hands. But he was so gentle with the movements that it was soothing instead of feeling forceful. As tall as he was, he had to bend his neck down to rest his chin on the top of my head. The gesture made me feel fully surrounded by his warmth and the tremors that were wracking my body began to subside.

"Shhh, it's ok. I'm so very sorry. I can definitely imagine what it was like to lose your best friend like that." I pulled back enough so that I could look up into those dark eyes of his but not so much that he loosened his grasp. I didn't want him to let go. Ever, I realized.

"So now do you understand?" I asked him with pleading eyes. "Now can you see why there could never be anything more between us than just friendship? Honestly, I'm not even sure if I deserve that. I need to be punished for what I did. And if God won't do it for me, then I have to do it myself. This is it. This is my future. Painful memories, suffering, isolation… all of it."

He stood there, jaw dropped open in disbelief, apparently taken aback by my confession to eternal torment. He slowly started to shake his head no and in a voice that left no room for argument said, "Brinley, it wasn't your fault. And you can't doubt your faith in God for not punishing you, or for bringing Annie to Him. He knew what He was doing that night, no matter how much we want to bicker about it. He obviously needed Annie with Him, to be a part of His legion. No one can blame you for what happened that night. That's why it was called an accident.

"And none of this means you should endure isolation forever. I am so very deeply sorry for what happened. But you are a strong, caring and beautiful woman who deserves to be happy as much as the next person. Just because you don't feel His presence does not mean He has been absent since the accident. God has been here with you every step of the way. And He will always be here with you, whether you want Him to be or not.

"You have to forgive yourself for what happened, for circumstances that were out of your control. You have to believe that God had a bigger purpose for Annie in Heaven than here on Earth. And He has a bigger purpose for you, too." I watched as he swallowed, his Adam's apple bobbing up and down with the action.

He carefully brought his hand to my face and wiped some of the tears away from my cheek with his thumb. With a look of wonder and a slight smile he continued to humble me with his words.

"I see that purpose. I've seen it since the night we met. You are so special. You need to have faith in that.
Trust in the Lord with all thine heart, and lean not unto thine own understanding. In all thy ways acknowledge Him and He shall direct thy paths."

I had been ready to argue everything he was saying. But in that moment, with Jaxson quoting one of the most inspirational bible verses from earlier in my life, the wind left my sails.

Proverbs 5:3-4 had always been the verse I turned to in times of skepticism, struggle and confusion. I felt the tenderness in his words and an immediate warmth washed all over me. My crying had stopped and my shoulders relaxed. I felt strangely at ease, at least about some of my problems.

I knew he was right about God having a larger plan for Annie. She always was worthy of so much more than what was offered to her here on earth. Even the amount of success she had wasn't enough, in my mind, for what was due to Annie and her gift. I didn't believe the part about my being special but that was another issue for another day.

I could feel understanding taking shape in my mind and heart. This anger I have toward God and myself starting to break free from my soul, like a moth breaking free from its cocoon. I understood that anger will never bring her back. And it's been making me miserable on top of everything so learning to forgive myself needed to become a priority. To try to be happy.

"Why is it that my entire family makes the same argument for almost a year and never makes a dent in my thick skull? But you, who I have known for all of fourteen days, can start to break down my barrier with only one discussion?" I asked him, honestly mystified with how the words from him could cut right through my wall. Not just cutting through but breaking it down with the force of an army tumbling over into enemy territory.

He smiled and there was a mix of emotions visible on his face. Approval, relief and a little bit of regret. He pulled me close into his chest again, cradling my head.

"You and I have a lot more in common than you know." He sighed. "Maybe the next time you come to Texas, I'll fill you in on *my* life experiences."

I stood there in the safety of his arms for several minutes, reveling in the feel of his hands continuing their soothing circles from earlier. I recalled something Jaxson had said before and finally broke the silence, warily seeking clarification.

"So, are you supposed to be a part of my 'bigger plan' that you said God has for me?"

He leaned back and gazed longingly into my eyes. I watched as those chocolate browns moved over every inch of my face–my nose, my cheeks, my mouth and back up to my eyes, determined.

It made my stomach flutter the way he looked at me with such intensity, obviously searching for the right words.

"I don't know." I felt my body cringe. He must have felt it too, and sensed my panic. He tightened his hold and quickly went on before my'flight or fight' had a chance to kick in. "But I do know that you are all of mine."

In that instant, with his words lingering in my head and over my heart, the cracks in my wall started to grow. With the least amount of pressure I knew the barricade to my heart could break open with this man. Just like a dam bursting with the force of a tidal wave, relentless in its effort to mold to dry land, Jaxson would be uncompromising of the opportunity to mold himself in my soul.

For the first time in a long time I welcomed the interference. Because with that interference I started to feel hopeful.

Chapter 11

"A man's heart deviseth his way: but the Lord directeth his steps." Proverbs 16:9

October 16, 2013

My nightmares have changed dramatically over the last six weeks.

I still woke this morning, as with every other morning, drenched with sweat and unable to breathe. But it wasn't the fear and remorse I always felt from losing Annie to death that set my heart to pounding.

No, now it was from her fading presence. It was not seeing her as clearly as I used to or being able to recognize my part in her death. She was still in these horrendous dreams of mine. Most of the time anyways.

Sometimes it was Jaxson who was suffering like that first one I had of him back in Lake Shores.

In my latest one, I had been walking along the beach hand in hand with Jaxson when I saw Annie in the distance. I ran to her. Desperate to catch her in my arms and hug her relentlessly. To tell her how much I missed her. But when I reached the spot on the beach where she had been standing, she was gone, nothing left except a pair of footprints being washed away by the tide. I spun in a circle and looked all around me but I couldn't find her anywhere.

Jaxson was there at my side in an instant, placing his work worn hands on my shoulders to still my movements and asking me what in the world I was doing. I told him about just seeing Annie. That he needed to help me find her. He stood there and looked at me with a dumbfounded expression, like I had grown a second head or maybe a third eye.

"Who?" he asked.

And then I woke up screaming for her, my gaze darting around the room for a glimpse of Annie. I closed my eyes and took some deep breaths, trying to calm my nerves.

It was just a dream… it was just a dream… I told myself over and over again.

Eventually I plopped back against the mattress with my head on my pillow, slowly coming back to reality. With my eyes still closed I tried to remember everything about the dream.

Happiness with Jaxson, shock at seeing Annie, panic at not finding her and Jaxson's loss for who she was. It all combined together to make me feel so, I don't know. So scared of losing Annie's memory.

And yet at the same time I felt so secure with my future. Anxious, yes, but in a good way. Because the anxiousness was mixed with excitement about seeing where Jaxson and I were headed.

For the first time in a long time I wanted to see what the future held.

Jaxson left two days after I told him about the accident that day on the beach. Getting that guilt and fear off my chest had been a balm to my heart. And his unwavering acceptance was just what my battered soul needed.

The rest of the visit had been both sweet and calming. I had originally planned on spending his last day here in LA at the studio, showing him my workplace. We never made it. Instead we sat around my house all day and talked. And talked. And talked for hours.

I told him about my life in California and how much of a struggle it was when Annie and I first came out here. He was holding his side laughing by the time I finished relaying all the horror stories of our various rat-infested, hole-in-the-wall living arrangements.

Filling him in on the different actors and actresses was fun, too. We made a game of him guessing who had the greater-than-thou attitude and who was genuinely down to earth. He did surprisingly well for a cowboy who isn't into much television and tended to stay outdoors.

When we switched the conversation back to him he told me more about growing up in North Carolina and working on ranches his whole life. About how he had always had the dream of owning his own place someday. Watching the animation on his face was fascinating.

But what I remember, more than anything, was him telling me about how he felt when he was on his horse.

. . . . .

September 20, 2013

"When I'm in the saddle, I'm able to handle the world like nothing can touch me. I can run my horse for what seems like forever just to feel free. Or I can sit there resting on him, watching the sun rise as a new day dawns, letting my mind get prepared for the tasks ahead. Or in the evening when the sun sets. That's one of my favorite times. I lean my arms on the horn of the saddle, watching the colors change from light to dark and let it all go. I can actually feel my worries disappear."

"It sounds like you really love your life." I whispered in response to his confession.

We were lying on a pallet on my living room floor, still dressed in pajamas. The sun was high in the sky, its rays leaking through the holes in the blinds to spotlight the beauty that was Jaxson. With the pillows scattered all around us we had both propped up on our elbows to make it easier to face each other. He watched me closely with heated eyes like he was waiting for something–some instinctual action maybe–to kick in.

Though whether it was for my benefit or his I didn't know.

"I love my job. But my life has always been missing something. I never knew what it was so I never really paid much attention to it. It was just a hole that I knew was there." He paused, searching for the right words.

"But when I met you, there was a warming in my chest and it happened so fast, like kindling when it goes up in flames. Somehow I knew deep down that you would be a challenge. I think it was probably because I could feel your torment in life. The grief was so obvious in your soul that it was almost visual. But I knew that you were the reason my life had been so empty before. It had to be. Because you were… no, that's not right. You *are* the one to fill that hole. You are the one to shut the door on my emptiness. The only one."

I was completely speechless. He was talking about the hole he had and it felt like he had taken the thoughts right out of my head.

I'm the one with all the emptiness…

Hearing Jaxson acknowledge impressions that so closely related to mine left me amazed. Sharing that kind of lonely depth with him brought out an emotionally intimate drive that was next to impossible to ignore. I wasn't supposed to feel this way, didn't deserve to feel this way.

But here I was feeling it anyway and I knew there was no stopping it.

Only enduring it.

And then he did it. He did the one thing that could possibly stand a chance at changing my entire view of my life. And the path it had taken since my best friend's death. With this one moment in time he changed my attitude from self-torture, morphing it into something much more self-gratifying.

He changed everything.

Slowly, almost at a crawling pace, he leaned in toward me, never taking his eyes off of mine. He paused just inches from my face. I could feel his warm breath on my lips. I could see the heat burning in his eyes. I could feel the strength in his hands as he tenderly reached up to stroke my cheeks.

I closed my eyes and could smell that invigorating sunshine essence associated with all things Jaxson, burning with excitement in my nose. I opened my eyes to find that he was watching my mouth.

Then he looked back up into my eyes, waiting for either rejection or permission. I was holding my breath, like I had a habit of doing when he was this close to me. When I forced my gaze from his mouth and into his eyes, they were locked onto me with a powerful emotion.

I licked my suddenly dry lips and ever so slightly nodded.

He took that as his cue. Keeping his hands in place on my face, he slowly lowered his head the last few inches and placed his lips on mine. Passionately but without any trace of urgency. Our lips moved together in perfect synchronization with the small pecks we placed on each other.

When I opened my mouth to take in a lungful of air, he lightly touched the tip of his tongue to mine. I felt the electricity burst through my veins like a lightning rod being struck with a fierce current.

My hands–in a move all on their own–wrapped around his neck to tangle in the strands of hair at his nape, holding on tight. He moved his hands from my face and placed them tenderly around my waist to pull me closer to him. When he began rubbing the small of my back with one hand and holding the back of my head with his other, my body melted into his.

Between the light strokes of his tongue against mine and the feel of his warm hand against my back, keeping me in place, I felt winded. Forced to come up for air again, I turned my face up and toward the ceiling, becoming transfixed by the way the blades moved on the fan above us.

He took the opportunity to move his mouth down to my neck. From the frantic beating pulse at the left of my throat to the identical one on the right, his lips moved across my skin. The touch of his tongue left a trail of warmth to run through my body, surging to a fever when he placed an open mouth kiss to the hollow of my throat.

When I could take no more of the sweet torture I pulled his head up so that my lips found his again. Our mouths molded together like two puzzle pieces being connected at last. He tilted his head sideways as our eager tongues took on a mating ritual as old as time, sliding in and out of each other's heat with no more effort than it took to breathe. That's how natural, and wonderful, it felt to be kissing Jaxson.

Our kiss–which could genuinely be called *the kiss of the century*–began to slow; not so much losing its momentum as it was just taking on a different manner. Less lusty desire and more passion. More intimate. Gone was the frenzied worship from a moment before. In its place was a slower, more reverent kiss, back to the small sipping of lips. I was relieved when he slowly pulled back to look into my eyes, afraid that I might not have been able to show the same restraint. Thank God he did.

"Brinley," he said with his deep voice in a sweet whisper, bringing his hands back to my face and leaning his forehead against mine, "I've made some mistakes in my life. With work, with women, family. Mistakes that I knew better than to make at the time but was either too young or stupid to care, maybe both. But I will not let you be one of them. I want to do this… us, I mean, right and with no regrets."

I sucked in a breath and knew, just knew, that was it. Those words were all it took for him to break down my wall entirely, crashing through my barrier like the storm surge from a hurricane. It took everything I had to not cry, from the guilt for Annie or the happiness with Jaxson.

Not trusting my voice, I smiled tentatively and nodded yes, hoping that Jaxson knew I was agreeing with his declaration.

The rest of the day, and that night, I laid there in his arms feeling blissful from the top of my head to the tips of my toes. Every now and then I would raise my face to look at him, almost like making sure that this wasn't a dream. He would smile and kiss me–my nose, my forehead, my cheeks, my lips–and then rest his head back on top of mine, stroking my back and arms softly.

When it came time for dinner, neither of us wanted to go out so we ordered a pizza and ate on my back deck where the salty air mixed with the smell of tomato sauce. We kept sneaking glances at each other like a couple of teenagers until we had finished the pizza and took our trash inside.

While I showered and changed into clean pajamas, Jaxson cleaned up from our al fresco dinner and straightened up the pallet. After showering himself we settled back down in our same spots, his arms protectively around me.

Reluctant as I was to close my eyes and miss a single second of my time with him, Jaxson's sure strokes on my hair and back, combined with the moonless night that allowed not a single fleck of light inside, lulled me into a deep sleep.

A sleep where, for the first time in almost a year, I felt content and safe.

When I dropped him at the airport the next morning, he kissed me one last time, intensity and yearning evident in the way he held me. He didn't tell me goodbye. He simply said that he would call me when he got in. He picked up his duffel bag from where it was resting on the ground next to his feet and stood tall, looking down at me. He grabbed my hand and lifted it to his mouth, kissing my palm gently. I got tingly again and had to suppress the shiver that threatened to run through my body at the touch of his lips against my skin.

"You know I'm going to marry you someday." It was a statement, not a question.

"I know," I whispered to him, smiling so greatly my cheeks were starting to hurt. With a look of satisfaction gleaming in his eyes, he turned and walked into the terminal.

. . . . .

I talk to Jaxson every night on the phone. I would call him when I got home from the set. He would call me while he brushed down his horse from the day of riding. We would talk into the wee hours of the morning, not caring that we were losing sleep and would be tired the next day. None of our conversations were ever about anything in particular, just the mundane things that made up who we were as people.

We shared our favorite foods (his was anything Italian), books, family, old flames. Although neither of us wanted to dwell too much on romantic history, figuring it would be better to let the past lie and not chance having jealousy rear its ugly head.

We never had a dead spot in our conversations and it was so refreshing. Especially because with each of our nightly talks, I felt closer to Jaxson than I had to anyone in my life. I felt that darkness and emptiness that had encased my heart fade more and more into the distance with each conversation.

Tonight, listening to the ringing on the other end, I thought about how valuable Jaxson has been in filling my loneliness. About how his talking with me has opened my mind up to embrace the world again, bit by bit.

A fleeting memory from my childhood church days flashed through my mind. Something about conversation and being content with what you have, from Hebrews maybe. Weird. I haven't thought about any bible verses since Annie died. Except for the one Jaxson quoted while he was in L.A. with me.

I shook off the past as he answered the phone. Just hearing Jaxson's deep voice on the other end of the line brought a smile to my face as I plopped down on my bed, leaning my back against the headboard. But even still, I was plagued about that dream and only half paying attention to our conversation. After telling me about his day he waited for me to respond with the events of mine. I guess he could tell I was somewhat distant (figuratively speaking since we were thousands of miles away from each other), despite my best efforts to cover it up.

"Are you going to tell me what's going on? I can hear the tension in your voice. I know something is bothering you."

I hesitated. I didn't want him to feel bad because of my issues. And I know he would. He always told me how much it had hurt him when he saw how heartbroken I was on that day at the beach. How seeing me cry had torn at his gut, making him want to slay any demons in my life just to see me shine.

But no matter how hard I tried, I couldn't keep anything from him. It was like he was my own personal diary, not including my journal to Annie. That one is special; no one knows about that except me and her. Telling him everything else though made me feel complete; like there was actually a reason for God bringing the two of us together after all.

Whoa! Who said anything about God having a hand in this? This was pure luck. But I'll still take it.

Sighing heavily, I finally gave in.

"Do you remember what tomorrow is?" He sat quietly on the other end, apparently trying to recall what the day meant. When I heard his sharp intake of breath, I knew he got it. "Tomorrow–" I held on tightly to the tears threatening my voice, "–is the one year anniversary of the day that I killed Annie."

"Hey now. You were doing so well on working to get past this. You know it wasn't your fault. You even told me last week you felt like maybe it was time to try to find a way to release some of that anger and guilt. I know this is a hard time, being the first anniversary, but you're going to make it through this. Tell me what I can do for you? To help you?" His voice was pleading.

Knowing I'd done exactly what I desperately wanted to avoid–made his heart ache right along with mine–kept me from trying to push him away and dodge his help.

I watched as my tears fell onto the comforter like fat raindrops and wiped at them with my hand.

"I don't know Jaxson. I felt like I *had* been doing better. Starting to at least try to move on. I don't know if all the anger was gone but I've been happier these last few weeks than I've been in a long time. It felt like it was fading and a lot of that is because of you. But being here in LA, alone, with this day tomorrow… it just makes me feel so depressed again. And the guilt trip I'm putting on myself is only making it worse. I know it's not logical, but there it is."

"Baby, its okay to be sad."

The endearment brought my head up and helped to stop the flow of tears. That's the first time Jaxson has ever called me anything other than my name. I liked it. A lot. And he didn't even seem to notice the difference in his words so I didn't interrupt him.

"It's okay to feel remorse to an extent. But it is not okay to blame yourself. And you are not alone. You have your parents and family, other friends… me. I will always be here for you. And God is always in your heart, especially when I can't be with you physically. You mean so much to *both* of us that you never have to fear being alone again." he said to me and it was heartening to hear.

"I think…" I hesitated, not sure what he would think of my idea. "Maybe I should come home for a while. To Texas, I mean. We finished shooting re-takes yesterday. The movie is in editing now so there's really nothing for me to do here but wait. And I really think that *you* are what I need if I'm going to make it through this day tomorrow in one piece."

When he fell silent I instantly wondered if maybe my suggestion was a mistake. Maybe he wasn't ready to see me again since our amazing weekend here. Maybe he needed more time to sort through these feelings I was sure he had about us because mine were in a whirlwind. But then I could hear the happiness as well as the eagerness in his voice.

"It's about time you come home and see me."

I sighed in relief. We stayed on the phone long enough for me to book a red eye flight. I didn't care that it would be after midnight when I got to Houston. I didn't want to be anywhere near L.A. for the seventeenth of October.

I had no problem renting car when I got in; but, Jaxson said he wanted to pick me up. When I argued that it would be too late he told me he didn't care what time my plane got in, he'd be there. He was obviously not taking no for an answer so I agreed.

I threw enough clothes into a carry-on bag to last several days and headed out the door to make it to LAX for my departure in less than two hours. Luckily the weather had cooperated in both cities; clear skies make for easier plane rides and less delays.

And now here I am, five hours after talking to Jaxson, walking out of the terminal at Houston Hobby Airport. I spotted him immediately; it wasn't really difficult to do since the pick-up lane was all but empty. He looked so majestic leaning against his big red truck with his cowboy hat just shading his face, so strapping. And so gorgeous.

I couldn't help myself when he stood up straight, took a couple steps in my direction, tipped his hat back and smiled.

I dropped my bag and ran straight into his open arms. He lifted me off the ground and spun me around in a move that was surely meant for a long lost love reunion. As he gently set me back down, he cradled my head in his large hands and whispered words in my ear that took my breath away.

"My beautiful baby. I feel so blessed to have you with me."

Chapter 12

"The Lord is nigh unto them that are of a broken heart; and saveth such as be of a contrite spirit."
Psalms 34:18

October 17, 2013

I stayed the night at Jaxson's house my first night back in Texas because it was so late when we drove into town.

Plus, my parents didn't even know I was here yet. Not wanting to face them today in case I lost it, and because I knew they would be overcome with worry, I decided to surprise them later. Probably tomorrow.

Jaxson had mentioned to me when I was here for dinner a few weeks ago that his home had four bedrooms. So when we got in he directed me down the hall to the room across from the spare bath, turning on lights as we went to bring the house out of darkness.

He casually mentioned, as he set my bag down on a stool at the foot of my bed, that his own room was at the other end of the hallway on the right in case I needed him for anything. Bending to quickly brush his lips across my cheek as he walked by, Jaxson bade me goodnight.

Stripping out of my travel clothes, I took a quick shower, brushed my teeth and collapsed into my 'own bed' thirty minutes after we got in. With the memory of Jaxson's soft lips on my face, I fell into a deep sleep.

It was late when I woke up; the sun was already very bright and shining through the window on the far side of the room, illuminating tiny dust particles drifting through the space. The clock on the night stand said it was twenty after eleven in the morning. Although I never slept in like this very often, it felt nice. And I was a little relieved that in doing so, almost half of this day–the day I had been dreading so much–was behind me.

Climbing out of bed, I took in my surroundings as I stretched. Beige carpet that was thick and soft cushioned my feet. Light honey-colored wood made up the matching headboard, footboard and dresser. There was a brushed nickel stool placed beside the dresser that also had a mirror resting on the surface. The room was clean, if a little sparse.

But then, it was a guestroom.

Grabbing my clothes for the day, I went straight to the bathroom. Despite taking a very quick shower before bed last night, my brain was fuzzy. I was hoping a nice long shower this morning would help clear the cobwebs from my mind. I took my time in the expansive stone shower, admiring the masonry talent it took to make the space so beautiful.

After rinsing the conditioner from my hair and giving my shoulders one last roll under the hot spray, I turned off the water and grabbed a bath sheet from the rack by the shower door. Wrapping the sheet around my body I blow dried my hair then got dressed in a pair of jeans and short-sleeved black cotton blouse.

I hung my towel back up on my way out of the bathroom and set my toiletry bag back in my room on top of my open suitcase. Finally ready for the day, I strolled into the kitchen, feeling famished, to find a note from Jaxson.

Brin- Had to go to work for a bit to get the guys lined out. Be back by two. Make yourself at home.
Always-Jax

Don't mind if I do Mr. Mathews, I murmured to myself. I rummaged through the pantry and the refrigerator looking for something to eat and decided on a ham and cheese sandwich.

Meandering through the house–sandwich in hand–I walked into the great room. I hadn't been able to really look at anything the last time I was here since we had spent the evening outside but saw that the room was overflowing with antiques.

From the vases on the entry table to an old tiffany lamp on the fireplace mantle. They were all beautiful.

A grandfather clock took precedence on the wall across from the front door and it especially caught my eye. The face was a faded cream color and the woodwork so intricate, so precise, that it looked to be done by hand. The brass accents along the face as well as the weights and pendulum were still shiny, even with the slight patina noticeable on the edges, likely where they had been touched by human hands. There was no way it was from this era.

I'm no expert but it definitely looked to be somewhere around a hundred years old.

Turning back to the living room, I saw that the two end tables were each draped with an off white lace doily. I couldn't tell if the color was originally off white, or if it had darkened from age. But judging by the age of the clock I would guess the latter.

There were two large, mocha leather chairs sitting opposite of a matching couch. A low glass coffee table with bull horns for legs stood separating them. I couldn't help the giggle that escaped my mouth looking at that table. *How did he find a table made with cow horns?* I wondered. Shaking my head, I turned yet again to inspect more of the space.

A large built-in bookcase to the right of the entryway took up an entire wall and was filled with hundreds of miscellaneous books and novels. I skimmed over a few–Huck Finn, Pride and Prejudice, The Great Gatsby–they were all first editions! I could spend all day curled up in one of the overstuffed chairs with these books and be in heaven. The entire scene was mesmerizing and I was only in the living room.

I finished my sandwich and made my way back to the kitchen to clean up. After putting the dishes in the washer and putting the meat and cheese back in the fridge, I decided to check out the bedrooms.

Well, really just one bedroom I admitted to myself… *out of simple curiosity.*

I walked into the master suite and was unable to move my feet past the threshold. Whether it was because of the sight of the stunning bedroom or the feeling of being an intruder, I didn't know.

In the far corner of the room, right next to a wall of windows, was an enormous four poster bed made of dark stained wood. The sheets were simple white with a lightweight white down comforter folded down and a plethora of pillows against the headboard. It sat up so high that the posters almost touched the ten foot ceiling. There was a large bench seat at the foot of the bed.

I'd have to use that just to get up there. What the hell?! No one said anything about you getting up there Brin. Turn away from the bed and calm the hormones!

On the perpendicular wall, next to another bank of windows, was a sitting area complete with a loveseat, table and chair with matching ottoman. It was trimmed with the same dark wood as the bed and made with red and white plaid cushion coverings.

Very country.

The windows faced the east and I could still see the sun's rays peaking through at the top of the window pane, a last ditch effort to light the room before disappearing over the roof.

The black and white cow skin rug in the center of the room was large enough to pose as a king size comforter.

Must have been from a bull... I thought.

Breaking me from my ogling, Jaxson's hand touched the small of my back. I jumped; startled because it was only one o'clock and I hadn't expected to see him for another hour or so. I blushed, very nervous and feeling somewhat ashamed for being in here, like I was invading his privacy.

"I'm sorry. I didn't mean to shock you." His deep voice instantly soothed my racing heart while the hand at my back started a new set of feelings tearing through my body. "I wanted to get back here as soon as possible. I didn't want you to be alone today, and I hated having to leave in the first place. Once I knew that my foreman, Blake, and the rest of the crew had their jobs lined out for the day, I headed home."

He leaned over and kissed my forehead, placing his free hand on the side of my cheek. It felt so comfortable to be held in his strong, masculine arms like this.

"Sorry for snooping but I was just admiring your place. All those first edition books in the great room are really something. And that clock. Oh my Gosh! They are all so incredible. How did you come across all those antiques?" I asked him without moving. I didn't want him to move his hand, either of them, or his lips that were still resting on my forehead, lightly placing tender kisses across my flesh.

He chuckled at my innocent curiosity, not seeming to be bothered by my nosiness in the least.

"This rug–" he turned me halfway around to face his room again, dropping the hand holding my cheek to point to the huge cow skin, "–was one of my prized bulls back in North Carolina. When he got too old to breed and I had to put him down, I kept his hide cause he was such a good looking animal."

I knew it was a bull. I applauded myself on my earlier assumption.

"Most of the furniture I got from an old antique store over in Brazoria. Hidden Treasures was the name I think. Anyway, right after I moved here my foreman told me about the place so I hit them up for furnishings."

He still hadn't said anything about the clock or the books.

Should I ask him for details again? Should I drop the subject? After a few seconds of being torn between the two uncertainties, I decided to ask him.

"What about the clock? And all those books?" I asked looking up at his handsome face that was shadowed by the cowboy hat he was always wearing.

"The clock was a gift from my mother. She and my Dad had gotten it as a wedding present from her grandparents, and she decided to pass it down to me. I was the only one who ever really enjoyed it, the ringing of it. When I was a kid, I could sit forever just waiting for the chime every hour. And…. the books…"

I could see the pain in his face as his eyes became hooded and his mouth tightened into a thin line. For whatever reason, the books were painful for him to talk about.

"The books were all given to me by my father, before he passed away. He and I both had the same love for reading. He put it in his will that they all come to me." His voice was strained, his brow furrowed.

Sensing how troublesome this was for Jaxson, I pulled him over to the sitting area and made him sit on the loveseat. Conveniently, he took up most of it himself so I crawled into his lap.

I removed his hat and set it on the chair next to me, stroking the hair at the back of his head with one hand and lightly brushing the five o'clock shadow that was already showing up on his face. I stared into his beautiful, dark eyes, looking for an opportunity to pose the question that had been hanging in the air.

"What happened to him, Jaxson? Your Dad I mean."

He sat there for a few minutes, looking down at his hands that were wrapped around my waist. I could feel his grip tighten like he was instinctively trying to protect me. From what, though? When he finally met my gaze again, he spoke with a soft tone that had hushed his normally resonant and spellbinding voice.

"Do you remember when I came to see you in LA, and I told you we had more in common than you knew?" He waited for my answer. Unable to find my voice, I slowly nodded my head yes, willing him to go on. "Well, what I meant by that, was we both felt responsible for killing someone we loved. Someone who meant a great deal to us."

I felt my heart speed up, racing like a horse fresh out of the gate. I knew what this story, his story, was going to be about and it hurt to think it. It hurt to think that he had endured the same pain once upon a time that I've been suffering from for the last year. I didn't want that for him. Not Jaxson.

Almost as if the weather was mimicking the change in conversation, dark clouds passed over the sun, shrouding the room in a gray shadow.

"It was the summer of 2007 and I remember how hot it was. Not Texas hot, mind you, but hot for North Carolina, in the low nineties. My Dad and I had been riding the hills for most of the day. Checking on fences. Looking for some lost cattle. They tend to roam farther when their calves start to gain more strength, looking for fresh grass.

"We had heard on the news a few days prior about a hurricane watch being in effect. But with the sun as bright as it was and with the dry heat, we didn't put much weight on the warning. Thought it would probably dissipate before it reached land and, ultimately, us.

"For about the last hour or so that we were out my Dad had been talking of calling it a day; looking for the rest of the cows later. Said we should be going home and bunkering down. Just in case. But I was insistent on not letting him talk me out of finding the rest of the herd. I told him I'd be fine out there by myself and for him to go on in but he said that if I was staying, he was staying with me."

He closed his eyes briefly and swallowed hard, taking a few deep breaths before continuing.

"The wind picked up out of nowhere. I mean it went from a light breeze gently rustling the fescue grass to these violent gusts blowing seventy miles per hour and laying trees on their sides, all in a matter of minutes. That's when we knew that the weatherman was right–for a change–and that the storm was not only heading in but gaining force.

"And then the rain came. Not just a light drizzle, though. It was coming down in sheets so thick, so torrential that I could barely see ten feet in front of me. You know, that kind of rain that feels like needles pricking your skin over and over.

"I heard my Dad call to me, said it was time to head in. I told him we were almost done. I had spotted the last cow and her calf about forty yards away from us through a break in the sheeting rain. I asked him to ride on over with me so we could get them in the gates together quicker and then we would move on in to the house.

"He rode up ahead of me. Man, he was faster on a horse than anyone I had ever met. Anyway, he was waiting for me next to this big oak tree the two cows were sitting under, trying to take cover from the downpour."

Jaxson's breathing had sped up and his hands were flexing around my waist again. Bringing my hands up to run soft circles around his shoulders, I waited patiently, silently trying to give him the encouragement he needed to finish what he started.

"I saw the light in the sky before it hit. It was like I was watching it happen in super slow motion, one agonizing moment drawn out over an eternity. The entire thing took all of five seconds, maybe. One instant he was there–my Dad–sitting all nobly atop his horse. And then the lightening hit that massive oak. The power behind it was so strong that it sent my Dad flying off his mare."

He paused, eyes closed, no doubt envisioning the horrific scene in his head.

His brow was furrowed, lips turned down slightly at the corners of his mouth. It was obvious how painful this was for him to think about and I wanted to kiss his lips just to see them curve up into a smile again. When he opened his eyes to resume his story, I could see the glossy moisture covering his eyes and my heart ached for him. Taking a deep breath, he went on.

"And then the tree cracked and fell right where he lay, crushing him in the process. I raced my horse over to him as fast as possible, hopping out of the saddle before I even had the gelding at a stop. But by the time I reached him he was already dead. I did CPR for probably half an hour, maybe longer. I don't know. Finally I had to sit back from his lifeless body and accept the fact that he was gone. The autopsy report said that the weight of the tree had crushed his sternum, sending bone splinters directly into his heart. He died instantly.

"I blamed myself for his death. If I had just gone home when he asked me to then maybe that wouldn't have happened. He always had a sixth sense about the weather and I knew that. I should have listened. But I was too stubborn to give in. Too sure of myself and the task at hand. My own thick skull killed my father."

"Jaxson, it was a freak accident. That was nothing you had control over. You can't blame yourself for an act of…"

My eyes widened as I trailed off, realizing what was about to come out of my mouth.

"An act of God?" he finished my sentence with a knowing grin on his face. "I know that. But knowing it and accepting it are two different things. I blamed myself for a long time. That's why I left. Bought this place in the fall of 2009 and moved away. Everything–the ranch, the town, my mother–reminded me of my Dad. I saw him every time I turned around, like a ghost haunting my conscience. I know that's not realistic but there it is. I just had to leave, to exorcise myself of all that torture before it ate me alive.

"When I got here, to Texas, I was finally starting to forgive myself. But in that process, I became very angry with God. For taking my father when *I* should have been the one that tree fell on. For leaving me here to try to fill the shoes of a man with more worth in his little finger than I had in my whole body. My faith was incredibly weakened because of it."

Everything he was saying made sense, seemed so recognizable. I had blamed myself. I had blamed God. I had been so angry with Him that I stopped believing in His wonder, His favor, as well. Hell, I'm still angry half the time.

I realized too though that he was so much more at peace with his 'incident' than I was with mine. Granted, he's had over four more years under his belt, but still.

How did he come to grips with it all, I wondered? *And how can I get my mind and soul to the place where his is?*

"But now you have more faith than anyone I know. What happened to ultimately give you that kind of serenity? What helped you chase away your demons?"

I was desperately hoping to get some insight and maybe find an answer for myself.

"About a year after I moved here, I had a dream. It was so vivid I thought it might have actually been real. Huh… I can still hear the wind blowing the way it did in that dream and the way the buttercups smelled. I was standing on that hill, next to the big oak tree. My Dad was there, leaning against the tree with a very concerned–and very pissed–look on his face. He told me, 'Son, I'm only going to tell you this once so by God you'd better pay attention. My death was not your fault. It was God's work. He needs me here to help watch over my family, to help watch over you. There will be no more blaming God. There will be no more anger. There will be no more sulking around like a lost puppy dog without his owner. Understand?! Bring back your faith in Him and He will bring you to your future.' And then he was gone.

"I woke up feeling so confused but for the first time since he had died, I felt relieved. So I opened my bible and went straight to Psalm 91. *He shall call upon me and I will answer Him: I will be with Him in trouble; I will deliver Him and honour Him.*

"Ever since then, I knew in my heart that God had always been and will always be with me. Even when I was so angry at Him, He was there ready to welcome me back into his fold. Because that's what He does, Brin. We get the chance to make mistakes but we also get the chance to make them right. That's why I said for you to not doubt your faith. I've been where you are, alone and angry. But you're not alone. You never were. And if I've got anything to say about it, you never will be again. Honor Him and He will deliver you."

Jaxson was right. I hoped to be able to let go of all of my pain and anger the way he has. Maybe, just maybe, I'll get there with his help. As for God, well, there are some things that I'm not ready to face yet and having undying faith is one of them. With all this still playing in my head, Jaxson gently set me off of his lap and onto my feet, stood up in front of me and pulled me into his arms. He felt so good, strong. And his sunshine smell that I loved made me almost dizzy it was so rich and invigorating. He gently pulled my head back so that I was looking up and we were staring into each other's eyes, green to brown.

Like the change of energy in the room, the clouds that had been blocking out the sun shifted, allowing its rays to once again shimmer into the place where we stood.

He leaned down to my lips and lightly brushed them against mine once, twice, a third time. Slowly moving down the left side of my neck, with his tongue giving teasing licks along the way, he crossed his mouth over to the right and made his way back up again to my lips. When he landed there, his innocent and sweet kiss exploded into something so much more. His tongue delicately slid across my lower lip, seeking entrance.

I gave it to him willingly, opening my mouth up to his sweet invasion as our tongues danced together slowly, not thinking of anything beyond this moment.

There was a feel of longing in his kiss; like he needed to feel me close to him. Or maybe, that he just *needed* me, period. I was utterly breathless and unsteady on my feet. But I didn't want him to stop. I was on a cloud that floated above all the harsh reality that the earth held, and I knew I needed to be close to him, too.

When he finally pulled away, panting as heavily as I was, the passionate expression in his eyes made my heart skip a beat.

"Come on." he said after giving me one last peck on my now flushed cheek. "Let's go for a walk to the lake."

Hanging on to what he had told me about his past, I began to feel relieved and hopeful all at the same time since Jaxson was with me. Connected in a way more deep than any partners in a budding relationship had a right to feel.

No matter what happened with my nightmares, guilt, anger, any of it, one thing was certain. I would not let him go, could not. I knew he was the best part of me and I'd be a fool to let him slip through my fingers.

There was still an important question hanging in the balance and plaguing me, though. With him being at that calm place and me still struggling with my past, where do we go from here?

Chapter 13

"I saw in the visions of my head upon my bed, and, behold, a watcher and an holy one came down from heaven." Daniel 4:13

With my hand firmly held by Jaxson's as we made our way outside, I was able to push the insecurities about a future together to the back of my mind.

'Enjoy the here and now' became a mantra for me. Because of that persistence the rest of the day was absolutely surreal.

Jaxson walked me to that lake that I had only so briefly seen before at my brother's wedding. It was even larger than I had first guessed it to be that night. Probably about the size of two Olympic sized swimming pools put together. The water was clear and I was able to see the striped bass and shad swimming in small schools around the water's edge. Reflections on the top of the water shone like mirrors, the oak and pine trees bordering the bank also guarding us in the water.

We went for a long swim and I giggled at the feel of the fish nipping at my toes. When my laughing caused me to go under the surface, Jaxson wrapped his arms around me and pulled me back up. Being held by him in the cool water helped to alleviate some of the heat his body sent racing through my veins.

I was mesmerized by him. Fascinated by the way the water rolled off his chiseled-from-marble chest, I traced the drops and watched others fall down his bulging biceps and his corded neck. It reminded me of the way rain looked as it glided down a hard window, so smooth and sure in its downward path.

So beautiful. I could have stayed there in his arms forever.

Needless to say, I was a little dejected when he adamantly pulled me out of the water and onto the grass. But laying there on my belly with a cotton blanket beneath us, letting the warm sun dry our bodies, was just as wonderful as being in the lake.

Hmm… maybe it's because I'm with him.

The fleeting thought had me wondering if I would always feel like this with him, happy and safe from demons.

Here and now, Brinley. Focus on the here and now.

He had one hand protectively resting on my lower back–like he always did–and the other was tracing the contour of my palm, which lay open across his bare chest. Even though his hands were rough through years of ranch work, they felt so tender against my skin. The callused strokes left pinpoints of electricity in their wake. That fiery stream his touch sent through me was only intensified by the already warming sun kissing my skin.

As we lay there continuing to dry out Jaxson opened up more about his father and how close the two of them were. It was obviously not as hard for him to talk about his Dad as it was for me to discuss Annie.

I could hear the pride in his voice when he told me how his Dad had been a cowboy all his life; along with his grandfather; and his great-grandfather before that. Ranching ran deep in his blood and he said he had wanted to be a cowboy just like the other men in his family for as long as he could remember.

He complained that his Dad was always a firm man, which was sometimes hard to grow up with. But as Jaxson got older, he said he began to appreciate that firmness for what it really was. Laying the groundwork for a solid set of morals and values.

His parents had been together since high school, despite a brief break after graduation to 'sow some oats.' Jaxson said it was truly tough on his Mom when his Dad died. He said his Mom suffered tremendously; like half of her had gone missing that day on the hill.

I understand how she feels, I thought to myself.

His sister and two brothers still lived in North Carolina, so they kept an eye on their mother, made sure she realized that even with their father gone she still had a purpose here on Earth. Jaxson felt guilty about not going to see her more often but said that she always told him she understood why he had a hard time with it. She was planning a trip to Texas for a visit after the New Year with his sister, brothers and their families.

"I'd love for her to get to know you," Jaxson said.

"Don't you mean for her to *meet* me?" Having only ever seen her in his pictures, the confession confused me.

"Actually–" his mouth took on a shy smile, "–she saw you at Aaron's wedding. Ha! She called me a few days after she got home and asked about you. I told her what I knew, up to that point anyway, which wasn't much. She said to me, 'Jaxson, that's the woman you will spend the rest of your life with.' She told me she had a dream about our wedding. At first I thought she was just being a hopeful mother who wanted a new daughter-in-law. But now I'm starting to understand what she meant."

Jaxson had been staring up at the sky with his eyes closed, almost like he was embarrassed by his mother's forward thoughts. But when he turned his chocolate eyes on me, I saw his belief in the words.

"You're what I never knew I always wanted."

I was completely shocked by his admission, speechless. More so about what his Mom had said since I was getting used to his wistful declarations. She didn't know me from Adam and yet she thinks her son and I will be together. Forever. I didn't know whether to feel triumphant for capturing the approval of his mother or terrified. I think it was a little bit of both.

Jaxson must have noticed the change in my expression and mood. He reached up and laid the back of his hand lightly on my cheek, chuckling.

"Hey, don't get all freaked out on me now. This will happen in *our* time."

Oh damn! What does he mean 'this will happen'? And what does he mean 'our time'? I'm just now starting to realize I can care for this man, but marriage? Am I even remotely ready for something like that? No...no I don't think so.

I veered the subject back to his family, trying not to dwell too much on what he had just told me. "Why doesn't your Mom come to see you more often?"

"She doesn't fly and she has never been much of a driver. She's got really bad knees and the pedals prove to be too hard on her. Since my sister's still in high school, she has to wait for one, or both, of my brothers to bring her down. And since they're busy running the ranch eight months out of the year, and spending time with their kids the other four months, they just don't get down here much. Luckily Alise, my oldest brother's wife, was able to bring her down for Aaron's wedding. Since it was branding season up there, my brothers and the kids had to stay behind to work. But my Mom really wanted to be here for me since your brother is my best friend. Ali really helped her out by driving her down."

"Wait, rewind a second. She doesn't fly?"

Despite everything else he had told me just now, my mind latched on to that one statement and I couldn't keep the surprised squeal out of my question.

"No." he laughed, "She has a debilitating fear of flying. Wouldn't even fly when my father was still alive. It's okay though; she's happier in North Carolina. I talk to her a couple times every week and that works for us. We both know how much we love each other. We don't feel the need to push that in unnecessary trips."

Nodding in understanding, I recognized that same quality between me and my own parents. Even though they could still be smothering about my emotional well-being, I knew it came from love. And I appreciated the fact that they didn't push excessive visits, either.

Evening was coming up quickly, with the bright blue sky molding into a deep teal and the shadows from the descending sun lengthening.

Standing and shaking out the blanket, which Jaxson wrapped around me like a cocoon, we casually walked back to the house. Not being in any type of hurry or feeling a need to fill the silence with forced conversation made the moment relaxing and nice.

Once inside we both went and took a shower, he in the master and me in the spare. After seeing Jaxson covered in lake water, it was hard to keep my mind from straying to what he would look like under the hot spray. Rushing through my own bathing to ward off those thoughts, I quickly soaped, rinsed and dried.

Dressing in some clean jeans and a long sleeve t-shirt, I walked down the hallway loving not having to get 'dressed up' here like I so often did in LA, even for a quick grocery trip.

Jaxson was waiting for me in the kitchen wearing his customary outfit of wranglers and pearl snap shirt, sans boots. Standing barefoot at the counter, busying himself with food, made the scene seem so domestic, natural. I asked if I could help with anything but he refused.

"You know, I'm actually a really good cook. I wish you would let me fix you something sometime."

He smirked at me and said that sometime I could do just that, but not tonight. So he cooked me dinner again but this time a more 'manly' meal–his words–of steaks and baked potatoes, which we ate by the grill on the patio.

After we were thoroughly stuffed, and I had cleaned the kitchen (I insisted), Jaxson suggested a late night ride on his horses. I was incredibly excited because it had been years since I'd been on the back of a horse.

Even without the presence of all the twinkle lights from the wedding, the barn and the pasture beyond was beautiful.

I watched carefully as he brushed down his horse, the beautiful buckskin I'd seen before. Then he handed the brush to me so I could start on the blue roan mare that he said would be perfect for an out of practice rider. Sending a scowl his way, I got to work brushing her shiny coat with perfect precision.

Jaxson went into the tack room and came out with two sets of riding gear; saddle blankets, bridles and saddles. He set the blankets down on the horses' backs, followed with the saddles and hooked the bridles up last. Giving me the reins for Misty, the roan, he took the set for his buckskin, Lakota. Walking out of the barn we saw that there was enough light from the stars and full moon to leave the flashlights behind.

Jaxson gave me a leg up, adjusted my stirrups to fit the length of my long limbs, then walked over and mounted his own animal. I could clearly see his chiseled face as he looked at me expectantly. Giving him a nod of my head, we took off toward the pasture at an easy trot, riding in silence with nothing but the crickets and frogs by the lake giving us an orchestrated song.

After a half hour or so–time seemed to pass differently here so it could have easily been longer–he unexpectedly hopped off his horse. As I started to do the same, taking a cue from him, he waved his hand at me.

"No, no. Stay where you are." Then he pulled himself up on my horse, with an ease that would be envious to the stuntmen in Hollywood, and sat directly behind me. He pulled his buckskin gelding behind us, turned the horses around a hundred and eighty degrees and clicked at Misty to take off into a full sprint back the way we came.

My eyes closed unconsciously and I held my arms out wide (cliché as it is, it reminded me of that scene from Titanic), enjoying the speed and the freedom that came with it. The wind was blowing my hair right into his face and I heard his sharp intake of breath as his arm around me tensed for only a second before loosening again.

"You smell like jasmine." he whispered in my ear. "It could become very addicting to me."

I smiled at that, glad that I wasn't the only one who had to resist an almost uncontrollable urge to inhale whenever we were around each other. I could smell him for hours. Sweet sunshine.

I kept my eyes closed while we rode, reveling in the touch of him behind me. The way his arms automatically pulled me tighter into his chest, like he was protecting me again. The way my back seemed to mold perfectly against his chest. The feel of his breath, cool and even, right next to my cheek. I had to fight the impulse to turn around in the saddle and throw my arms around him, kissing him until we were both breathless. Instead, I just brought my arms down and linked my fingers with his, holding on tight while he guided us back.

Too quickly our ride had ended and Jaxson was halting the horses outside the barn doors. He dismounted and held his arms up for me. Swinging my leg over Misty's neck, I placed my hands on his shoulders and let him guide me back to the ground. He leaned in and kissed my lips gently before taking the reins and leading the horses to their stalls.

While he placed all the gear back in the tack room, I brushed the two animals down and filled up their feed buckets with a healthy dose of oats. It was almost midnight when we walked out of the barn. We made our way back to the house with the full moon directing us like a guiding light.

Once we were inside he stopped me, pulling my back into his chest again and resting his hands on my waist. Again it was like we were two puzzle pieces fitting together perfectly as I laid my head back on his shoulder. I could literally stay in this spot, in his hold, forever. My arms reached up behind me to hold his head in my hands. His breathing sped up as he brought his hands to lightly rub the under-side of my upper arms. He spun me around to face him in a move so fast, it felt like we could have been salsa dancing.

And then he kissed me, taking my breath away, again. It was a very slow and intimate kiss, a joining of our lips with no roughness or urgency behind it. Nothing but pure passion and it made my whole body feel giddy.

Have I ever been kissed with so much love and infatuation before?!?

No, not love. No one said anything about love. Caring. And tenderness. I couldn't bring to mind any past instances and that made this, the here and now with Jaxson, all the more invigorating.

He brought his hands up from the grasp he had on my hips and held my face as he slowed his kiss even more to a crawling speed. I savored the little nips his teeth gave my hypersensitive lips.

"You should get some sleep." he whispered in between biting kisses. "We've had quite a day, and you're supposed to go see your parents tomorrow. Would you like me to tuck you into bed?"

His question was perfectly innocent; no hidden meaning behind it whatsoever despite the heat lingering in his eyes. I sighed heavily in response, letting my forehead fall to his chest.

"Probably wouldn't be the greatest idea. My hormones are now in raging overdrive thanks to you."

"Okay then. Sleep sweet and I'll see you in the morning."

He chuckled as he kissed my forehead, spun me out of his hold in another dance-like move and strolled off to his room with a gait that seemed far too controlled for what we had just experienced.

I walked down to the opposite end of the hall, making a quick stop to brush my teeth along the way. I didn't feel exactly sleepy, but my body was exhausted. Changing into my pajamas, I laid down and replayed, in detail, the fantastic day I had spent with Jaxson.

Somewhere around our eating steak, my mind lost its battle to stay awake and I was dreaming.

October 18, 2013

I was riding the beautiful blue roan, Misty. Only I was alone, no Jaxson riding beside or behind me. But it was very peaceful in the pasture so I didn't mind. I was casually scanning my surroundings, taking in the beauty that is the Burnt Aggie Ranch.

I looked to my right and could see a big oak tree. Not just any oak, the one that Jaxson had described to me from his father's ranch in North Carolina. Odd that I'm seeing it here in Texas, in my dreams. There was a part of my conscience that was trying to tell me the presence of the tree was supposed to mean something.

Then again, maybe I'm reading too much in to something that's probably just coincidental.

I felt myself blink–heavily–and then I was no longer in the pasture but on the PCH, coming up on the crash site. It was daylight with white, puffy clouds drifting over the cliff and down to the ocean like a waterfall; unusual because normally my dream happened at night like it had in real life. I was still riding the horse, not in my car or standing on the cliff like I usually was in these dreams. Strange that I'm able to see this as a dream and not let it hold power over my mind and heart like it typically does.

I pulled her to a stop as I approached the exact spot from the collision. When I dismounted and turned around, I saw Annie standing there with her arms crossed over her chest. She looked so beautiful. And so pissed!

I started to run to her, afraid she was going to disappear like she had in my other dreams. She put her hands up in front to stop me. I did but was confused as to why.

Why was she pissed? *Why* did she make that gesture? *Why* did I actually stop?

When she spoke, it was like hearing an angel–no pun intended–and it made me realize how much I truly missed being able to hear her voice. The records she'd made while she was alive had not done her justice. Her voice rang out like church bells on a Sunday morning.

"Do you know why I'm here Brinley?" she asked.

I was having a hard time finding my voice and all I could muster out was a garbled, "No, I don't."

"First of all, I'm here to rip into your hide because you have been making a mess of my best friend's life. *Your* life."

Whoa, she really is mad. I've never seen her yell at a fly, much less a human. She took a deep breath, calming herself.

"Secondly, I'm here to let you know that it's okay to be happy. I'm here to tell you that the accident was not your fault. I'm not upset with you so you shouldn't be upset with yourself. I'm happier than I have ever been! I had only been running through the motions on earth. But in Heaven, singing brings me more joy than I thought was possible."

It was overwhelming to hear what she was saying. It was even more difficult to try to understand it. Is Annie honestly telling me that dying was the best thing for her? Because that's exactly what it sounded like to me only in not so many words.

How could someone be happy to die?

"I've seen you with Jaxson, Brin. I've seen the warmth in your heart when you are around him. It wasn't a coincidence meeting him when you did, you know. This has all been part of God's way to show you how to love again. He's given you Jaxson as a way to re-enter the land of the living with more love than you ever had before. The tree, the big oak?"

The thought ran through my mind that there was no way she should have known about that.

"Seeing it and his father in his dream was Jaxson's way of letting go. And this–your dream and this highway and *me*–this is me showing you that it's time for you to let go. I'm not saying you have to forget me. In fact, I'd prefer that you didn't. But you have Jaxson in your life and he knows how to help. This is how you two are tied together; loss and love. So go and be happy and love. And please remember that I love you Brinley."

And then, like a mist being swept away with the wind, she was gone.

I woke up immediately and for the first time since Annie died, my heart was beating regularly; my breathing was unlabored and steady. I felt peaceful, calm with this knowledge that Annie was happy and wanted me to be happy too. Even though it was barely seven in the morning, I couldn't help my eagerness.

I ran into Jaxson's bedroom–after a quick stop to brush my teeth in the restroom–so I could tell him about the dream. The revelation!

I was expecting to find him still asleep, but he wasn't in his bed. I froze, looking frantically around the room and found him in his sitting area. He was in the chair, still wearing his pajama pants, with his bare feet resting on the ottoman and a newspaper sitting in his lap. A cup of coffee rested on the table next to him and he was gazing out the window at the dull red-orange sun starting to rise over the horizon.

My breath caught at the sight of him sitting there, outlined in the early morning colors of purple and a yellow similar to butternut squash, he was so handsome.

He turned when he heard me and smiled charmingly, causally got up from the chair and walked over to me. I kept my gaze focused on his face, not daring to look down at his bare chest and get side tracked from my reason for being here, in his room, this early in the morning. As he put his arms around my waist and lowered his face to mine, he spoke to me in his rich and ardent voice.

"Good morning beautiful."

Jaxson kissed me like it was the most natural thing in the world; him and me, first thing in the morning. I wrapped my arms around his neck and held on, feeling dizzy in his arms. For long moments we stood there in our embrace, not wanting to break contact. My arms around his neck, his arms holding me tightly to his chest. It was a memory I wanted to hold close to my heart for a long time.

The sun rising behind us, the scent of coffee floating through the air, the feel of being wrapped in Jaxson's warmth. I forgot about the dream and everything else in the world. It was only us.

Chapter 14

"If we confess our sins, he is faithful and just to forgive us our sins, and to cleanse us from all unrighteousness." I John 1:9

Jaxson walked me backwards until I felt the edge of the loveseat hit the backs of my knees. All the while still kissing me, he turned, sat and pulled me with him so that I was half-on, half-off his lap.

It was amazing how comfortable it felt to be here in his room, in his arms, when not so long ago I didn't feel worthy of this kind of connection.

I hadn't gotten around to telling him about my dream. The urgency wasn't there because it was just that, a dream and not a nightmare like those that usually plagued my sleeping hours.

We were too preoccupied with each other. And it was wonderful. I didn't want to do anything to interrupt this moment. My legs were intertwined with his and I couldn't help giggling at my first thought.

Thank goodness I shaved last night.

One of my hands was tangled up in the dark hair at the nape of his neck. The other desperately trying to find something to hold onto but finding only his bare, hard chest.

His hands were not as still, not as content to stay in one place. They were roaming all over my body; my back, my neck, my head, my hips. Strong and free in their movement, his hands reminded me of wild horses journeying wherever they felt compelled to go. The friction his wandering caused against my skin left fire trailing in its wake; lighting me up with pure excitement from the inside out.

His lips sealed tightly to my own. His tongue traced the contour of my neck every time he broke away. I knew he felt the pounding pulse there, brought on by his touch, and didn't care.

And then his hands–his dominating and protective hands–were lifting me so that I was sitting directly on top of him. With his arms around my waist he held me so tightly into him that our upper bodies touched, heart to heart. I couldn't tell whose heartbeat was whose.

The quiet moaning that escaped from my throat proved to me how intense this moment was. How is it possible to feel this intimately close to someone with only kissing?

I didn't know. And I didn't care. All I cared about was that I was here, with him.

After an immeasurable amount of time–one I didn't want to end any time soon–our kissing and petting finally slowed until we were barely moving. Trying to slow my breathing, I felt the light kisses he trailed along my jaw line, up to the lobe of my ear and across to my lips. When he pecked me one last time and leaned back against the loveseat, he smiled and it was full of pure male satisfaction.

"Good morning to you, too."

I returned his grin with a flustered and sheepish one of my own. Jaxson laughed so hard that my entire body, which was still perched atop of his, shook underneath him. But he didn't utter a word, just regarded me with eyes that were both deep and adoring; a reassuring expression that was full of awe.

I'm the one in awe, I thought to myself before remembering why I came bursting in here in the first place.

"I wake up this morning actually being able to breathe and come in here to tell you about my dream. And then you go and do that. Catching me completely off guard." I took a deep breath, still trying to get my oxygen level back to normal.

"So much for my first day, in a year mind you, of waking up not breathless."

"I'm sorry. I guess I got a little carried away when I saw you run in here, all sleep rumpled and sexy." he said as he kissed my neck, stroking his fingers along my cheek. "Would you like to tell me about the dream now?"

"Hmm." I thought about it, regarding him for a second. I was still surprised that my emotions were so calm and composed this morning. Definitely a far cry from where I'd been. "I think I might need to take a nice cool shower first. How about over breakfast?"

Again he laughed only with more enthusiasm. His whole body surrounding me quaked, completely reiterating my need for the shower.

"I think you need to consider one too." I pecked him once more as I hopped off his lap and practically danced down the hall and into the bathroom. "I'll meet you in the kitchen in about twenty minutes." I called back to him and softly closed the bathroom door behind me.

It took me almost the entire twenty minutes in the shower just to get my pulse back down to a normal rhythm. Once I was out and dried off, I wrapped the towel around my body and pulled my still damp hair up in a clip. After throwing on a white t-shirt and some cut-off blue jean shorts I quickly made my way to the kitchen.

Jaxson was already in there with a supply of food from the fridge on the counter next to him. His back was to me and he was standing barefoot by the stove in a tight pair of faded wranglers with no shirt on.

Could he be any more irresistible?

I tried really hard not to imagine an answer to that question, afraid that those errant thoughts would lead to a sequel of our antics from the bedroom. I really wanted him to hear about my dream which meant I needed to stay focused.

"Do you like your eggs sunny side up or over easy?"

He glanced over his shoulder at me, a particularly playful tone in his voice, smiling with gratification.

"Is there anything you can't cook?" I asked him before answering. "I like sunny side up as long as there's bacon to go with it."

"Of course there is bacon." he scoffed, almost shocked that I even suggested otherwise.

I watched him while he went to work on the bacon, placing the cooked pieces on a plate.

The muscles in his back flexed as he moved the cast iron skillet around with ease. His tan body sparkled like caramel from the sunlight that was drifting in through the windows.

My eyes were glued to him, mesmerized by the domestic tranquility of the moment.

After fixing the eggs and setting two each on separate dishes, he set our plates down at the breakfast bar across from each other with the plate of bacon in between. I shook myself out of gawking and grabbed the coffee pot to fill up our mugs that he had already laid out.

We ate in a comfortable silence for a minute before he finally brought up my earlier declaration.

"So what's the deal with your dream? Tell me what had you running into my room this morning like a bat out of hell."

He leaned over the bar so that he was merely inches from my face.

I could smell him, my sunshine.

"I saw Annie, which isn't anything new. But it was so different from all the other times. Before they were always nightmares; me trying to save her, me seeing the accident from the outside as it happened, me losing sight of her altogether. I was always reliving the pain. And I always woke up screaming, gasping for air with my heart about to beat out of my chest."

He nodded his head to show that he was still listening.

"Last night though, or early this morning depending on how you look at it I guess, it was… peaceful. I was riding your horse, the blue roan, in the pasture. I saw the tree you described to me; the big oak, the one with your father. Which was weird. I didn't understand what the significance of it was to me."

I paused to see how he would handle this bit of information. I was afraid it might bring up some painful memories from his own past.

But his face was indisputably at ease. He showed no signs of worry or pain. He was obviously more comfortable with his history than I was with mine.

So I went on to tell him about everything that happened, starting with the change of scenery. I told him about everything that Annie had said to me, as well as what she said about Jax.

"And when I woke up this morning, for the first time in a year, it felt like a massive weight had been lifted off my chest. My heart didn't hurt so much. My lungs didn't have that burning feeling of being underwater for too long, making it difficult to breathe. Everything inside me just felt quiet, the way a church is in the middle of the night when the world is resting. That's when I ran in to find you.

"Don't get me wrong. I still ache for Annie and her not being here. I still feel remorse because I had been driving the car. Or maybe it's just because of the fight we had. But, I don't feel mad at myself anymore. And I don't feel angry with God either. I think seeing her, how happy and healthy and vibrant she was, broke that grief up inside me. Without anything to hold onto, the pain just kind of disintegrated. And seeing how obedient she is made me come to grips with the fact that there's no blame to be placed.

"The accident wasn't about a life lost… it was about an angel gained."

He was grinning at me, his gorgeous smile stretching from ear to ear. It made my insides melt like butter in a sizzling pan knowing that I had inadvertently put that smile on his face.

"Okay." he said, "So what do you want to do now?"

"Huh… I think…"

This was the hard part. Knowing what I needed to do and actually doing it was going to be my ultimate test, like Abraham's test of sacrificing his son, Isaac.

"I want to go to church. I want to confess my sins–the anger, the guilt, the hate, all of it–and ask for God's forgiveness. I know, really know, that my lack of acceptance to God's will has been what's made me so miserable since Annie died. Maybe then I can really start to move forward without any qualms or regrets."

Jaxson had been studying me closely as I relayed what had happened when I slept and what my plans were now. His brow was slightly furrowed as he stood straight up. Leisurely, at a creeping speed, he walked around the bar, grasped both my hands in his and lifted me from my stool. He pulled me against his shirtless chest, wrapped his arms tightly around my waist and kissed me.

His lips were hard and insistent against mine but felt so reassuring at the same time. This one kiss, even without his tongue teasing me as I had come to expect, had so much force behind it. Like he was trying to convey with his mouth what he wasn't able to with words. This was the kind of kiss you see when a loved one goes off to war, never knowing when the two will meet again. The kind where two lovers are reunited after a year-long separation, anxious for their private reunion.

It was absolutely mind-blowing and made my knees buckle.

Had Jaxson not had such a strong hold on my body, I surely would have melted to the floor in a puddle of pleasured woman.

He tore his lips from mine and whispered in my ear, "Well in that case let's get you to the chapel." I giggled at the double entendre behind his statement. Jaxson unwrapped his arms from around me and headed off in the direction of his room, for clothes I hoped.

Before he made it out of the kitchen, he did something that sent a jolt through me. I didn't know whether to be annoyed or feel cherished. He slapped my rear end playfully. But what had me warring between my feelings was the fact that his hand fit perfectly. And my embarrassment over wanting it back there. *Strange.*

An hour later I was walking into my childhood church, St. Timothy's. Standing inside the chapel, just beyond the doors, brought so many memories forth to flood my mind, like a levy breaking under the pressure of a massive wave. Lock-ins, weddings, confirmation, funerals. Surprisingly none of the memories I pictured, even the funerals, brought up sorrow.

For the first time since Annie died, I felt at home in church again.

The warmth that radiated from the top of my head to the tips of my toes was a miraculous sensation. I hadn't felt the presence of the Lord in me that strongly since the day I was confirmed and the Bishop had laid his hands on my head. The affection from God was one that I had definitely missed.

I walked candidly up to the alter, admiring the myriad of colors gleaming on the tile floor from the stained glass window depicting the downward dove. Looking up from the ground, I knelt down directly in front of the vast cross hanging on the back wall.

Closing my eyes and bowing my head gave me a sense of comfort rather than the panic so common over the last year. Clutching my hands together and taking a deep, fortifying breath, I did something I hadn't done in a very long time.

I prayed.

Most Gracious Father… I come here today first in thanks. Thank You for the health and happiness of my loved ones. Thank You for my own health. Thank You for always being with me during this last year of self-loathing and misery, even when I didn't believe You were there. I would like to confess that I have sinned against You; in thought, word and deed. I did not believe in You when I should have. I did not believe in Your greater knowledge and plans. I didn't spread Your word like I should have. I am so very sorry and I humbly repent. I ask that You have mercy on me and forgive me. I ask that You continue to be with my family and friends. I ask that You continue to be with me. Help me to regain the strength–emotional, mental and spiritual–that I have let falter for far too long. And lastly Lord, I would like to give You an immense thanks for Jaxson. I know that his coming into my life was not by chance. I know that his presence is a gift from You. I ask that You continue to nurture our relationship and help us to guide it according to

Your will. All this I ask in Jesus' most precious name... Amen

I finished confessing and looked up at the cross hanging before me, watching the cathedral lights play with the shadows of the cross like a game of tag. The voice was so subdued, that I wasn't even sure if I was actually hearing it. And I could see the words before me but then again not. The words were just there. If I hadn't been paying close enough attention, the message that I was sure was from the Holy Spirit would have been missed.

Fear thou not; for I am with thee: be not dismayed; for I am thy God: I will strengthen thee; yea, I will help thee; yea, I will uphold thee with the right hand of my righteousness. Trust in the man I have sent to you and you shall find your happiness.

I was so taken back at first that I literally leaned away from the alter, afraid that I was hallucinating and needed an escape. I had never heard the voice of the Lord before.

And I knew, without a doubt, that the words given to me were from the Spirit.

I recognized the verse from Isaiah almost immediately. And the rest... well, it was exhilarating! I stood and rushed out of the church to the courtyard, watching my steps so as not to fall in my haste to get outside.

Jaxson was waiting for me by the small pond that my Daddy had helped build when I was in grade school. He looked up from the Oscars swimming around just as I got to him and practically knocked him down when I leapt into his arms. Of course he was so strong there's no way that would have happened. He swiftly lifted me and spun me around, burying his face in the side of my neck. His warm breath tickling the skin there felt fantastic. Mixed with the warmth from the sun on my upturned face, the feelings distracted me for a moment. At least until he set me down and took my face in between his warm hands.

"I take it you had a good conversation?" he asked me with a curious voice, his dark eyes soft and nervous as if he'd been worried about how everything would go.

I smiled outrageously at him, tears brimming my eyes but not falling over. I genuinely felt happy. In my heart, my spirit, my mind. It felt like everything that had been holding me down the last year was slowly fading, allowing the light to come take its place back in my life.

"I did." was my only manageable response before the tears of joy choked me up.

A small wind blew through the courtyard and it felt like arms reaching out to envelope us in a curtain of security. I reached up and held his face in my hands. Staring into his deep chocolate eyes I saw the same brilliant emotions mirror those that were currently overtaking me.

And then I kissed him, my heart filling up with happiness at the touch of our lips and I felt the rest of my angst melt away.

Chapter 15

"And Mizpah; for he said, The Lord watch between me and thee, when we are absent from one another." Genesis 31:49

November 22, 2013

Whoever came up with the phrase '*absence makes the heart grow fonder*' must have been smoking something illegal. Since coming back to California from my all too short of a trip with Jaxson, my heart has been aching. I missed him terribly, despite talking to him every day on the phone. Usually multiple times a day, in fact. And all it does when we hang up is make my heart feel that much emptier. Hearing his voice and yet not being with him in the flesh makes my life feel less fulfilling.

It's strange how quickly my soul adjusted to having Jaxson in my life and how now I want to be with him always. Ending my phone conversations with him every day makes me remember the amazing time we spent together only a month ago. I replay the memories from our time together constantly, hoping they will beat down the doubt that tries to bubble up in his absence.

. . . . .

October 19, 2013

After my soul cleansing confession, Jaxson and I spent the rest of that day together. Alone. I needed to be with him, only him, to reflect on what God had shown me.

Once we made it back to his house we walked the short trek to the barn. After saddling the same two horses from the day before and leading them to the gate, we both mounted, aimed toward the pasture and rode. There was no talking, just the sun kissing our skin while the wind cooled us at the same time. Reflection. That's what the time meant. I never fully understood that before but now I get it.

We swam in the lake that rippled its protest at having us invade the stillness of the morning. We napped under the shade of one of the pine trees wrapped in each other's arms, listening to the woodpecker beat a tune on a perch high above us.

And we talked. Oh my, did we talk, more than any normal conversation should have allowed.

I explained some of what I had confessed to God without going into detail about his name being brought up. I guess I'm still trying to guard myself in case something goes wrong.

Jaxson listened, really listened. That, in and of itself, was a huge treat for me.

All my family ever wanted to do was tell me what I should be doing and how I should be going about it.

But Jaxson was letting me set my own pace for healing and being supportive in the process. I could only hope and pray that he would stay supportive. But more importantly I needed to try to remember to trust in the Lord. After a year without my connection to God it was definitely going to take some work.

When the light started to fade behind the horizon and the crickets began the evening ritual of waking up, we made our way back to the barn.

While Jaxson took care of the horses, I took care of a quick dinner. Once the frozen pizzas were done, we carried paper plates stacked high with pepperoni and supreme slices into the living room. Deciding to eat on the floor by the Austin stone fireplace had kept the atmosphere comfortable but romantic.

There was a front moving in so Jaxson lit a wood fire and we stared at the flames as we ate. They were licking up to the ceiling, looking for an escape from their confinement. I couldn't help but feel like those flames. Searching for a way out of the darkness that has enveloped me the last twelve months.

At his insistence, we decided to call it an early night. I watched him while he banked the fire then he stood and took my hand. Separating from Jaxson was easier than it had been the night before. After such an emotional day filled with spiritual breakthroughs, he knew how exhausted I was. Jaxson saw me to my door, gave me a chaste kiss goodnight and told me he'd see me in the morning.

I had stripped down to my t-shirt and fallen into bed. I hadn't cared about the blinds being open as the moonlight streamed bright and unhindered through the windows. I went straight to sleep.

Today he was taking me to my parents' house. I knew they would be upset if they were aware that I had been here for two and a half days without calling them. I decided to omit that detail when we pulled up in the driveway, bargaining with myself that I had not been in the right state of mind upon first arriving.

Funny that as soon as that thought passed through my mind, the sky darkened with gray clouds as though un-approving of my decision.

My mother must have heard Jaxson's truck since it's a Ford F350 diesel that makes a lot of noise. She came running out of the front door to grab me just as I hopped out of the passenger side. Her hug was warming and felt much more real than it had the last year. Maybe it was just that my heart was opening up again. Whatever the reason, my Momma's hug finally felt like home again and I was glad of it.

"Brinley!" There so much sparkle in her voice and eyes as she pulled back to look at me, "What are you doing here? Why didn't you tell me you were coming? This is so unexpected!"

"Well, we finished shooting the movie earlier than was originally planned. So while the producers are doing the final touches, I decided that I needed a break. I had Jaxson pick me up so I could surprise you."

I sighed to myself with a combination of relief and a little guilt. Everything I said was true. She never asked me when I got in and I prayed she wouldn't. I couldn't lie to my Mom.

But a lie by omission is still a lie, my conscience nagged at me yet again, just like the last time.

Resigning myself to tell her the whole truth once we were alone helped erase the guilt and focus on the here and now. As suddenly as they had appeared, the clouds vanished and the sun shone bright in the sky once more.

Signs from the Lord, I thought to myself.

She smiled so joyfully at me and grabbed my arm to link with hers.

"Come on, let's go inside. Your Daddy will be so thrilled." We walked up to the front door with Jaxson following close behind carrying my bag.

"I'll leave you three to visit." Jaxson said as he set my bag on the doorstep and turned to head back to his truck. My Mom caught his arm and scolded him, giving him her 'Don't you argue with me, son!' glare that booked no room for argument.

"Don't even think about running off, Jaxson. After all, you were in on this little surprise. So you had better come and join us. Are y'all hungry? I can whip us up some pancakes for breakfast."

"Yes ma'am, Mrs. Lambert. Thank you." I smiled my appreciation back at him as we followed my Mom into the house. He was respectful and sweet, the South having a big impact on manners.

It proved to be challenging for me to not run into his arms, kiss him for all I was worth and cradle him close to my heart.

This is neither the time nor the place, Brinley.

We spent the entire day at my parents' home. First a pancake breakfast as my Mother promised, then a light lunch of cold-cut sandwiches. Lunch was spent on the patio, listening to the dove as they swooped down to nibble at the bird seed Daddy methodically put out every morning. As the day progressed and the four of us carried on idle conversation, I kept wondering if Jaxson was really okay with being here or if he was simply humoring my mother.

But every time I looked at him, at his gorgeous face, he was smiling. Not a coy or shy smile that held secret meaning like he so often bestowed on me, but an authentic one. One that reached his eyes and showed his relaxation. It was what I had come to think of as *my smile.* He was genuinely enjoying himself. It made me feel fortunate to know that he was so secure around my family, just like I'd want him to be were we thinking of forever. What a turnaround my life has taken since meeting Jaxson.

My parents had insisted on taking us all out to dinner and we decided to go to Wilken's Café where we could relax and enjoy some delicious home cooking.

We walked into the quiet one-room restaurant where yellow votive candles lit the tables and white Christmas lights that hung from the crown molding lit the rest of the room.

Other townspeople smiled and waved as we made our way to an empty table. Some shaking my Daddy's and Jaxson's hands; others giving me or Mom a hug, saying how good it was to see me. It felt good to be seen.

None of us had to look at the menus wedged in between the candles and condiment holders. My Mom and I both had the toasted turkey-avocado-swiss subs with side Caesar salads. My Dad and Jaxson both went for the rack of ribs with roasted potatoes.

I couldn't help but to watch Jaxson as he ate. My Dad, being older and not giving a damn, was devouring his dinner. But Jaxson ate with such composure, carefully chewing each bite so as not to look like an animal.

When he finished his ribs and glanced across the table to see my studying gaze, he slowly licked his lower lip of the remaining barbeque sauce. He was doing it intentionally and I suddenly felt the urge to have those lips, and his tongue, dancing around with mine. It was very unnerving to have these thoughts while sitting in between my parents. But what choice did I have? He made me feel alive!

When the waitress came and set the check on the table, Jaxson snatched it up before my Dad could get his bearings. I giggled at the disgruntled look he got from my father and sat back to watch the battle of masculine wills take place.

"Please Mr. Lambert. Allow me?" Jaxson asked. "You've already fed me twice today. This is the least I can do."

Daddy seemed poised for an argument but then simply caved, much to mine and my mother's surprise. Despite the confusion on Momma's face, I knew exactly how Daddy felt; he apparently had as hard a time as me when it came to denying Jax.

After dinner, as we walked out into the chilled night and the parking lot full of cars and trucks that had been washed for the weekend, my mother asked if I was riding home with them. I told her Jaxson and I were going to take a walk and get some ice cream but that I'd have him bring me home in a little while. She seemed pleased with the plan–if her knowing grin was any indication–and gave us both a sweet kiss on the cheek before getting into the truck. Daddy hugged me with one arm around my shoulders while he shook Jax's hand and thanked him for dinner.

A quick wave at the door then he got in the driver side of his own shiny Ford and drove off. I turned to find Jaxson staring at me with an inquiring glint in his eye.

"What?" I asked timidly, pulling my lightweight barn coat a little tighter around my shoulders.

"Ice cream, huh?" he smirked, taking my hand as we walked along the sidewalk down Main Street. "I'm not sure I can watch you eat ice cream, especially of the cone variety. I'm trying very hard to be good with you. But ice cream might put me over the edge and make it too difficult to keep my promise to myself… and you."

His tone was teasing but with a seriousness ringing underneath.

"We don't have to eat ice cream. It just seemed like a harmless excuse to give my mother so that we could have a little more time alone. She's been very protective and wary over me since Annie died. I understand why. My depression lasted for so long."

He squeezed my hand tightly at the mention of my depression and I got the feeling he was trying to reveal some feelings of his own. Empathy, security, pity? I didn't know which was the cause and tried not to dwell on it. His reassurance by way of hand holding felt nice and I didn't want to tarnish it by getting upset over something as silly as pity.

We walked slowly in silence for a few minutes, looking into the windows of the barber and floral shops, the western boutique, the dollar store at the corner that sold a little of everything; a small town's version of Wal-Mart. We turned and started to head back to the Café when I stopped as I got my thoughts together about my mother.

"But–" I continued, "–what she doesn't know yet is that I don't feel that way right now. With you, I feel… free, relieved. Safe from harm, you know? I feel hopeful."

He stopped walking too and we stood in front of the Discount Dollar. He pulled me tightly into his arms, swaying back and forth to the beat of a silent song. He reached up and placed one hand on the back of my head, pulling me closer to his own. I was beginning to love this feeling.

That determination and dominance he showed in giving me comfort.

I thought he was going to kiss me but instead leaned down, brushing his warm breath across my ear as he whispered a sweet pledge.

"You will always be protected with me. I promise."

And *then* he kissed me with such need, such forcefulness that I knew he meant it. Like he thought he could push the truth into me by way of my lips. I knew in that moment that I would be his.

Only his.

I left Texas, miserably, two days later.

. . . . .

My mind was wandering at a rapid pace, replaying everything that happened on my last trip home. The photographer had to yell my name three times to get me out of my trance and I had to blink away the spots blurring my vision from the flash.

We were doing the photo shoot for the movie posters today; the last bit of business to attend to before the premiere next week. I just wanted to get the entire session over and done with. I finally had something other than work to look forward to and smiling at a camera was keeping me from it. Reiterating to myself that the fastest way to finish was to cooperate, I forced my smile to remain in place while the camera clicked, clicked, clicked away.

Four hours later I walked in the front door of my home, poured a glass of white wine and went onto the deck to call Jaxson, knowing he would be wondering how the shoot went.

"Hey, baby." He answered the call with affection, no doubt seeing that it was me on the caller ID.

"Hey you." I was quiet, abnormal compared to my usual demeanor.

He knew something was bothering me. Either from my lack of talking–which was rare–or the tone from the only two words I had uttered. Maybe both. But it definitely put him on alert.

"What's wrong, Brin? Did everything go okay today? Did something happen at the shoot?" His concern was evident in his voice and it made my heart soar, like a bird taking flight toward the sun, to know that it was for me.

I still didn't know how I deserved him, but I was learning to accept it more and more each day.

"No, no. The photo shoot went great once I got my head on straight. The producer and photographer both think we got some nice shots and that the poster will be amazing."

"Well then what is it baby?" he pleaded with me for an answer.

I loved when he used that endearment. It made butterflies tremble in my belly, spreading joy throughout my body. And the way he worried for me; no one has ever been so fearful for my well-being, aside from my parents of course. To some women it might be smothering but to me, someone who has been independent for so long, it made me feel cherished.

I watched the moonlight play over the ocean like an old time movie reel, debating on whether or not to tell him what was going on. Honesty won out; the time for hiding was over.

"It's just… ugh! This long distance crap is for the birds!" I blurted out angrily. He laughed wildly. I'm not sure if it was at me or at my outburst itself.

"If you're laughing at me–" I warned him, "–so help me I'm going to hang up on you right now, Jaxson!"

"Hey, hey now. I'm not laughing at you, baby." he said, his voice sobering and turning soothing. "I'm laughing because I feel the same way. I'm making the people of Lake Shores, not to mention my crew here at the ranch, crazy talking about missing you all the time. I hate not being with you. It makes me afraid of breaking my promise. About protecting you."

I could feel the tears threatening to surge over my eyes, my heart starting to ache. But this time it wasn't because I was sad. Well, maybe a little sad from missing him and not seeing him first thing in the morning. Our time together before I went to my parents' house had really spoiled me for his presence.

But, mainly, that ache was because this man truly cared for me.

For whatever reason, he wanted me and I definitely needed him. That wanting and needing made this distance that much harder to tolerate, though.

"You don't know how wonderful it makes me feel to hear you say that Jax." I took a sip of my wine, giving myself time to fight back the water works.

"Listen. Maybe, if it's okay with you, I can come over for another trip. Try to be there right after your premiere. When is it?" he asked.

I sighed with sweet relief when he made the suggestion, knowing I wouldn't be able to get back to Texas for a while. Too many interviews and other appearances scheduled.

I was so caught up in that relief that I didn't even register the fact that Jaxson already knew when my premiere was. We had talked about a few days before.

"It's six days from now, next Thursday. I know it's on Thanksgiving. The publicists are hoping that might bring out a good crowd. Typical entertainment personnel; they think no one has familial obligations. Anyway, I'm slated to be walking down the carpet for interviews at six and then the showing starts at nine. I should be home and ready for company by midnight."

"You're not going to the after party?" he questioned me.

"Nope. If you think you'll really make it that night then I'd rather come home and wait for you. But I'll probably leave the gown on. I don't want to waste all the hard work that goes into making me beautiful that night." I teased, sipping my wine and watching a couple stroll down the beach hand in hand while the stars guided them along.

"I've got news for you, Miss Brinley Lambert. You're at your most beautiful when you first wake up in the morning. And I speak from experience."

I blushed at the thought of the nights we had spent together. Thoughts of the things that had taken place between us that had nothing to do with his horses, the lake or cooking.

Or even sex.

We never did anything more than kiss and cuddle, with some petting thrown in on occasion, but always clothed.

And always so intimate and genuine.

When he didn't get a response to his statement, not that he really thought I would say anything as I'm sure shock value was his incentive, he told me he would call me the next day. Let me know his flight details. Reluctantly, I said I'd talk to him then and hung up the phone, watching as the tide pushed the waves onto the beach with force, wetting all the surrounding sand.

And couldn't help wishing I was watching the water ripples from the banks of a private lake at the Burnt Aggie.

November 27, 2013

Tomorrow is the day of my premiere. There are enough jittery nerves flowing through my body that it feels like I've been drinking coffee nonstop for a week. Or maybe waiting to ride a rollercoaster for two hours and the anticipation has me on edge. Funny that it's not about the movie at all but the excitement over seeing Jaxson after the showing.

At precisely five o'clock (seven in Lake Shores time), Jaxson called and dropped a bomb I was not prepared for. And had my anticipatory 'before the rollercoaster' feeling swiftly change to a sinking 'I'm going to be sick in the middle of the ride' feeling.

"Brinley… baby. I am so sorry, but it doesn't look like I'm going to be able to come see you after the premiere tomorrow." He turned as silent as I was, waiting for my reply. To say I was disappointed would be an extreme understatement. This distance between us has been brutal and now what had been my only hope for a break in the loneliness has fallen through.

"Is everything okay?" I cleared my throat, trying to get rid of the frog lodged there and to regain control without sounding too distraught. "I mean, no one is hurt or anything, right?"

"No baby, it's nothing like that. Everyone here is fine. There's just some professional business that I need to tend to. Plus, I couldn't get a seat on any of the flights arriving after seven tomorrow. I am planning on coming first thing Friday though. Maybe…" He sounded nervous and I knew I needed to get my crap together. Some things were beyond our control and I couldn't hold that against him. "Maybe you should go ahead and go to the after party. It could help keep your mind occupied, at least for a while, until I get there." He was quiet again and when he went on I could hear the pain in his voice.

"Please say something, Brin."

"I'm not upset with you, Jax. I'm just upset at the situation. Upset at the thought of having to wait for another day to go by before I can see you. I'll be okay though. I might go ahead and go to the party after all but I make no promises. We'll see how it goes." I was fighting back the tears and really didn't want him to feel guilty or responsible for them. I gave an excuse to get off the phone as quickly as possible, before Niagara Falls made an appearance with my eyes.

"Listen honey, I'm really tired so I'm going to go take a hot shower and head to bed. Call me tomorrow?" I asked.

"Sure thing, baby. I am so sorry, Brin. Try to get some rest and I'll call you tomorrow."

The soft click when he hung up was like the flipping of a switch to let the falls free. I looked out the windows at the back of my house and noticed the lightening. Then the rain came down so hard that it sounded like sledge hammers on my roof, trying to beat its way in. I cried myself to sleep.

November 28, 2013

I was sitting in a dressing room at the Beverly Hills Hotel. My hair was already finished, styled by the magnificent Raúl from the Rodeo Salon. I had opted for a simple and elegant French twist and he left a few ringlets framing my face.

My make-up artist, Isabel, was putting the finishing touches on my blush and lipstick. After she thoroughly scolded me for showing up with dark smudges under my eyes and red-rimmed eyelids, Isa had done her magic on me.

With shades of purples and mauves, she said it was to bring out my green eyes. The thought brought back memories of my first dinner date with Jaxson and made me miserable.

Don't think about it, I thought, not wanting to mess up the great effort that had gone into making me look beautiful tonight. So instead, I told myself that the colors were to match the plum and white sequined gown I would be wearing.

Not letting my daydreaming get the better of me throughout the 3 hour long session was difficult. When my mind did stray, I was reminded that Jaxson would not be here until tomorrow.

I can't cry! I can't cry! I told myself over and over again; hoping the mantra would take root in my psyche and work. At least he was still coming. And they say, 'Better late than never.' But really, who the hell is they and what do they know?

Breathe... Breathe.

Soon I was all dolled up and ready to go. I stood in front of a gilded mirror hanging on one wall to take in what the people would see. My strapless dress was fitted through the bust and waist. It fanned out at the knees to float over my four inch black stilettos. When I turned in circles, the dress looked like the seeds of a dandelion floating in the breeze.

My matching black clutch felt heavy in my hand, hanging down at my side with my lipstick and phone inside. The diamond studs in my ears winked at me in the chandelier light. The teardrop diamond necklace reminded me of the tears I shed last night and that I had a job to do today.

Forcing on a smile, I turned to walk away, determined to keep real teardrops from falling. The black Lincoln Town Car that was reserved for me for the night was waiting to pick me up at the valet station. With a small smile and a nod to the driver, he put the car in gear and drove me to the premiere.

The streets surrounding the theater were already filled to the brink with fans. Black and white limos and town cars lined up on the right side of the street and I flashed back to the night Annie died. Only this time I didn't feel disgust, just a need to get this over with and get home to wait for Jaxson.

When the usher opened my door and I stepped out, I was blinded momentarily by the onslaught of flashing cameras. Screams filled the air as I smiled and waved, regaining my sight before making my way down the carpet with the same usher who had opened my door right by my side.

At precisely six o'clock, the interviewers were allowed to start throwing their questions in my direction. I would stop every five feet or so to take a picture or answer another mundane query.

What's next on the agenda? Are you going to the party tonight? When are you going to bring a man around? Anymore gifts in the name of Annie Cross?

Most of them I ignored when I saw they were with the tabloids. When I was with my fourth interviewer, a young woman with kind hazel eyes and blond hair from US

Weekly, I glanced around at the crowd in answer to her question of *'Does fame ever get lonely?'* I was going to say something along the lines of *'How could I ever get lonely with all this support'* but stopped cold in the middle of my response. The reporter probably thought I was crazy the way my mouth hung open and my eyes bulged out. Or maybe that I was on drugs and hallucinating. I didn't care. I couldn't help myself.

On the other edge of the carpet, just *inside* the roped off area, was Jaxson! He was absolutely stunning in a plain black tux with matching bow tie. He held a black felt Stetson by the brim in his hands which were resting in front of his waist. I unabashedly looked him up and down, pausing only a second on the black caiman boots peeking out from under his dress pants. I was grinning at my cowboy's wardrobe when my eyes met his. He was watching me carefully.

When he smiled–*my* beautiful smile–and winked at me, I couldn't pretend to be engaged in the interview any longer.

I politely excused myself and ran in those four inch stiletto heels straight into his open arms. He lifted me from the ground and when he spun in a circle, my arms wrapped around his shoulders. He bent his head down and nuzzled his face into side of my neck, inhaling deeply like the scent of my perfume was the air he needed to breathe. My eyes were closed but I could still feel all the camera flashes going off around us, capturing the moment that had my world righting itself once again. Those pictures would probably be on the front page of every newspaper tomorrow.

Again, I didn't care. He was here.

When he set my feet back on the ground I tried to step back from him but he caught my face in his strong hands. The waning sun cast a glow around his head like that of an angel. His eyes glittered like chocolate diamonds. His grin was full of thrill and arrogance, like he had just given me the surprise of a lifetime. Of course he had, but he didn't need to look so smug about it.

He slowly leaned in and whispered in my ear, "You look absolutely beautiful, baby."

And he kissed me gently on my lips. At first. His kiss increased ever so slightly, in speed and passion, until his tongue was lightly caressing my own back and forth, in and out. I should have worried about the paparazzi, at least the unrespectable ones, and what they would do with something like this.

But he was the only thing on my mind right now. Which brought to the forefront the fact that I needed answers.

I broke free easily and asked him, "What are you doing here? I thought you had work?"

"No, I said there was some professional business to tend to. I never said *who's* professional business."

Again with that arrogant grin. Lucky for him it's also sexy.

"But how did you get here… on the carpet, I mean… past security?"

"Easy. I gave your Mom a buzz a couple weeks ago, asking her to help me set this up. She made a call to your agent, Tom Something-or-other, and gave him all the details of what I wanted done. He told your Mom he'd take care of everything and that all I had to do was show up."

"Wait… so you've had this planned since before my freak-out moment last week?" His smile was so conceited that I had my answer.

I knew we had already talked about when my premiere was.

But being here in his arms again, with my heart about to burst out of my chest, none of that mattered. Jaxson had taken everything I said about this distance between us being a problem to heart. And found a way to ease my blues, even if only for a short time. He shook his head in disbelief.

Did I say that last thought out loud? No, no I didn't but he obviously knew what I had been thinking.

Smiling he said, "Baby, you're not the only one who has been miserable about the distance between us. I just decided I needed to close it."

He kissed me on my forehead and turned, placing my arm inside the crook of his elbow. My eyes remained locked on his beautiful chocolate ones as Jaxson walked me down the rest of the aisle.

Chapter 16

"Owe no man any thing, but to love one another: for he that loveth another hath fulfilled the law."
Romans 13:9

November 30, 2013

"Brin-ley… baby… come on, time to get up," Jaxson whispered into my ear, trying to coax me out of my tranquil sleep.

I always slept more soundly when his arms were around me, despite the fact that our 'sleepovers' remained PG. I didn't want to let go of the amazing slumber this morning, so I fought his attempt. Hoping that if I kept my eyes closed and my body unmoving he'd think it was a losing battle.

"Hey, open your eyes baby." he whispered again adding soft and sweet kisses along my jaw and down to my neck. I resisted the urge to turn into his lips but then his tongue delicately touched the hollow of my neck. That did it. My eyes, unwilling though they were before, popped right open.

"Good morning. What's so important that you have to wake me up at–" I glanced at the clock on my nightstand and groaned. "–half past seven in the morning? Can't you just come back to bed?" I asked sleepily, trying to pull him back onto the mattress with me while stifling a yawn.

"I have a surprise day planned. So you need to get up and get ready. We need to be leaving in no more than forty-five minutes."

He stood up to escape my grabbing arms. His smooth voice was deep and full of persistence, leaving no room for argument. I recognized it as his ranch voice. The one he used with his ranch hands when they were giving him a hard time about following orders.

"How are you planning surprises for me in my town?" I asked with a mix of sarcasm, astonishment and drowsiness.

He grinned at me, rubbing my cheek with the back side of his hand, melting me inside and out with his dark chocolate eyes. He leaned in and kissed me sweetly on the lips before pulling back but keeping his face close to mine. He answered in a manner someone might use to explain right from wrong to a child.

"First of all, this isn't *your* town. You just reside here for the time being. And secondly, it's because I know how to make phone calls and get things done." His smile was both beautiful and cunning at the same time.

He stood up and walked to the windows, throwing open the curtains to let the bright California sun blind me with its intensity. On his way out the door, he slapped my butt.

"Now get up so we're not late."

Forty minutes later, Jaxson was driving us in my Mercedes down the coastal highway, the ocean stretching out to our right like a never-ending pool. I assumed we were headed to the beach and smiled to myself, recalling the last time we were there together.

My confession to him of my past, his comforting me with his embrace. His words. I felt giddy at the memory and silently thanked God for having him in my life.

I had given up on trying to get clues out of him. He said that his lips were sealed and I would have to wait patiently to see what he had planned. All he informed me of was that I needed to wear jeans and bring a light jacket. I put on a sad face but was really thrilled at the surprise. Jaxson taking charge like this opened up a place in my heart that had been vulnerable for so long.

Trust.

"There." he pointed over to the distance in the right, "Do you see where we're headed?"

I looked in the direction his hand was pointing, seeing nothing at first. But then, almost as if it appeared out of nowhere like those silver carp fish jumping up from a lake, I spotted the massive red, white and blue reverse tear-drop hot air balloon.

Blown up, fire blazing underneath with a large basket attached, it sat on the beach regally among all the scattered picnic tables and umbrellas.

My mouth plunged open and my heart started to race with anticipation. I turned to him quick enough to catch the wink of his right eye before he focused on the road and turnoff lingering just ahead.

"You set up a hot air balloon ride?" I asked, completely stunned and still unable to close my mouth. It's a wonder some bug didn't fly in.

I was bouncing up and down in my seat like one of the kids from Lake Shores getting ready to go on their first horse ride. He didn't look at me but I still saw his beautiful smile again. Grinning from ear to ear, obviously pleased with my reaction, he quickly shook his head yes.

He parked my car in between a Chevy truck and one of those smart cars in the park-n-ride we pulled into. Grabbing a bag off the backseat that he had packed this morning while I was getting ready, he quickly got out, obviously as excited as I was. After coming around the car to help me out, he locked the doors and took me by the hand.

As we walked along the sand and approached the balloon, he released my hand and put his arm around my waist instead, pulling me close to him. The move sent chills of desire down my spine that were hard to ignore. His arms–strong and tender–were always so welcoming and promising, making it easy to rest my head on his shoulder and really put my trust in his protection of me. It felt like I was walking straight into the pages of a fairytale. My fairytale.

Once we got to the balloon the pilot, who looked like a native Californian with dark tan skin and cropped bleach blond hair, shook Jaxson and my hands and introduced himself.

"Good morning! My name is Samuel Martin and I'll be flying you two around today. Are you ready to go?"

I instantly answered yes, jumping up and down. My sudden burst of excitement threw Jaxson into a fit of hysteria. He laughed loud and hard and hugged me into his chest as he caught his breath. He swayed me back and forth for a few minutes. Taking a deep breath and obviously more composed, he turned to the balloon pilot.

"Yes sir." he said to Samuel, always the gentleman. He tossed the bag into the gigantic basket.

And then, so swiftly I didn't even see it coming, he swung me up in his arms as if I weighed no more than a feather. Squeaking at the sudden move, I locked my arms around his neck just in time to catch his lips as they crushed down against mine.

The kiss was quick, hard and over before it had really began. The look in his eyes showed a struggle, like he was debating whether to follow through with the ride or take me back home.

Good manners won out and he placed me inside the basket. Sitting on the rail, he swung his legs up and over in the same action he used to mount his horses. We stood off to the side and watched the waves crash against the shore while Mr. Martin finished his last minute checks, making sure the propane tanks were full, the drop line and fire extinguisher were all in place.

After about twenty minutes of checks he turned and gave a thumbs up sign to four other men I hadn't noticed before. They were untying lines from stakes in the ground and another ten minutes later we were ready for 'take-off'.

"Hold on guys, here we go." Samuel said to us as he turned up the propane and the flame came to life, pushing the balloon higher and higher toward the sky.

Soon we were floating up above the sand, water and city; away from reality. This was the physical adaptation of the way I felt when Jaxson kissed me. And held me. And told me the most heartfelt things. Pretty much anything that happened when Jaxson was around made me feel as weightless as we were right now. This was my own personal dreamland.

We had been drifting between the ocean and the Pacific Coast Highway for what seemed like an eternity. In actuality, we had only been up here for about a half an hour. But it was so serene and relaxing that the time felt like it was flying too.

I imagined the rabbit from Alice in Wonderland and the way his pocket watch hands went round and round, time meaning nothing.

I was standing at the railing of the basket and Jaxson stood directly behind me. His arms were locked securely around my waist. His chin gently rested on my shoulder with his cheek just grazing mine and his beard that he neglected to shave this morning tickled me there. I leaned my head into his and caught a whiff of his amazing sunshine scent.

Impulsively, I lifted my right hand up to run my fingers through his dark hair that was blowing with the wind since he left the cowboy hat at home. He rivaled my ministrations by nibbling on my earlobe. I shivered as he kissed my neck and spun me around in an instant to face him, unable to stop my giggle at his rapid movement.

"It's so beautiful up here." I told him, hoping my gratitude showed in my eyes.

"Yeah, the view is amazing. But–" He looked out toward the ocean, squinting at the strengthening sun for just a second before bringing his gaze back to me, "–it's a dark day compared to you. You, Brin, are what makes this entire experience so incredible for me."

I blushed at his words, though I don't really know why; they weren't inappropriate. Maybe because no one ever said anything to me like he does.

Truthfully anyways.

Maybe because his words made the butterflies that were always present in my belly go into overdrive yet again. Maybe because I felt the same way.

This view, this ride–literally and figuratively–none of it would be worth anything if it weren't for Jaxson being here to share it with me.

Thank You Lord, I prayed silently, still amazed at how easy my prayers came out, looking for a way to the Lord's ears.

Another fifteen minutes later and we were coming up on lunchtime. The balloon was beginning to descend at a leisurely pace. I asked Jaxson if there was something else going on because we were nowhere close to the park-n-ride that held my car.

"The balloon ride was only part of the surprise." He quirked his eyebrows and beamed at me with his beautiful, calculating smile.

How many tricks do you have up your sleeve Jaxson Mathews?

I was mock glaring at him and knew that he saw right through my façade, but didn't push the issue. Our day had been splendid so far and I didn't want to take a chance on changing it.

Samuel decreased the flow of the propane and gently set the basket on the beach. The same four men who were at our take-off site were there to catch the ropes Samuel tossed to them. Jaxson released me from the embrace he'd held me in since we first took off from the beach. He hopped nimbly out of the basket to help the men settle the balloon on the ground and get the stakes in the sand.

When he came back to where I was, he reached inside and picked up the bag he brought with us, setting it on the beach at his feet. I still had no idea what was in it and my curiosity was really starting to get the best of me. I was dying to know its contents.

Jaxson lifted me from the basket, grabbed the bag and thanked Samuel and the other men for the ride. Then he steered me with his hand on my back toward a rocky alcove about forty yards away. I tried to lean around him and take the bag but he jerked his arm up and away at the last minute, making me fall flat on my butt in the sand.

I was laughing at myself because, honestly, it was funny. He stood with his feet on either side of my legs and leaned down so he was directly over me, blocking the sun so I could look at his face.

"Don't you be trying to ruin my surprise." He kissed me innocently on the tip of my nose as he grabbed my hand and lifted me back to my feet.

I crossed my heart and held up three fingers, promising with scout's honor that I wouldn't try any more funny business.

He insisted on holding both of my hands just in case so he slung the strap of the bag over his shoulder and walked behind me. Reaching in front to hold my hands in his much larger ones against my belly sent tingles spreading out to my body from that spot, like the roots of a tree spreading throughout the ground below.

As we came around the corner of the alcove, my breath got trapped in my throat at the other shocker waiting.

There was a large red and white plaid blanket that I recognized as the same design that's in his bedroom sitting area. It was laid out on the beach complete with candles around the border, my favorite flowers–yellow roses–and a bottle of white wine sitting in an ice bucket. It was a breathtaking sight and my heart swelled with gratitude for the man behind me.

I turned my upper body around and grinned ridiculously at Jaxson who was biting his lip. Maybe nervous that I wouldn't like it but more than likely to keep from laughing at me again.

He released his grip from behind me and we strolled over to the blanket hand in hand. He no longer needed to keep my hands restrained; I was too overcome with awe at the scene in front of us to worry about what was in his bag anymore.

We sat down on the blanket and Jaxson casually opened the duffel to remove the contents. He brought out different sized Tupperware containers, each containing an assortment of cheeses, crackers and fruit. After laying it all out neatly on the blanket next to the wine bucket, he reached over and pulled me into his arms.

"Are you happy with this?"

"Oh, Jaxson. More than I could ever express." I said to him.

For a while we just laid there cuddled together, watching the waves crash into the shore and the seagulls fly overhead, swooping down in a nosedive to snatch up the fish at the surface of the water. The sound of the rushing ocean and friendly squawk of the birds was therapeutic in itself. But having this amazing man beside me, cradling me like I was a piece of fine china, was the icing on the cake.

When he heard my stomach rumble, he reached across my waist and grabbed a bushel of red grapes from the fruit container. I was taken aback when he started to feed them to me; no one had ever fed me before.

But one by one I became more relaxed and decided to reciprocate, breaking a red morsel off its stem and placing it inside his waiting mouth. I followed the fruit with a soft kiss, enjoying the taste of sweet juice on his lips.

Never had anyone felt as pampered as I did in this moment.

I brought my hand to his face, gently rubbing the stubble on his cheek. It made my hand tickle. He closed his eyes at my touch and leaned into my hand. My whole body began to tickle in tune with the feeling in my hand, mingling energies like a bunch of power cords connected together. *He is so gorgeous,* I thought to myself.

I leaned in, taking advantage of his eyes still being closed, and whispered closely to his ear, "Thank you."

He opened his eyes to look at me and they were full of both passion and adoration. He sat upright and tenderly placed his hands on either side of my face. Studying me for only a moment, he brought his face close to mine and kissed me.

First my forehead, then my nose, followed by each of my cheeks. Sweet, barely there kisses that only teased at what lay hidden behind his restraint. He moved down my chin, across to the left side of my neck, slowly trailing a path to the right and finally, finally, back up to reach my lips. His movements were romantic in their rhythm and his lips were sensitive against my skin.

Shivers worked their way up my spine and down throughout my arms and legs. He must have mistaken my trembling for me being cold as he pulled his lips away and brought me into his chest.

"I'm not cold." I murmured into his neck. "You give me these shivers. You make me feel nervous with an eagerness that's hard to contain."

"I don't mean to make you feel nervous." he said softly against my head, placing his lips against my hair.

"It's not a bad feeling. It's a mind-blowing feeling. When your arms are around me, when you kiss me, I feel… well…" I swallowed hard, not knowing whether or not to continue. "For lack of a better word, I feel loved."

He pulled away slightly and I immediately regretted my choice of words.

Please don't let my poor articulation scare him away. It's not what I meant.

He studied my face with his chocolate eyes, searching. He stroked my cheek gracefully with his left hand and placed his right firmly on the small of my back, holding me close. His expression was that of both confusion and… longing? Sympathy? I just wasn't sure and I was awfully tense waiting for his reaction.

"Brinley." he quietly responded, "It's because you *are* loved." He waited, maybe to see if I would have any remarks. But when my brow furrowed in uncertainty and I shook my head, he went on.

"Baby. I love you. The truth is I've loved you since that night we met at the rehearsal. You… you're the love of my life."

Stunned into silence, I could only stare at him. The sound of the crashing waves faded until they were only a faint echo in my ears. The birds' squawking stopped. The sun dimmed, only briefly, from a bright canary yellow to a more subdued shade. All the elements around us paused, waiting just like the man in front of me for a response.

I care for Jaxson so much. He's helped me spiritually, emotionally and physically; making me remember what it feels like to be alive in mind, body and soul.

But, are my feelings love? Am I even capable of giving this kind of love? Can I actually love so soon after my own personal forgiveness?

I wasn't sure about any of it. The only thing I *had* been sure of was that I wanted Jaxson to be a part of my future.

Now I knew, though, that I had to find out my own truth.
Find out if this feeling is something I can reciprocate.
Not only for myself, but for him.

Chapter 17

"Be ye also patient; stablish your hearts: for the coming of the Lord draweth nigh." James 5:8

December 7, 2013

How long is the time frame for getting over shock and marching into avoidance? I wondered as I stared out the passenger car window at the passing buildings. Street lamps were flickering to life at the same time as the lights in windows of the high-rises went out. Men and women walked along the sidewalk; some going home from work, others on their way for a night out on the town.

All seeming to be in perfect harmony with their company and their surroundings while I struggled inside my head.

It's been a week since Jaxson told me those three words that have shifted my entire existence. I have gone from self-loathing to self-forgiveness to facing a future with this man in a matter of three months.

Is that even possible? Or am I avoiding? Is that why I haven't been able to respond to his 'I love you' in kind?

Jaxson was still here in California with me. He said he was going to stay until I kicked him out of my house. Like that was even a possibility.

The ranch was in its off season; all the cattle sold to be butchered, except for what the Burnt Aggie was keeping as stock for next year. He hasn't pressed me for a response to his confession and I was grateful for that. But I still feel the burden of knowing that he's told me he loves me and that I need to tell him something. It just feels heartless of me to not to.

For some unknown reason, though, I haven't been able to tell him that I love him back yet.

When he's with me it feels like the world, which had been crashing down around me, is now at a stand-still, the pause button of life pushed to wait for our next move. I feel alive, able to accomplish any obstacle that might be set in our way. Inside me there's a sense of complete satisfaction.

I feel whole.

But do I love him? Is that what this is for me too? I just didn't know.

We parked my car in an overnight garage by a large cement pillar on the first floor and walked several blocks until we were standing outside Las Países for dinner. I was hoping some Mexican food and margaritas might be just what we needed to relax. And to forget about the proverbial elephant in the room at least for a while.

I tried to keep the conversation easy going as we ate our cheese enchiladas and enjoyed the music from the Mariachi band. Sharing trés léches cake right before we left might not have been the wisest choice on my part. I don't know if it was Jaxson's feeding me, his taking a bite from the same fork, or a combination of both that had me so worked up, emotionally and physically.

But by the time we left, I was wound tighter than a cheap department store watch. I thought walking the five blocks to the garage where we had parked my car would give me some much needed time to cool down my overactive thoughts. But the night had chilled considerably while we were eating.

Jaxson's arm was draped protectively over my shoulders. The heat his body radiated was keeping me warm in the cool December night air. When a strong breeze plunged down on us from the north, his arm around me tightened, pulling me closer.

Unable to resist the urge, I lay my head on his shoulder and leaned up to snuggle my face into his neck. He smelled so wonderful, my sunshine. He felt so strong and secure, my knight.

He stopped walking and wrapped both of his arms around my waist, waiting patiently for me to look up at him.

When I drew my eyes up past his Adam's apple–I don't know why that part of him is so appealing to me–to his mouth and landed on his eyes it was to find him gazing intently at me.

My heart dropped to the pit of my stomach because I thought I knew what he was going to say. And I was still so unsure. How unfair was it for him to keep professing his love and me not reciprocating the words?

"Brinley, I need you to understand something." His voice was pleading, begging to be taken seriously. "I love you. I do and that's not going to change. But I don't want you to feel like you have to rush into saying something that you aren't comfortable with yet. I just need you to know that whatever you think might happen–with you taking your time to find your feelings, taking your time to express those feelings, whatever–I am not going anywhere. I told you in the beginning that I would always wait. I promised you that I would always protect you. My intention wasn't to scare you away with what I said, so please don't be frightened." He paused, taking a deep breath and giving his words a chance to sink in.

I noticed that he had reached up and was holding my face in his hands–*When did that happen?*–his own face only a few inches from mine. The look in his beautiful dark eyes was so demanding, like he was willing to do anything to make me understand, to make me believe him. But they were still soft as he stared into my own eyes.

"I just need you to know that I'm here for the long haul and I will *never* leave you. No matter how long it takes."

The words were barely out of his mouth before he pulled my lips to his own and kissed me with such power, with such passion, that I knew he meant every word. What my ears didn't want to hear, my soul gladly accepted with this version of a pact, one as old as the first couple on Earth.

One hand was on the small of my back, caressing through my thick cotton sweater but holding me in place. The feeling never failed to send quivers up my body. He held the back of my head with his other, keeping my mouth in place, his own latched on and not letting go.

He kissed me so deeply that it felt like we were giving each other our dying breath.

The butterflies again went crazy with my insides, banging against my belly and chest and searching for a way out to fly. The pull from him was so eager, almost maniacal. I wrapped my arms around his neck, no longer willing to hold anything back.

Running my fingers through his hair, down his cheeks to rest on his chest felt instinctive to me. It was so natural. Elemental in the most primitive ways sure; but, this went beyond anything just physical. I felt him in my head, my heart. I felt him in me.

We stood there, both needing the touch of each other and kissing for so long that we were both out of breath when I finally pulled away.

"Jaxson… I–" my words tried to get caught in the back of my throat, "–I care for you so much. More than I have about anyone before. You know that. But I do need you to be patient with me. You've had a lot of time to deal with your past 'beasts', such as they are. I'm just now starting figure out how to let go of all of mine. I'm still so unsure as to whether or not I'm even capable of love. Unsure as to whether or not I deserve to have the kind of love you've given me." He opened his mouth to speak but I quickly placed my finger over his lips. I was not done explaining myself and by God, I needed to get this out.

"No, I need to finish this. Please. My faith and my heart are so much stronger with you, *because* of you. But for twelve months I was completely shut off; a recluse perfectly content to stay crawled up in her spun web. I'd been going through the motions of life without ever really paying any attention. Now, feeling so alive with you, it's a little awkward and unnerving for me. I need to learn to acknowledge these feelings you've ignited inside me again. And how to give them back to you the way you deserve, because they've been absent for a long time for you, too."

I paused, now giving him a chance to comprehend my words. There was nothing but sincerity and understanding in his eyes. He didn't speak but the slight grin on his face told me what I needed to know. When his hold tightened around me it allowed the breath I'd been holding while waiting for a response to be released in a long sigh.

"I don't want to lose you." I went on, feeling encouraged. "So, if you really are willing, I ask that you do wait. I need some more time. But I need you, too."

He gently placed his forehead against mine and we stood in silence; neither of us wanting to let go of this powerful and meaningful moment between us. Other pedestrians walked around us, most of them quiet but some giving us a few choice words for blocking the path. We were oblivious to them all.

Eventually he took my hand in his and pulled me alongside him into the garage until we reached my car. He opened the passenger door for me and waited patiently as I slowly got in, folding my body up into the seat. Fighting these emotions had been draining and now that most of them were out in the open, I was exhausted. He walked around to the driver's side, got in and started the car. Giving me a quick wink, Jaxson put the car in reverse and pulled out of our spot. As we pulled up to the exit lane of the garage, he pulled my hand up to his mouth. He kissed each of my fingers lightly, sweetly, and placed my hand over his heart as he said to me, "This… is yours. Of course I'll wait."

December 8, 2013

Sitting in the glider in Annie's room, I marveled at the fact that not so long ago, I wasn't able to sit in this room without feeling numb inside.

My 'Annie Journal' was sitting in my lap, unopened for the time being. It's strange being in here and not feeling the pull to write, to pour my heart out to her in the form of words.

Jaxson had been staying in this room for the last nine days; the exception being his first night in California, when we slept curled up in each other's arms but separated by the blanket on my bed.

In here there was evidence of him in all corners of the room.

His duffel bag lay open at the foot of the bed, which was unmade. There were several shirts hanging up in the closet, my favorite western ones with the pearl snaps. His boots sat side by side next to the door.

I smiled to myself at how much progress I've made since meeting Jax. Allowing him to stay in Annie's room, my sanctum, was proof that yes, I was healing.

I glanced up as the object of my thoughts came walking through the door, towel wrapped snugly around his waist.

"Hey. Nice shower?" I asked, desperately trying to keep my eyes on his face.

"Oh yeah. As relaxing as the beach can be, it always feels good to get the sand out of your nether regions."

We had spent the day on the beach off the back of my house, opting for a quiet day together instead of crowds. Giving us a chance to come to grips with everything that was said last night.

"I see you already finished yours." He looked me up and down, noting my cotton night shirt and wet hair.

"Like you said, de-sanding my body was a priority."

"Whatcha doing in here? Not that I mind seeing you all cute in your pajamas." He lay down on his belly across the bed so that his head was close to where I sat.

Shrugging my shoulders by way of an answer, I just smiled at him. He glanced down and saw the journal resting, still untouched, on my lap. He didn't need to say anything; the question was evident in his eyes as he looked back up at me.

"This is my journal. Actually, I call it my 'Annie Journal'. I write to her in here about once a week. Tell her what's going on in my life and things like that." It wasn't until I stopped talking that I noticed the frown marring his beautiful face. "What?" I asked, worried about what had changed his mood.

"How long have you had that journal?"

"Well… I went to a shrink, sorry, a therapist. Anyway, it was about three months ago. Right before we met, actually. He suggested that I keep a journal to document my feelings so that I knew what was triggering any depression or anger. It helps."

Why did it feel like he was judging me? Maybe it was the look on his face, almost like disappointment.

"Did he tell you to keep a journal, as in something generic? Or was he specific about it being directed to her?"

Can he not even say her name? Annie. Her name is Annie. See? It's not that hard. At my silence, he continued.

"Since you're not answering, I'm going to assume you made the call to make the journal a devotion to her." Suddenly feeling the need to defend myself, I sat up straighter and hitched up my chin.

"Yes, it was my decision. But the doctor never specified that it couldn't be directed toward Annie. It helps." I stressed to him again. "I'm healing but it keeps me connected with her. And why is it such a big deal to you? Who gave you the authority to judge how I deal?"

My voice rose as my rant continued until I realized I was yelling. But it's not right for him to make me feel bad about what happens to be my best coping mechanism.

"I'll be right back." he said tersely, grabbing a pair of jogging pants and t-shirt from his bag and heading off down the hall to the extra bathroom. Not two minutes later, he was back and dressed. Instead of sitting down on the bed, he stood facing me with his arms crossed over his chest and looking mad.

What did he have to be pissed about? It's not like I was the one criticizing him about how he dealt with his father's death.

"Brin, you keeping this journal, this passage to Annie–" *Aha, so he can say her name.* "–it's not going to help you heal. All you're doing is masking reality. Do you think that by writing to her you can bring her back?"

Well now I was mad too and I'd be damned if I was going to sit here, letting him tower over me, and not fight back. Standing up to my full five foot eight inches, I got right in his face.

"Who are you to tell me that what I'm doing isn't right? Who are you to tell me that I'm 'masking' reality? I'm here, aren't I?" I slung my arms out wide to envelope the space around us. "In reality I'm right here, with you, in Annie's room. What's been going on between us has been real hasn't it?"

Apparently something I said set him off because now he was right back in my face, raising his voice as much as I'd raised mine.

"I'm the man that loves you, dammit! That's who the hell I am! I'm the one who's trying to build a future with you, trying to help you see that we belong together. But you've been fighting me every step of the way! Holding back a huge part of yourself from me. Your love, your trust. That's all I've ever wanted from you. Your love and trust to know that I'm here and that I'll protect you."

His chest was heaving with his own anger now. Somewhere in the back of my mind was a small and niggling persistence that what he was saying was true. But I wasn't ready to throw in the towel just yet and the blame has to go to my Italian pride.

Just as I was about to argue my own point, he cut me off.

"Now I know why it's so hard for you to give me that part of yourself. Why you can't entrust your heart to my care. You've got it wrapped up in white pieces of paper with a leather binder." He pointed to the journal I still had clutched in my white knuckled hands, glaring at it for a moment like it was something horribly offensive.

"That. That has your heart. Until you can let it go we can never move forward. Because you won't be able to give me your love as long as you keep it written on those pages to someone who's not here anymore. But I am. I'm here, Brinley. Love me. Trust me. Let me give you what those pages never can. Let me give you our future."

Jaxson's image blurred in front of me as I fought to keep the tears from escaping onto my face. The man was begging for me to give him this and I wanted to. God, how I wanted to.

But it felt like a betrayal. Even though Annie told me to move forward with him, I still needed to keep her here with me. The journal was my only connection left with her. If I lose it I don't know what I'd become.

Yes, Jaxson has been a life saver for me. Pulling me back from the edge of a cliff to help me re-enter the land of the living. He's helped me to see that God has always been a constant in my life. And he wants to be my constant now. He wants to be what I hang on to in place of my journal.

Tears finally spilled over my eyelids and onto my cheeks as I shook my head no. Whether it was to deny him his request or deny the knowledge that he was probably right, I didn't know.

Jaxson's shoulders slumped as he stepped back from me and hung his head. When he looked up I could see the defeat in his eyes and I hated it.

"I think it's time for me to go back to Texas." His words hit me in the gut like a sucker punch, my breath whooshing out of my lungs the way a balloon does when you let go of the top.

"You need to figure out what you want Brinley. I love you. God only knows how much. And I'd like to spend the next fifty years showing you. But until you decide to let me in, I'm stuck." He wrapped his arms around me in a bear hug and kissed the top of my head.

"I'm going to go home tomorrow and give you some space. Just know that my heart will stay here with you."

December 9, 2013

We headed to the airport in silence. I was driving and Jaxson sat quietly subdued in the passenger seat. I could feel his gaze on me but was unable to say anything to him.

The weather outside the security of the car seemed to match the mood inside. Black clouds had rolled in right as we drove away from my house, shrouding the sky in a sinister looking blanket. Lightening flew around us in brilliant streaks reaching down from Heaven.

After twelve days of being in LA, he was finally going back to Lake Shores. He had said he really needed to start getting preparations in order for Christmas and his mother's visit right after. But after our heated argument last night it was pretty obvious that that was only a side reason. Especially seeing as how Christmas was still three weeks away.

I appreciated the fact that he hadn't brought up last night. What was there to say? He was asking me to give up something that's been like a life line. As much as I wanted him in my life, I wasn't sure I could give him this. Wasn't sure I could let go of Annie like that, so finitely.

He was definitely being patient with me even though that patience felt unfair. *God, how do I deserve him?*

I pulled up outside the 'Departures' gate underneath the awning and we both got out of the car. I walked around the front and came to stand by him just as he grabbed his bag from the backseat and closed the door.

He linked his hands with mine and wrapped our arms together around behind my back. He leaned in to kiss me and when his tongue lightly touched my bottom lip my entire nervous system went on full alert. Would I ever be able to live without these feelings Jaxson had awakened inside me?

His kiss was reinforcing as he delved his tongue deeper inside my mouth and his hold around me grew stronger. I was helpless in his arms and I melted like ice on a hot summer day.

Not wanting him to leave but knowing I needed this time gave me the strength to pull back from him. Staring into his chocolate eyes, looking for a sign that we were ok, I couldn't shake the feeling that this kiss felt like a finale. It scared me.

He let go of my hands and grabbed the sides of my face. He pecked at my lips, nose, cheeks, my forehead. He kissed me once more on my quivering mouth before he leaned in to my ear and whispered, "I'll see you at Christmas. I love you."

He picked up his bag and started to walk away, calling over his shoulder, "I'll call you when I get home."

I watched him, waiting for him to be fully out of sight inside the glass doors.

Then I got back in my car and drove off with no intention of stopping until some answers came.

The rain came down in steady, heavy drops as soon as I pulled away from the curb. I couldn't help feeling as if God was crying along with me.

Jaxson's plane wasn't scheduled to arrive in Houston until eight my time tonight which meant that I wouldn't hear from him until after nine, at the earliest. It was only two in the afternoon now. I knew that if I just kept driving somehow, someway, the answers I sought would come.

I cracked the windows just enough to let my hair blow all around my face, ignoring the water that snuck inside. My mind roamed free and the scent of the rain and ocean mingled together in a clean, salty aroma to waft up to my nose.

The radio was blaring my Joe Cocker Greatest Hits CD and I was lost in thought listening to *Bird on a Wire.* When *Let It Be* came on–originally recorded by the Beatles but covered by Cocker–my mind strained as I heard the words in a new light.

And when the broken hearted people
living in the world agree,
There will be an answer; Let It Be
For though they may be parted there is
still a chance that they will see,
There will be answer; Let It Be

It hit me in the face, or rather the heart, like a ton of bricks. I've been so caught up in my own insecurities, in what would happen if I lost this last thread I had with Annie, that I didn't see the answer staring me straight in the face.

Yes, I've been broken hearted from her death. Yes, the journal was a way to cope with my depression and give me something to latch onto.

But I've been given a chance to see love and happiness in the face of Jaxson.

God's words to me were '*trust in the man I have sent to you and you will find your happiness.'*

And now that we're parted, even though it had only been a short while, I could see it. I could feel it as if it was reaching out of my body and grasping at every beautiful thing in the world, looking for a way to share. If it had a voice, I'm sure I would have heard it too.

My love for him. Love that was as tangible as the steering wheel I was gripping so tightly.

I have to let my past be what it is. The past. And I have to let my future be what it will be. Jaxson.

I made a u-turn at the next park-n-ride and drove straight home, unable to contain my joy at this new epiphany. He said he'd call tonight. I needed to tell him how sorry I was that it took me so long to figure my feelings out. To figure out what he and Annie and God had known all along. I needed to tell Jaxson how I felt. I needed to tell him that I am irrevocably and utterly in love with him. I needed… him.

As soon as I pulled into my driveway, I threw the car in park and ran inside. Showering in record speed and dressing in one of Jaxson's undershirts that had been left here, I lay on my bed and placed the phone in my hand.

Waiting to hear from *my love*.

December 10, 2013

I was walking down a dirt road. It was dusk and eerily quiet out, not even the sound of waking bugs breaking the silence. I came to a fork in the road.

The left side was pitch black, the right side was bright white. My insides were torn on which way to go. My head was telling me to go right, into the white light. But there was a loud ringing that had started in the left side, the side that held an unknown, and it was so hard to ignore.

I tried to walk to the right and the light but my heart was trying to push my body to the left side, into the dark. I couldn't make my feet move but I just knew that I needed to get there, to the right.

The ringing got louder, relentless in its effort to pull me down the shadowy road. Louder still until my ears could take no more.

I slammed my hands over my ears and started screaming for it to stop!

I sat straight up in bed to find the phone, still clutched in my hand, shattering the silence of my room with its insistent ringing. I glanced at the clock.

Three in the morning. I never heard from Jaxson.

My mind was still screaming at me from the dream. Trying to understand what it was about was making it hard to concentrate on anything; much less answering the phone. I looked down again at the device and it felt like a foreign object in my hands. When I was able to focus and saw that the caller ID said it was my mother, my mind started to click back into the present.

It's five in the morning in Lake Shores. Why is she calling? I thought to myself. The question cleared the rest of the confusion from my mind and gave me enough composure to pick up the phone.

"Mom." I said sleepily, "What's going on?"

"I woke you. I'm sorry I woke you up. Did I wake you?"

She was babbling. Momma never babbled.

I waited to give her a chance to settle down and heard her take a deep breath on the other end of the line.

"Oh honey." she was talking quietly, cautious even. Something was wrong. "There's been an accident." she said.

"What is it Mom? Is Dad okay? Aaron and Jessica? Alex? What? What Mom?! What is it?"

I was pleading for an answer. But in her silence, I realized that I already knew who it was and held my breath, waiting for her confirmation.

"Oh sweetie… its Jaxson."

"What happened? Tell me what happened." My voice sounded hollow, like a yell in the distance that's indecipherable. My mother sounded like she was fighting tears as she told me about the accident.

"When he left the airport, an eighteen wheeler ran a red light and t-boned his truck on the driver's side. He's at Memorial Hermann Hospital and the doctors had to put him in a medically induced coma. He's got some broken ribs, one of his femurs has been shattered and there is quite a bit of internal bleeding. Honey, it's really bad. I knew you__"

I cut her off.

"I'm booking the next flight out. You tell him I'm coming! Tell him I'll be there soon. Tell him!"

The last words to my Mom hung in the air like a heavy fog as I called the airport to book a flight while racing to my bedroom.

Please God, no! Not Jaxson, too! Please, no, No, NO! I love him! Please help him! I begged to God as I frantically threw some clothes into a duffel bag and zipped it closed right as I got my flight confirmation number.

I thrust my legs into jeans, shoved my feet into a pair of sneakers and yanked on a Longhorn sweatshirt. Jotting the confirmation number down quickly on a notepad, I threw it into my purse, picked up my bag and ran out the door.

Two hours later I was on a plane heading to Texas. To demand Jaxson to fight. To demand him to stay with me.

Staring out at the dawn just making its appearance over the horizon from my seat by the window, I knew what Jaxson was really going to need to hear. What he needed to know, finally.

I had to make a promise to him. Promise that I love him, will always love him, and am never letting go of him again.

Chapter 18

"Jesus said unto her. I am the resurrection, and the life: he that believeth in me, though he were dead, yet shall he live." John 11:25

Journal Entry Twelve – December 14, 2013

"Dear Annie, Well I've really gone and thrown things in the gutter now haven't I? Let me just say that everything you told me in that dream, everything, came through loud and clear to me. Believe me, nothing was taken for granted or at face value. Especially after confessing to the Lord and having that amazing, incredible, divine message from him. I tell you, that's not something I'll ever forget.

Between Him and you, I got it. I got that Jaxson was here for me.

But seriously, was I actually supposed to cut you out completely? How was I to know that by keeping my journal to you I was jeopardizing my future with Jaxson? I didn't know. I couldn't because he didn't even know about it.

He does now, though. Boy, does he ever.

Just thinking about the fight we had–wow, not even a week ago–makes me so sick to my stomach that I lose whatever I ate last. That fight gave me a kick in the butt. Maybe that's what had been missing from the dream. You were mad but unable to really do anything about it. If you had been here, in person, you probably would have smacked me upside the shoulder and told me to face the reality of the situation. That I love him.

Funny. We argued about my reality not being 'real'. All this time I thought it was. But that was an illusion wasn't it, Ann? Writing you never gave me a sense of healing. It was never real. All it did was give me an escape. From family, friends, feelings. From reality.

I don't want to escape anymore, Annie. I want to be present for the here and now and have a future. If that makes me a bad friend, I'll deal with it when we meet again someday.

But that's the God's honest truth. I don't want to relive everything that happened in the past. From our fight to the wreck, you dying. It's had a huge impact on my life but it's been those events that's led me here.

Right now my 'here' is an uncomfortable, under-stuffed hospital chair next to a cold and silver hospital bed. Jaxson is still being kept asleep.

God Annie, he's in such bad shape. This amazingly strong and virile man that's become everything to me is lying here in this cold bed.

The tubes are everywhere, his nose, his forearm, the catheter. At least they took out the breathing tube. It's not much but being able to press my lips against his gives me hope.

I haven't even told him I love him yet.

I'm surrounded by these machines that do nothing but beep-beep-beep. I guess it's good since they let me know he's still alive. But the sound reminds me of an alarm alerting me that time may be running out and it's starting to drive me crazy.

Our time can't be out yet, can it?

My parents and the nurses have tried to get me to leave, go get some rest. But I can't. I won't leave him. He promised to protect me. The very least I can do is to sit here in this uncomfortable and under-stuffed chair to protect him. To watch over him.

Huh.

That's what you've been doing isn't it? All this time you've been protecting me, watching over me. And I've been hanging onto you, keeping you alive in this journal like the sustenance my body needs to survive.

Oh, Annie. Jaxson was right. I don't need this journal. Jaxson, he's my sustenance. He's my future. And I can't grab that dream while I'm still living in the past.

There's always going to be a part of me that wishes things had happened differently that night last year. I can't change that and I'm not sure I even want to.

But I have to let it go. I have to let this journal go. Anything that's going to stop the progress of mine and Jaxson's relationship isn't something I can have in my life.

There was a time when the thought of not having these words with you, to you, probably would have sent me into a full blown anxiety attack. But these last few days, watching Jaxson fight for his life, has made me realize some important things.

I love you, always have and always will. But it's like he said, you're not here to love me back anymore.

He is, though. And for whatever reason he wants to.

I don't need these words and these pages and this leather binder to stay connected to you. I have our memories. I don't need to hold onto your presence to feel strong enough to make it through the day. I have Jaxson.

And he's going to have me too.

I realize that our future is precious. From now on my priority isn't going to be keeping you alive. You already are alive, eternally in the arms of God. I need to focus on living for myself. And Jaxson.

Yes, I'm going to focus on him and me and where we go when he wakes up. When, not if. Starting now. It has to start now. I'll talk to you soon… maybe. I love you, Annie.

Chapter 19

"The Lord will strengthen him upon the bed of languishing: thou wilt make all his bed in his sickness." Psalms 41:3

December 16, 2013

It has been almost a week since Jaxson's car accident.

The rain that had started in L.A. when I realized I loved him had finally made its way east to Texas. It's been raining for five days now with no sign of letting up. The deluge that was coming down outside seemed to put a damper on everyone's spirits. But I was determined not to let the gray, thundering skies dampen my faith or keep me from my vigil by Jaxson's side.

He's had two surgeries on his right leg, the doctor trying to repair the puzzle that had become of his femur. Plus, he's had two abdominal surgeries for his internal bleeding; one to remove his ruptured spleen and another to repair his lacerated liver. Both the orthopedic and general surgeons have high hopes that the surgeries went well. But until he wakes up we won't know for sure.

I spoke to his mother, Beth, the day after the accident. She was terrified for her son and wanted to be here with him. Unfortunately, both of his brothers had taken early Christmas trips with their wives and children so that they could be back for Christmas Eve and Day. And his sister had gone skiing with some friends.

I tried to talk her into getting on a plane; even offered to buy the plane ticket. But I knew as soon as I brought it up it was a lost cause. I vividly remembered Jaxson telling me of his mother's fear of flying. I promised to call her several times a day, every day, to keep her informed as she was praying and fasting for his recovery.

The anesthesiologist, I don't remember her name, there's just too many people to recall them all. But she was beginning to gradually ease him off of his propofol (the medicine keeping him unconscious so that he could heal).

I refused to leave his bedside. Terror struck through me, right into my heart, at the thought of not being here when he woke.

Because you will wake up, I warned him over and over again.

Every morning during the seven o'clock shift change I would force myself to go the hotel across the street.

Grabbing a quick shower and putting on some fresh clothes was the only respite I would allow myself from the uncomfortable and under-stuffed chair by Jaxson's bedside. And even then, it was only a brief fifteen minutes.

I would read to him, usually from some of his Dad's first editions, for hours on end. And even though my voice was not of the caliber that Annie's had been, I would sing to him, too. Different classic hymns that I knew were some of his favorites. *Amazing Grace, Just As I Am, Come Thou Fount.* Judging by the decrease in his blood pressure when I sang, he seemed to enjoy it. So I kept singing to him.

Other times, I would just lay there with my head resting on the bed, stroking his arm gently, waiting.

December 17, 2013

There hadn't been much of a change in Jaxson's status over the last twenty-four hours. He was now completely free of the propofol and the feeding tube had been removed from his nose. I sat here resolutely, waiting for him to wake up, willing him to wake up.

Doctor Thomas Roberts, the general surgeon that had taken Jaxson on as his patient, said it would happen in his time and to be patient. He was an older man in his late fifties with a shock of white hair and a pair of rectangle glasses that were constantly perched on his long nose. He was the only one who kept me up to date on Jaxson's condition.

The surgeon that had worked on his leg, a young man probably only a few years older than my twenty-eight, was a man named Doctor Amil Patel. His dark mocha skin and eyes gave him an air of inaccessibility. I didn't see him much. Only when he had given me a cursory report right after surgery but that was it.

But Dr. Roberts' kind smile and compassionate eyes said that he understood what I was obsessing about.

Still, the longer it took for him to wake up, the more concerned I got about his condition. I was reassured at every opportunity, by the nursing staff as well as Dr. Roberts, that he had no brain damage and would recover fully in that aspect.

It didn't matter what they said though. As painfully mind-numbing as it was to sit here and idle away the hours, waiting to see for myself, I wouldn't leave him. I promised him I wouldn't be going anywhere.

During the seven o'clock shift change that night, I walked down to the cafeteria to stretch my legs and grab a cup of coffee. I was used to getting kicked out of the room twice a day, every day so that the nurses could assess Jaxson and change any linens.

But being away tonight made me nervous. I wasn't sure why but there was an undeniable urge in the pit of my stomach pushing me to hurry and get back to Jaxson. Twenty minutes after I had left, I was briskly walking back into the intensive care unit.

Mandy, one of the registered nurses who I had become well acquainted with over the last week, met me outside Jaxson's curtain. With her larger, squat frame she blocked me from entering every time I tried to wiggle around her.

I finally gave up and stared at her in exasperation, waiting for an explanation.

"Brinley," she said to me with a sympathetic tone and I was instantly petrified. "Someone has been asking for you." She smiled timidly and I knew… I knew he was awake.

I rushed inside to find Jaxson lying in his hospital bed with his eyes wide open. That bed didn't look so cold anymore. He looked in my direction when he heard the curtain being drawn back forcefully.

He smiled his big, beautiful smile–my smile–that crinkled his eyes.

My breath hiccupped in my throat in a rush of relief as he reached out for me. I ran into his open arms.

"Hello, love." he said, folding his hands together around my waist and resting his forehead in my neck. His voice was hoarse and weak; a combination from the respirator and not talking for a week. But it still had that deep, velvet ring to it that made my heart melt.

I immediately began kissing his face all over–forehead, cheeks, nose, lips–and held his face so tightly that he winced.

"I'm so sorry. I didn't mean to hurt you," I apologized to him through the tears clogging my throat and carefully placed my hands on the bed on either side of his face. "I'm just so thankful that you are awake. Don't you *ever* scare me like this again! Do you hear me?" I chastised him.

"What? This?" he asked waving his hand over his shattered body. "This is nothing. You act like you were worried or something."

I hated that he was trying to make light of the situation, hated that he was somehow even in the frame of mind to make light of it. He almost died for crying out loud!

But I was so happy that he was awake that the rest didn't matter. I chose instead to take it as a good sign that his sense of humor was prevailing over any pain.

Gingerly, I placed my hands back on either side of his face, being mindful of the bruises and cuts. Staring into his delicate, russet brown eyes, I finally whispered what I'd been waiting over a week to tell him.

"I love you."

He smiled, closed his eyes and sighed heavily as a lonely tear ran down the left side of his face, apparently as relieved to hear those three words from me as I was to see him awake.

I carefully kissed the tear away and leaned back just as he reopened his eyes. He watched me closely but didn't speak, so I continued.

"If I would have known that you were going to go to all this trouble just to make me realize it, I would have told you back in LA. I'm so sorry it took me longer to recognize what you already knew. I'm so sorry we had that fight because everything you said was true. I didn't realize that by writing to Annie I was keeping that part of myself locked away.

"But I realize it all now. I love you so much. I don't want to live another day without being able to love you."

I kissed him, very tenderly. Our lips molded together like they were made for each other. I didn't need his possession or his roughness to tell me what I knew. This sweet, nibbling of lips conveyed what our hearts felt and everything around us faded into the background.

December 20, 2013

As the days cleared from their endless gloomy storms into clear blue skies, so did the haze that had been surrounding my heart and mind.

Since Jaxson had woken up three days ago, he has been working so hard with his physical therapy. I worried that he might be pushing too hard too soon. But Dr. Roberts guaranteed me that the bone in his leg was healing properly and that his abdominal incisions were well on their way to closing too since the surgeries had been done laprascopically. And also because of the amount of time he had spent unconscious.

Just that word–unconscious–had me shuddering with the memory of sitting by, helpless, waiting for Jaxson to wake up.

They said as long as he could handle the therapy and that the stitches held, he could keep working. Reluctantly, I went along with their rehabilitation plans.

I went down with him to the physical therapy room on the first floor every day, twice a day. I was his personal cheerleader; sitting on the sidelines, encouraging him when seemed flustered and praising him when he managed to lift up from the wheelchair on his own. I didn't mind much that I wasn't able to physically help him because the emotional and spiritual support I gave him would help just as much (if not more) than the physical.

But every time we made it back to his room, I still tried to get him to back off a little.

"Jax, you don't have to push this so hard you know." I told him after he was settled in his bed following his morning session.

He just snorted at me like I had said something funny or ridiculous. I scowled.

"Baby, I am *not* going to spend our first Christmas together in the hospital." How he managed to sound so optimistic and ornery at the same time was beyond me.

"But you know I'm not going anywhere, right? If this is where we have to spend Christmas, then so be it. I don't mind. We'll be together and that's all that really matters," I reassured him.

He tilted his head to the side and grinned at me with admiration in his eyes.

"I appreciate that. Really. But I have other plans for Christmas, and they do not involve hospital beds or machines or doctors or nurses. And definitely not bedpans. Dr. Roberts and the physical therapist both told me that as soon as my upper body is strong enough to lift myself from the chair to the bed on my own, I can be discharged. So I'm going to keep working until that happens."

"Well–" I looked sideways and gazed appreciatively over his body, "–I guess it's a good thing you had some decent muscle mass to begin with. So, you're already ahead of the game."

"Decent? Humph. It's nice to know where I stand with your scale of masculinity. Gives me something to work towards when this is all finished." And then we were both laughing at the absurdity of my statement as well as his response.

Yesterday Jaxson had moved from the ICU to a room on the medical-surgical floor, where they send patients who are recovering from surgeries.

After fluffing the pillows behind his back, acting oblivious to his protests, I plopped down in the chair next to his bedside while he rested in bed. We were watching T.V., quietly enjoying the absence of all the excessive beeps from the ICU.

I was only halfway paying attention to the news channel he had settled on, more content to daydream about his last visit in California, before the dreadful call from my Mother.

I hadn't noticed that the television was muted until I felt Jax's eyes on me, staring intently.

"What?" I asked him, fidgeting in my seat and feeling a little self-conscious.

"Tell me something, please." His voice was quiet as a mouse, like he was scared of what he was about to ask. "Did you figure out you loved me before or after you found out about the accident?"

I hesitated at first. Not because the answer was unknown to me but because I was searching for the right way to go about answering his off-the-wall question.

"Does it matter?" I finally responded.

"I was just curious. Sometimes tragedy can make people feel crazy things. I guess I was wondering if that was the case with you and me." I watched his Adam's apple bob up and down as he swallowed thickly, clearly nervous.

"Because from what I've witnessed, more often than not, those feelings will end up fading over time. I guess I just want to know what to expect."

The look in his eyes–which was normally so bold and beautiful–was so torn and worried. And full of a longing that showed how much he hoped that wouldn't be the case with me. With us. Like he was afraid my love might not be genuine.

Rising from my chair, I kept my eyes focused on his face and sat down delicately beside him on the bed. Reaching with my right hand to stroke his hair, I rested my left tenderly, lovingly on his chest, splaying my fingers over his heart. Feeling the frantic beating under my palm, I leaned in and gave him a long, intense kiss. I tried to leave no room for doubt concerning my feelings.

However, just in case, I gave him some extra affirmation.

Lifting his hand to place over my own heart, I pulled away from his lips and whispered in his ear, "This… is… yours." Then I kissed the side of his neck below his ear.

His breath caught and released in a long sigh and I knew it sank in. From the first touch to his lips, to my words in his ear, to the kiss where his pulse throbbed erratically.

That was his proof.

"Stealing my line now, huh?" he responded as he leaned back to look at me in the eye.

Then I saw that bright twinkle that I loved so much in his beautiful, dark eyes as he pulled me onto the bed to curl up by his side.

December 23, 2013

After Jaxson's evening physical therapy session, we decided to have dinner in the cafeteria. Despite the fact that he was in a private room now, the space was still becoming tedious and we needed a change of scenery.

Other patients from the various wards throughout the hospital were there with their family or friends. Some loved ones sat huddled in corners with exhaustion evident in their faces. I could definitely empathize with them and while their sorrow was heartbreaking, I couldn't help but be so thankful that I wasn't in that place anymore. Thankful for how far Jaxson has come in the last almost two weeks.

While we sat there eating our dinner–he with a burger and fries, me with a chicken Caesar salad–I decided to compliment him on how well he had been doing with his therapy. He could lift himself off the bed and into the wheelchair, as well as out of the wheelchair and onto the shower seat by himself.

"Jax, babe, I am so proud of you and your progress. You've shown so much strength and determination, inside and out. Despite my objections to how much you were doing, I just wanted you to know how happy it makes me to see you accomplishing your goals."

"Well thank you love." I grinned at his new sweet name. He always knew how to make me feel so treasured. "I'm beyond ready to get out of this place so that has a lot to do with it. However–" he eyed me cautiously over his drink as if judging my mood, "–you'll probably have to give me my sponge baths when I leave. You know, since I won't get my cast off until the end of January."

I flicked the water from my bottle on him, causing him to jump back a little from his chair, laughing. In spite of his cheeky suggestion, I laughed with him. Although on the inside I couldn't hold back the tingle of excitement at the thought. Jaxson with no shirt–chest and arm muscles even more defined now because of all the therapy–slick with soapy water. My nerve endings were on fire just picturing it.

We finished our dinner in a comfortable silence, content to just be in each other's presence. After throwing away all our trash and returning the trays to the food line, we headed through the lobby to the elevators.

I pushed the button for the fourth floor and when the doors opened, led the way down the hall to room 423, waving to the handful of nurses and aides behind their station on the way.

The doctor was waiting for us when we got back, sitting in the chair that I usually occupied. He was filling out some paperwork at the bedside table and set his pen down to look up at us as we entered.

"Hey you two!" Dr. Roberts said.

He had a mischievous smile playing at his lips. The kind you expect to see on a child when they've just set up a prank on their teacher and can't wait to see her sit on the pushpin.

"How are you guys this evening? Did you go down to dinner in the cafeteria?" At our nod he carried on his one-sided conversation. "I don't know about you, but I never was much on the food here. You'd think nationally ranked hospitals would have a better menu selection."

Finally, Jaxson saw fit to interrupt his rant on the provisions of the cafeteria.

"Was there something you needed, Dr. Roberts? Not that it's not good to see you but Brin and I are pretty tired and were going to get ready for some sleep."

Dr. Roberts just grinned again as he picked up his pen and resumed his writing. "Listen, Jaxson, I've been going through all your reports from PT and the latest CT scans of your belly. Your ribs are healing nicely, but they'll still be tender for about another month and you'll need to be careful so you don't aggravate the breaks. Your abdomen looks good; the incisions have stayed closed well since the removal of the stitches. Your leg is obviously still mending but, from what I've seen and heard, you've done an exceptional job at physical therapy and your orthopedic doctor agrees with me. So," he clicked his pen closed and put it back in his lab coat pocket as he looked up at us again.

"If you think you're ready, and if you're going to have round-the-clock assistance at home for the next few weeks…" he glanced in my direction before going on, "I think you can go home tomorrow. I'll make sure all prescriptions and discharge orders are ready for you first thing in the morning and you'll be free to go. I'll want to see you at my office in about four weeks to check out those ribs. I'll also have Dr. Patel there to look at the updates from your therapy on your leg as well. If he thinks it's ok, we'll see about getting that cast off then." He stood, shook mine and Jaxson's hand and strolled out of the room with a 'just another day at the office' aura about him.

I walked over and closed the door then turned to stare at Jaxson. While I was completely shell-shocked, he was so excited I thought he might try to jump out of the wheelchair he was still confined to. Instead, he wheeled over to me and pulled me down to his mouth for a crushing kiss.

"See?" he smiled at me, "I told you we would be out of here and headed home for Christmas."

Home for Christmas. It had a nice ring to it.

"Looks like I'll be staying with you for a while then. I need to call my manager back in LA and have her watch over my house until sometime after the New Year. Seeing as how you're going to need help with those baths and all." I grinned and blushed, remembering my earlier thoughts on the sponge bathing.

"I love you, baby." he said to me, his voice barely above a whisper. I put my arms around his neck and leaned in so I could whisper back to him in his ear.

"I love you more."

December 24, 2013

Being discharged from a hospital, any hospital, is never as easy and quick as the doctors make it sound.

Once all the forms were signed we had to go down to physical therapy so Jaxson could get fitted for the crutches that he'd be starting to use in a few more days. Then we had to listen to the instructions from the respiratory therapist on deep breathing exercises to make sure Jaxson didn't get pneumonia.

After a run through at the hospital pharmacy–so we wouldn't have to make an additional stop on the ride home–we finally left Hermann Hospital and all the personnel behind.

My Mom had brought her Toyota Camry sedan up yesterday for me to drive Jaxson home in. We all agreed that his truck, as well as Daddy's, were too tall for him to get into.

The weather continued to cooperate with clear skies that were dotted with white clouds that looked like cotton balls floating in the air. We pulled onto the dirt road leading up to Jaxson's house at just after five in the evening. The sun was starting to set and as I got out of the driver's side door I admired those beautiful shades of dark orange and deep purple blazing over the pasture's horizon.

Getting the wheelchair out of the trunk, I popped it open and pushed it to the passenger side for Jaxson to get into. Once he was settled, we headed up the walkway. My brothers, Aaron and Alex, and Jaxson's friend, Blake, had built a makeshift ramp leading up to the porch to accommodate the wheelchair.

"This is ridiculous!" Jaxson grouched in regards to the ramp as we headed to the front door. "I feel like an old man. Can't even walk up the steps to my own house. I can't wait to get this damn cast off so I can walk around on my own again. And ride my horse! How's a cowboy supposed to make a living without being able to get on his horse?"

I knew he was more upset about his horses than anything. The wheelchair, ramps and cast all put together were nothing more than a minor inconvenience. But riding was a huge part of his livelihood.

I opted to not add to the conversation, letting him have his rant. Maybe all the therapy he'd been doing was finally catching up to him. I didn't want him focusing on the negative and I was afraid that putting in my two cents would do just that. He was here, alive, which was more important than anything else.

So I just kept my mouth shut and opened the door. I went back to push Jaxson the rest of the way in only to have him tell me that he wasn't an invalid. He could push himself the rest of the way.

Biting my tongue to keep from laughing at the childish way he was acting, I walked into the foyer. I vaguely heard Jaxson wheeling in behind me as I gasped in bewilderment. The house was completely done up for Christmas.

Two stockings and green lighted garland covered the mantle on the other side of the room. Mistletoe hung from the archway leading past the foyer into the living room. Nutcrackers of all shapes and sizes were scattered on the end tables. A nativity scene was set up on the coffee table and there was a white light bulb hung from the top, acting as the North Star shining over a baby Jesus.

In the far corner of the living room was a massive nine foot fir tree, sending a rich aroma throughout the house that brought up memories of Christmas' past. It was simply gorgeous.

Jax took advantage of my speechlessness and spoke first.

"You didn't really think I would let us spend our first Christmas together without all the holiday cheer, did you?" His smile was full of pride and yes, arrogance. He had yet again surprised me.

"How did you…?" I trailed off, powerless to even find the right words.

He just sat there chuckling at me as I slowly made my way around the room to admire all the decorations.

"In case you haven't heard, your new sister-in-law is quite ambitious and intense when it comes to Christmas decorating. I called Aaron when you were showering a couple days ago and asked him to see if Jessica wouldn't mind helping me out. Even told him I'd pay her, which of course they instantly refused. She was more than willing to oblige."

He wheeled himself around the couch when I stopped in front of the stunning tree. All of the ornaments looked so old, real classic antiques, and most of them were hand made. They just had that air of deep-rooted familial bonds that was almost palpable. All the colors of the rainbow and then some winked at me under the glow of the lights.

Baby blue and pale pink beaded balls glistened like candy gumdrops. Sea green threaded teardrop ornaments made it look like the tree itself was crying. Square ones covered with deep purple sequins reminded me of the gifts brought by the three wise men to Bethlehem. It was amazing the way they all sparkled under the white lights.

"My Great-Grandmother had a knack for making ornaments. I told Jess where to find them when she agreed to do this." Jaxson said as he came up beside me, noticing my curiosity with them.

"They're beautiful. I've never seen anything like them before."

"This one here is my favorite." he said as he reached to a branch in the back that I hadn't seen yet and held one out for me to hold.

It was made of iridescent white pearls and it resembled a three dimensional star. I delicately took it from him and held it up by the metal hanger so I could take a closer look, slowly spinning it in a circle with my fingers.

The bright sparkle at the top of the ornament caught my attention and I stopped it mid-spin.

There, hanging from the hook and resting on the top of the star-like ornament, was the most elegant diamond ring I have ever seen.

A solitary princess cut stone of what I guessed to be around two carats was set high in white gold. My mouth fell open and despite my best attempts, I couldn't do anything to close it. Once again speechless. Once again caught completely by surprise.

How does he do that?

Before I could answer my own question, Jaxson's voice broke through my thoughts.

"If I could I would get down on one knee. But seeing as how I'm stranded in this chair, sitting will have to do." Jaxson said, staring at me intently as I brought my gaze back to him.

"Brin, baby, love… since you walked into my life, I have finally begun to understand what it feels like to love someone so much it hurts. You make me feel whole. You make me feel alive. You make me feel humbled." He swallowed hard and took a deep, fortifying breath.

"You make me want to spend the rest of my life loving you. My heart has always belonged to you. I would like to give all of me to you. Forever. I ask that you do me the honor and privilege of becoming my wife. And I will spend the rest of my days being the kind of husband you can rely on, be proud of, and always believe in for the love and support you deserve. Brinley Lambert… will you marry me?"

My heart was beating so fast I could hear it pounding in my ears. *Bump Bump Bump Bump Bump.*

My breathing was downright erratic.

My eyes were full of tears that ran in unheeded streams down my face.

I sank down to my knees in front of him and swallowed thickly, twice, before finally finding my voice.

"Jaxson. You have helped to set me free of so many demons I carried around for far too long. In doing so, you've opened my heart so that I can love again. So that I can accept love again. You are the one who's made me whole. I couldn't dream of spending another minute without you by my side and me by yours. Of course, yes, I will marry you!"

I threw my arms around his neck and kissed him with a fevered passion and immediately felt the electricity between us surge through the roof and into the open skies above. As Jaxson caressed my back and head, holding me still for him, I had a new mantra playing in my mind and heart.

He is mine. I am his. Forever his.

Chapter 20

"Every man shall give as he is able, according to the blessing of the Lord thy God which he hath given thee." Deuteronomy 16:17

Most women have the kind of proposal that involves flowers and candles, maybe dinner. Definitely an 'on bended knee' approach.

But like Jaxson said, we weren't under normal circumstances.

It's really frustrating when you've just been proposed to and all you want to do is crawl up in the lap of the one you love and, for lack of a better phrase, make out. It's what I so desperately wanted but couldn't do because of Jaxson being in a wheelchair with a full leg cast.

Instead, we had made our way to his room where he parked his chair by the nightstand and pulled himself up onto the bed. I stood at the foot of the bed to take off my boots before crawling up from there to lie beside him. I was very careful not to get too amorous; keeping to our agreement about wanting to do things 'right' and also afraid that I might hurt him.

He was less concerned for his own wellbeing if the fire in his eyes was any indication when I slowly made my way up the bed. As exciting as it was to see the expression on his face that said he was as powerfully affected by me as I was him, I had to force myself to be the prude one for once.

In reality, though, it was rather romantic. There was no fear of the unknown with certain expectations, like this is where we move to the next level of intimacy. Our relationship hadn't gone down that road yet and we didn't plan for it to.

Regardless of the fact that he was physically unable to right now.

We lay in bed together just staring at each other and I saw in his eyes the same devotion rolling throughout my body. The quiet determination that we remain abstinent. The passionate gaze that spoke of the intense struggle to do just that. The loving smile that showed a future with endless possibilities. We never spoke a word and several times we both dozed off. We were content to just… be.

In the midst of our exchanged looks I would run my fingers through his hair, enjoying the silky feel of it curling around my grasping hands. Every now and then I'd lean over to kiss him sweetly only to slap his shoulder lightly when he tried to deepen our kiss into something more sensual.

Feigning innocence, he rubbed my back gently under my sweater. The soft touch of his fingers against my skin would send the ever present butterflies battling to break free. Tingles would race up and down my spine and I'd forget about why I'd been trying to scold him.

It was around midnight when I finally kept from being distracted by his hands long enough to ask, "How long have you been planning this? The proposal, I mean."

"Well…" he began, "before I came to see you on Thanksgiving for you premiere, I took your Dad out to dinner."

"You did what?" I sat up quickly with alarm and he placed his finger over my lips; his turn to keep me from crossing a boundary.

"Do you want to hear this or not?" I nodded because his finger was still over my lips. "Okay. Like I said, I took your Dad out to dinner the day before Thanksgiving. I explained to him how much I love you and what my intentions were for our future. I asked him for your hand in marriage because, as I told you in the beginning, I didn't want to make any mistakes with you. I needed his blessing. He graciously gave it to me. Obviously."

"He wasn't mad or skeptical or anything? I mean because we've only known each other for three and a half months?" I asked.

"Not at all. He said that he knew there was something special between you and me when you were here in October. He could see it in the way we watched each other because it's the way he and your Mom have always looked at one another. He said he knew then it would only be a matter of time. And then he informed me that he'd be tickled to have me as a son-in-law.

"Actually, I believe his exact words were, 'Ah, hell son. You didn't have to ask. I'll be glad to hand her over to you.'"

His smug smile was back as he blew on his nails then rubbed them along his shirt collar. All I could do was grin and shake my head at him. Despite what Daddy had said, I knew Jaxson's asking him meant a lot and I was incredibly grateful.

How did I end up so lucky and blessed? Thank you, Lord! But the mention of my parents brought up another question.

"What do you think your Mom is going to say?"

I was really more worried about her reaction than Mom and Daddy's because at least my parents had known Jaxson for several years. They knew how wonderful of a man he is and like he said, they've seen us together.

But Jaxson's Mom, Beth, doesn't know anything about me aside from our brief conversations on the phone. In addition to keeping her informed of his progress while Jaxson was still being kept comatose, I had talked to her about his Christmas present. Maybe it was just me trying to remain optimistic and faithful that he'd be waking up or my way of being close to him in a different aspect of his life.

Regardless of the reason, she and I had talked about a dozen times and I promised a 'girl dinner date' when she was here next. But that didn't mean she knew me or believed in us.

"Do you not remember what I told you she said after Aaron's wedding?" he waited and I racked my brain, trying to recall what he had disclosed to me. I slowly shook my head because my mind was coming up empty; too focused on the rest of *this* day's events.

"Jax, so much has happened over the last few months. I'm drawing a blank. Help me out here." I laughed nervously.

"Awe, baby. I'm sorry. I know how much you've been through."

Me? I thought to myself. *You're the one who almost died and you're worried about me?*

He interrupted my inner deliberations.

"She told me that you were the one I was going to spend the rest of my life with, remember? And, that she had had a dream about____"

"–our wedding. I remember," I finished, feeling a heat sneak up my neck at the thought of our wedding that was now a future fact; not just a future dream. I know there was one of those stupid, goofy grins on my face. The kind that teenage girls get when they think of going on a date with some A-list stud.

But I didn't care. My own stud was laying here with me and would be my date for forever.

"So, did she happen to tell you when this wedding of ours took place? Was it sometime soon?"

"Nope. Just that there'd be one," he laughed at my obvious eagerness then eyed me carefully. "When would you like to have the wedding? My only request is that we wait until after this cast is off. I want to be able to dance with you on the night you become my wife."

His voice softened as he ran the backs of his knuckles down my cheek, past my throat and landed on the small of my back. His hand felt at home there and the perfect fit made me arch myself closer to him, wanting to fit everywhere.

"Hmm. How about if we have it in April? The weather is warm but not too hot and humid yet to be uncomfortable. Plus all the spring flowers will be blooming and their perfume will add to the ambiance. It will be perfect."

"April? You know that's only four months away, right? Can you actually plan a wedding that fast?"

"Oh ye of little faith." I smirked. "Don't you know that every little girl has a fantasy about her wedding? Most details have been planned since I was six. It doesn't matter that for a while there I never thought I'd get married. The specifics never changed."

"Well then April sounds good to me. But–" he still looked a little confused, "–you said something about humidity. It's not humid in LA. At least not like it is here so, does that mean you want to have the wedding in Lake Shores?"

"Of course I do! It wouldn't feel right having it anywhere else. Lake Shores is my hometown and all my family is here. I might have strayed from my faith for a little while but I'm back on track now and it would be a dream come true to get married in my childhood church. And maybe…" I self-consciously chewed my lip, unsure how he would react to my next request. "Maybe we could have the reception here. Like you did for Aaron and Jessica. Would that be okay?"

"Absolutely baby. Whatever you want. As long as I get to say 'I do' to you at the wedding, the rest is just details. My brothers always said that the wedding is for the women and the honeymoon is for the men." He winked and I laughed.

That would be all he'd have on his mind.

But when I sat up in bed and held his head in my hands, gazing into his eyes, I knew there was so much more. Anticipation, yes. Love, definitely. But it was the last thing I saw that was a treasure beyond anything.

His faith in me. In our future.

"I love you so much, Jaxson. I can only hope and pray that I'll be the kind of wife you deserve."

Before he had a chance at some kind of rebuttal I kissed him deeply. Our lips molded together so completely that we could have been permanently fixed on one another, sharing each other's breath, for an eternity. He stroked my face tenderly with one hand and rubbed those tantalizing slow circles on my back with the other. We were exploring in that perfect synchronization, my head moving left while his tilted right to take more of me.

We were both panting as I tore my mouth from his, suggesting we get ready to go to sleep. I helped Jaxson pull the scrub pants the hospital sent him home in down and over his cast, thanking God for boxer briefs.

While he took care of the rest, I went into his closet and changed into one of his long-sleeved shirts. I ignored the heated look and pouting groan Jaxson gave as I emerged and crawled back into bed beside him.

When we fell asleep sometime later it was forehead to forehead, holding each other's hands at our hearts.

December 25, 2013

Sometimes a feeling comes that pushes me to wake up. It used to be the accident in my nightmares. Then it was my insatiable craving to check in with Jaxson. For the last two weeks it's been the maternal instinct that needed to know he was actually here and alive.

This morning was no different.

I groggily opened my eyes expecting to see Jax still lying beside me, just like when we had gone to sleep. The barely risen sun hadn't rid the room of the gray light that hung on from the last remnants of night. It made the atmosphere seem that much more disturbing when I realized that he wasn't there. I sat up quickly, terrified that something had happened. I ran down the hall and into the living room, calling his name as I went.

"Jaxson! Jaxson, where are you?"

Just as I turned around to go look in the other bedrooms the storm door slammed shut at the back of the house by the kitchen. I raced in there to find Jaxson wheeling inside, looking panicky at me. Me!

"Hey, hey love. I'm right here. What's wrong? Did you have a nightmare?" he asked as I sighed heavily with relief.

"No, no nightmare. I was worried when I woke up and you weren't there. I was afraid… I thought you…" I was so flustered that the right words wouldn't even come out. On a deep breath in and out, my thoughts finally got themselves in order.

"I was worried that you might have tried to do something you aren't supposed to be doing and hurt yourself."

I walked over on shaky legs and knelt down beside him on the kitchen floor, laying my head across his lap that was covered with a blue and black plaid wool blanket. The morning sun poked its rays farther up in the sky and they streamed through the windows, warming my bare feet and face.

"Baby, I'm fine. Just sitting on the porch enjoying a decent cup of coffee. That stuff the hospital served tasted like burnt water most days and was really making me miss the good stuff. You looked so peaceful this morning that I didn't want to wake you, so I came out here. I'm sorry. Next time I'll tell you first."

He smiled down at me, tucking my wild bed-head hair behind my ear.

"Merry Christmas, Jax." I grinned back at him.

"Merry Christmas, baby."

He leaned down to kiss my forehead. But I stopped him before he could make it anywhere close to my lips.

"I was a little frantic when you weren't in bed a few minutes ago and haven't brushed my teeth yet. Let me go do that and throw some clothes on real quick. Then, I get to give you *your* Christmas present."

"Number one, I prefer you in that shirt of mine you're wearing. You look damn stunning. Number two, you've already given me the only present I could ever ask for. You."

His tender words made my heart swell.

"Well, number one–" I mocked him, "–it's too cold to go out in just a t-shirt, long sleeves or not, so I need to get dressed. And number two, you already have me so that's a moot point. Please, Jaxson. Let me give you the present that I've worked so hard to get for you."

He made a show of sighing heavily like he was really put off by the whole situation. I smiled and kissed his cheek before rising from the floor and skipping off to the bathroom.

I made quick work of brushing my teeth and hair, throwing my unruly mass in to a low ponytail. After slipping on a pair of gray flannel pants and my lucky Longhorns sweatshirt, I walked back into the kitchen holding a red bandana in my hands.

Jax eyed me skeptically before finally giving voice to the offensive fabric I twirled between my fingers.

"What's that for?" He asked suspiciously.

"I don't want you peeking."

His weak protests fell on deaf ears as I tied it around his eyes and wheeled him to the back porch.

The weather had enough of a bite to it that I was glad I'd opted for the sweatshirt and that Jaxson had the blanket over his lower body. But with no wind it wasn't so cold that I couldn't give him my surprise outside.

"Just sit there and give me two minutes."

"Fine. If I must." He tried to pout but knowing that he couldn't go anywhere only made the action seem all the more silly.

I quickly ran to the barn and pulled the old red radio flyer wagon back as fast as I could, smoothly making it up the ramp without losing its contents. When I got up to the porch, I was battling a myriad of feelings–exhilaration, anxiety, apprehension, compassion–they all rolled together in my stomach making me a little queasy.

Lord, I hope he likes it.

"Okay." I told him once I was settled on the deck a few feet from where he sat, "Open your eyes."

He pulled down the blindfold but kept his eyes closed at first, making a show of peeking them open one at a time. When he glanced down at the present sitting in front of him, his facial expression went from one of childlike excitement to stoically blank.

Shit! He doesn't like it!

His brow furrowed, his mouth tightened in a straight line and I could tell he was holding his breath. He wasn't giving anything away. His reaction could have ranged anywhere from furious to miserable.

When my apprehension got the best of me and I couldn't stand the silence anymore I spoke.

"Jax… babe. Say something please."

Still nothing. Minutes passed, could have been two or ten. Time was at a stand-still as I watched the muscles in his jaw clenching and started to become worried.

"I'm sorry. I thought you'd__" He sharply held up his hand, effectively stopping me from talking.

"Is that…" his voice came out raspy and thick with some unnamed emotion. He cleared his throat before trying again.

"Is that my Dad's saddle?" he whispered, not taking his eyes off of the dark brown, *Billy Cooke* saddle in front of him.

The taupe colored hand stitching woven in intricate swirls stood out in stark contrast to the dark leather and the initials *L.M.* took reign proudly at the base of the skirt.

I was too terrified to speak. As he shot a penetrating glance in my direction I nodded instead.

"Oh… my… Brinley," his voice caught in his throat only this time he didn't try to clear the emotion. As the tears slowly started running down his cheeks in thin rivulets, I saw his lips slightly turn up at the corners; a hint of a smile.

I breathed a sigh of relief and walked the few steps to close the distance between us. Kneeling down beside him, I placed my right hand on the back of his chair and my other hand on his chest.

"Yes, it is. I spoke to your Mom while you were in the hospital. We talked quite a few times actually. After everything you told me about your Dad, I knew this was what I wanted to do and she thought it was a wonderful idea. Said that it was just sitting around collecting dust up there. So I wired her the money to have it shipped down here. For you. Do you like it?" I asked, still feeling a little on edge because he hadn't actually said anything to reveal to me he was pleased.

Again, minutes passed as he merely gazed at the deep-rooted saddle.

"I know I didn't spend the money that you–" he turned and pulled my face to his, silencing me by crushing his lips against mine.

I could taste his salty tears on my lips and my heart swelled. When he pulled away he held my face inches from his own. I saw so much gratitude and love in his glistening eyes and felt my own start to tear up, too.

"Baby, this is the most thoughtful gift anyone has ever given me. It's second in line to the best present. You. Thank you. Thank you so much, my love."

I felt his breathing speed up through little puffs of air as he pulled me back to his mouth, claiming my lips as his own.

Two hours later we were headed over to my parents' house for lunch. The day was turning out to be beautiful. The chill from earlier had dissipated, sucked up into the warmth of the sun like a vacuum.

As we pulled into the driveway, I couldn't help but remember Christmas as a little girl. Daddy would always put those fat colored lights around the roofline of the house and down the sides of the brick. All the bushes lining the front windows and the magnolia tree standing tall in the yard would be covered from top to bottom with white lights, making them look like they were covered in snow. And always, always, there was a large, ten foot cross with a bright spotlight shining directly over the center in the middle of the yard. Appreciation for my parents filled my insides because everything was the same. I loved that happiness was the first feeling to so often bubble up from me these days. And so much of that had to do with the man beside me.

I glimpsed over at Jaxson. The rays from the window highlighted his golden skin and the tips of his hair that were peeking out from under his silver belly Stetson. Even in his profile, he looked gorgeous. His eyes were relaxed, the crinkles at the sides evident from happiness instead of stress. His mouth was curved upward in a half smile. He looked fulfilled and I felt my pride grow knowing that I had done that.

"I have one more present for you." I said. He looked over at me, head cocked over to one side, like he was taken aback.

"Baby, you've already given me the best presents. What else could I possible need?"

I grinned at him and placed my finger on the side of my nose, thrilled that I was finally surprising him for a change.

"You'll see." I walked around the back of the car to get the wheelchair from the trunk and locked it into place by the passenger side. He refused my help so I stood by on guard as he maneuvered his was from the Camry to his chair. Slowly, we made our way up the walk and to the front door, which was standing open for us.

Before going in, I leaned down and kissed him quickly on the side of his neck, whispering in his ear, "I love you."

He winked up at me as we walked into my childhood home.

Mom and Daddy were standing in the entry way waiting to greet us both. Momma gave us both a hug and kiss on the cheek. Daddy shook Jaxson's hand and wrapped me in a big hug. I hadn't made it home for Christmas last year and it was nice to be back with my family to celebrate the birth of Jesus.

My brothers and sister-in-law were all sitting on the couch when we walked around the corner. They all jumped up to greet us, trying to hide their sneaky smiles as they said the usual "Hi" and "Merry Christmas."

Everyone was anxious for the surprise to be revealed so as we came into view of the kitchen, my family parted like Moses and the Red Sea and Jaxson saw his other present.

There, standing at the bar with tears in her eyes, was Beth, Jaxson's Mom.

"Merry Christmas," I said softly to him.

He stared up into my eyes for a minute with a mix of confusion and… admiration I think?

"I love you, baby. Thank you."

And he wheeled into his mother's open arms.

The reunion was emotional and heartfelt. Beth sat down in a chair at the rectangle kitchen table with her arms tightly held around Jaxson's neck and her head resting on his shoulder. He laid his cheek on top of her head and hugged her closely into his chest.

They were both sobbing softly as I stood idly by and watched.

It wasn't until I felt the arms of both of my parents come around me that I realized I was crying too. Laying my head on my Daddy's shoulder, I listened to part of their conversation.

"Oh sweetie, I'm so sorry I couldn't get here sooner. I hate to see you this broken up. I hate that I wasn't here for you. Are you okay? Of course you're not okay. Look at you!"

Beth apparently babbled when she was nervous just like my Mother did. He assured her that he was doing well as he took her hands in his much larger ones.

"I'm fine Mother. Really. I've got a wonderful woman over there." he nodded his head in my direction, "And she's helping me get through this. She's got the mother-hen thing down for sure. It's good though. Because she's my motivation. What I don't understand is how you're here. How did you…" He choked up again and couldn't finish his sentence.

My own emotions felt raw just from watching their encounter.

"Well, son, that *wonderful woman* of yours sent her father and brothers to come and get me. We left Charlotte two days ago and got back last night." She studied Jaxson for a minute, scrutinizing like only a mother could. "Brinley is something special, isn't she?"

I blushed, tears continuing to roll from my eyes at her words and the pleasure they made me feel. Jax turned halfway around in his chair and looked back at me over his shoulder with love in his gaze.

"Yes… she is."

"Well then." Beth said, "Let me go formally meet my future daughter-in-law." She let go of her son, albeit reluctantly, and stood slowly. I remembered what Jax had said about her knees so I walked over to meet her halfway and she immediately pulled me into her arms.

"Thank you, my darling girl. I couldn't have asked for a better Christmas. Nor could I have prayed for a better woman for my Jaxson. I'm honored to be able to call you family." she said and kissed my cheek.

"Excuse me, Mother." Jaxson was right behind us. We both turned to look at him quizzically. "I'd like a moment alone with my fiancée if you don't mind." Beth smiled knowingly and shook her head no as she released me.

Jaxson wheeled himself out to the back patio and I followed closely behind him. When we were both outside with the door closed safely behind us, he turned his chair around quickly and grasped my hips forcefully.

"I need you to get down here." he demanded. "Now."

Without hesitation I brought my face to eye level with him and he latched onto my lips with such authority, such dominance, that I knew not to stop him.

As if I would!

His tongue encircled itself with my own, fighting for a place inside. His hands came off my hip to firmly hold my head in place as he tilted his head for deeper access. His breathing was as ragged as mine, little pants barely breaking through the tight seal of our lips.

Seconds–maybe minutes, hell if I know–passed by before he leisurely stopped and pulled my body close to lay his head on my belly.

"My baby, you are the most incredible woman I know." He looked up into my eyes. "And I'm going to call you my wife."

I knelt down beside him and sighed in absolute joy, "And I get to call you my husband."

Chapter 21

"Ask, and it shall be given you; seek, and ye shall find; knock, and it shall be opened unto you."
Matthew 7:7

February 12, 2014

After the Christmas and New Year's holidays, Beth was taken back to North Carolina by both of my parents. Momma had said that since she'd never been to that part of the country, they'd make a little vacation out of it on the way back.

Jax had taken a few days off from physical therapy–except for the exercises he did at home–so that he could spend time with his mother.

Once Beth was gone, he was determined to get back on track with his recovery. Dr. Roberts had scheduled his follow-up visit for January 24, one month after his hospital release, and Jaxson didn't want to give him or Dr. Patel any reason to put off the removal of his cast.

I was with him at every PT session as well as observing him at home, never interfering but keeping a watchful eye just in case. Of course sometimes I just enjoyed the sight of him, glistening with sweat, muscles straining under the intense battle they fought against invalidity.

On the day of his appointment, Dr. Patel was more than pleased with the progress Jax had made–thanks in large part to his tenacity–and sawed the cast off without hesitation. He did get fitted for a full length leg brace to help keep the strain at bay during therapy. Other than an advisement to try not to overdo it, Jaxson was released from Dr. Patel's care with the order to call only if any problems arose.

Dr. Roberts was even easier to please. The incisions on his abdomen from the two surgeries had completely closed up. An x-ray showed that the fractures to his rib cage had healed remarkably well. The doctor had said something along the lines of 'having an angel watching over your recovery because these kinds of breaks never healed this fast.' Jax and I exchanged a knowing smile at his statement but didn't say anything.

He gave us similar instructions to call if there were any sharp pains in his chest, and to not push recovery too hard but released Jaxson from his case load as well.

Now, for the last three weeks, Jaxson's physical therapy has been focused on leg strengthening. What had started as simple ankle and knee flexing and pointing has quickly progressed to stretch band exercises to work on range of motion.

He's still been confined to the wheelchair because the therapist said that since his leg had been shattered instead of just a clean break, it wasn't strong enough to walk more than eight to ten steps at a time.

The therapist says that. But I can see the muscles flex and swell in his leg; they look great to me. But he is a determined man so when we were at home he would push himself to the brink of exhaustion every day. It worries me that he's trying to go too far too soon but he insists he's fine, so I let it go.

When the time came for me to fly back to Los Angeles to settle some issues, I asked him to please take a break until I returned.

He reluctantly agreed; though it was very obvious he was not happy about it. Spouting some argument about how he could walk just fine with his crutches and that was something he would not stop doing while I was gone.

But easing up on the at-home therapy was enough to satisfy my 'mother-hen tendencies', as he liked continue joking about since he made the statement to his Mom.

My own Mother, who had gotten back from her mini vacation with Daddy about three weeks ago, had taken me to Hobby Airport on this unseasonably warm day. While temperatures rose to the upper seventies and the sun heated the morning chill away, Mom dropped me off at the departures gate and promised to look after Jaxson for me.

After an uneventful flight amidst a two hour time change, I walked out of the LAX terminal and into the parking garage to fetch my car. I was surprised at how it felt to be back here. I was expecting to feel some relief–joy, maybe–since I'd been gone for just over two months. It came as a shock to feel lonely. And homesick. LA had been my home for the last ten years.

I thought it would be forever.

But now, as I paid the astronomical fee for having my car sitting idle for eight weeks and drove out of the garage, it just felt vacant. Even the throng of people walking down sidewalks, full of excitement at being in the entertainment capital of the world, made this life feel like a lie. It was too pretentious. Too busy. Just too much, period. My heart was in Lake Shores.

Who'd have thought after all these years, I'd be ready to move back. Huh.

I pulled into the drive at my house on the beach at just after two in the afternoon. My manager, Melanie Moore, was coming over at four for an impromptu meeting. I was going to inform her of my engagement–that one word still made me grin like a school girl–and have her help me work out a game plan for my residence here in California.

I tossed my keys on the entry hall table, set my bag down by my bedroom door and walked through the living room out onto the deck overlooking the ocean. Standing with my hands on the porch banister and the sea breeze blowing a salty spray in my face, I realized I didn't want to sell the place. This was mine and Annie's home together. I liked having it. But my reasons weren't as obsessive as they might have been a few months ago.

Yes, I had many memories of this place with Annie, because of Annie. Before, keeping the house was kind of like that journal; holding on to some sort of connection with her and maintaining my self-torment, never forgetting that she was gone because of me. But I know that's not the case anymore.

Through Jaxson and my reawakening with the Lord, I get that she's where she is supposed to be and I have nothing to feel guilty about. This house brings peaceful memories now and it will be nice to have this place to come to whenever I worked. Or maybe just for a vacation from Texas.

Yes, definitely keep the house. But my home is with Jaxson.

Jax didn't know my plan was to stay in Lake Shores with him. He thought we would keep going back and forth like we'd been doing until we figured out a more permanent solution.

But that's not what I felt was the way to start a marriage. I wanted to be with him, always, once he was my husband. I was going to blow him away with the news of my bombshell on Valentine's when I flew home. I just had to think of a way to do so.

I turned away from the ocean that had been a refuge for the last sixteen months and made my way back inside. While I waited for Melanie, I wanted to start packing all the mementos, clothes, etc. that would be coming home with me.

I sat down on the living room floor in front of the coffee table to start with the photo albums there. Pulling them onto the ground next to me, I reminisced while looking at all the pictures. There were so many photos of Annie and me from various events and trips over the years.

I was flipping through the second album when I realized this was the first time I'd been able to look at these without crying. This was the first time since she died that these albums made me feel happy and blessed for the time I'd had with Annie, instead of that overwhelming pain at her absence.

And the gratitude, despite everything Jax has done for me, ultimately came down to one.

Thank you, God.

I didn't realize how long I had been sitting there, recalling the good times, until the doorbell rang at quarter after four.

So much for packing, I thought as I got up from my spot on the floor and went to open the front door.

Mel walked in full of life and energy. At five and a half feet with light blond hair, eyes that could range anywhere from a sea green to a sky blue and a body that made most men look twice, she was a woman admired and envied by many. I was grateful for the friendship I had gained with her since Annie's death. I didn't realize that's what she and I had until now.

"So," she spun a hundred and eighty degrees to look me in the face after she surveyed the room. "What's with all the boxes lying around? Are you planning on going somewhere? Last time I saw you, you were skipping off down the carpet at the premiere with some hot cowboy on your arm. You haven't been keeping me informed." She was tapping her toe in impatience but I knew it was all a front.

Mel was twenty-five and had more patience than a mother with her newborn baby.

I should introduce her to my brother, Alex… Nah, he'd kill me for interfering in his love life.

Besides, I didn't really know a whole lot about her. Other than the few glimpses into her personal life that she's let out. Like not dating anyone at the moment and wanting to meet someone with a 'strong hand', whatever that meant. As fun and energetic and sweet as Mel was, she was also strangely closed off.

"Oh, Mel. I'm not even sure where to start."

"How about with something to drink?" she suggested.

In full agreement, I grabbed a bottle of pinot grigio and two glasses from the kitchen and she followed me to the couch in the living room. We sat down at opposite corners with our glasses, sipping casually while I filled her in on all the details, starting with Aaron's wedding. To my extreme surprise, she didn't ask a lot of questions, just listened intently. When I told her about the proposal and everything Jax had set up and said to me, she was crying almost as much as I had been that night.

"Oh my God, Brinley." Hearing her say that one phrase made me a little uneasy but I chose not to dwell on it. It just kind of reiterated the fact that I didn't know much about her history. She kept on, seemingly oblivious to my discomfort.

"That has got to be one of the most romantic stories I have ever heard. But it's not a story, it actually happened! This is your real life! Oh, what would you think about a documentary? I mean really, this is the stuff that sells!"

I was already vehemently shaking my head no before she even finished her proposal.

"Absolutely not, Melanie! Like you said, this is my life. It's time I start living it. I'm not leaving the business for good. Just taking a break for a while. But I'll be back, you can count on that. In the meantime, I'm going to need someone to keep an eye on my house for me, so…" I raised my eyebrows at her, hoping she would accept the unspoken question.

"Of course I'll watch over things for you. God knows I'm not going anywhere. I'm a Cali girl through and through."

Huh. I thought to myself. *I never knew she was from California.*

Yet another piece to the Melanie Moore puzzle.

By six that evening, Melanie was getting ready to leave and she had all my contact information in Texas, including what would be my new address at Jax's house. She turned to face me at the door, holding on to the knob as she spoke.

"If you ever need me for anything, you know how to reach me."

"I know. And I really appreciate everything, Mel. It means a lot to have a friend in my corner over here."

I told her that I'd be leaving the day after tomorrow and would only come back for auditions and vacations. We walked down the driveway to her little red Audi coupe. After she was settled in the seat and buckled, she leaned out to grab the door and informed me with a wink that the thriller I had starred in was doing very well at the box office with a gross income of over forty million worldwide thus far. I realized that I hadn't even given it a second thought since Jaxson's accident.

To be honest, though, the money didn't mean anything. My job was acting; which was what I loved. The money was just an extra perk.

Now, I'd give all my resources and the cash in my bank account away to be able to spend the rest of my life with Jaxson. Lord knows, by His blessings, Jax's ranch is successful enough to support us.

I gave a little wave to Melanie when she tooted her horn as she drove off. Staring up at the sky, watching the stars start to peek out in random shimmering little specks, I couldn't help but think of the future of my career.

Maybe I'll give it up. Be a wife. Maybe even a mother someday.

I spent the rest of the night packing up as many photos, books, mementos, knick-knacks–whatever–as I could. All of the framed pieces in Annie's room would be staying. The only thing I was taking from her room was that big stuffed dog.

I'm not sure why but it just felt like that needed to go with me.

Tomorrow would be reserved for clothes and shoes because I knew those would take the most time. Of course, the ball gowns would be staying since I had no use for them in Lake Shores. But everything else needed to be boxed. And then I'd be headed home to my love. When I finished taping up the last box for the night, I decided to call him before I went to bed to let him know how everything was going.

It took four rings before he answered.

"Hey baby." He greeted me when he picked up the phone.

"Hi." Just hearing his deep voice made me melt.

"How's everything coming along? Are you getting all of your stuff taken care of?"

"Yeah. Melanie left a little while ago. She told me the movie is doing really well and that there haven't been any problems here at the house since I left."

"That's good news. Are you going to tell me what it is that you're doing over there?" he questioned me.

"Nope. But you'll know soon enough. How have you been feeling today? Are you taking it easy like I asked?"

I hoped that by changing the subject he wouldn't keep asking me about my plans. I'm terrible at keeping surprises a secret.

"I'm feeling pretty good, actually. I was thinking about running a marathon."

"Jaxson, don't mess with me." He only laughed. Who knew it was such a funny thing to tease your fiancée.

"Yes, I'm taking it easy. I miss you though." Now that he had his joking out of the way, he sounded weary.

"I know. I miss you too. You need to get some rest. I can hear how exhausted you are in your voice. And don't try to deny it. I just wanted to call and tell you that I love you. I'm going to be busy around here tomorrow but I'll call you in the evening."

I needed to get off the phone before the crying started. I didn't know how it was possible to miss him this much when I just saw him this morning.

Yes you do. It's because you love him so much. Add to that the worry that I had a suspicion he wasn't taking it as easy as he says and my emotions were going haywire.

"Okay love. You try to get some rest too, though. I know you need it after everything you've been doing for me here. I'll talk to you tomorrow. I love you." he said.

"Me too, Jax. Bye."

"Bye baby."

I heard him hang up as I switched off my phone. Deciding to forego the shower, I curled up in bed wearing one of Jaxson's shirts that I snuck in my suitcase this morning. Giving myself a pep talk to suck it up and quit acting like a big baby, I closed my eyes and fell into a deep sleep full of sweet, sunshine dreams.

February 13, 2014

When I woke up this morning, the sun was just starting to rise. I stretched lazily and rolled out of bed to head to the bathroom. After brushing my teeth and braiding my hair to keep it out of the way, I went into the kitchen for a cup of coffee.

Luckily, I'd managed to remember to set the timer last night and the pot was full, sending off a rich Columbian scent. Taking my mug to the back windows, I looked out over the horizon that was full of brilliant shades of dark yellow, amber and golden orange.

Sipping my coffee, I was amazed at how well rested I was. I hadn't realized the amount of sleep I'd lost since Jax's accident. Being so concerned over him hadn't allowed me the time needed to pay enough attention to my own well-being. But today I felt great so I turned from the ocean view and went to get dressed, definitely anxious to get started.

I didn't want there to be any reason for me to not make it home tomorrow.

Home.

Getting all of my clothes packed up was not as easy as I had anticipated. Aside from the formal clothes, there were many suits, cocktail dresses and the like that I didn't figure would do me a whole lot of good on a ranch. Sorting through them all and boxing what was going with me took almost five hours and a full pot of coffee. By the time I was finished, it was close to noon so after grabbing a quick shower and throwing on some jeans and a UT t-shirt, I drove down the highway to get some quick lunch.

Uncle Pat's is a little hole in the wall restaurant–if you could even call it that–right off the coastal highway, nestled inside an alcove of trees. If you didn't know about the place, you'd never think that the small building with chipped white paint and a faded blue roof served the best fried catfish in California.

After getting a basket loaded with fish and chips, I took a seat at one of the picnic tables out front to watch the people coming and going. There was a group of motorcyclists that pulled up shortly after me. Their bikes that were sitting in the sun were shining reflections of the Chinese lanterns hanging on poles around the patio.

A handful of young college kids in bathing suits pulled up in a van and raucously made their way to the front door, obviously grabbing a bite to eat before they hit the beach.

But what grabbed my eye more than anything was the elderly couple sitting two tables down from me. They sat across from each other with an empty basket pushed off to the side. They were holding hands and simply gazing at one another with the look of long time lovers. I couldn't help but to hope and pray that Jaxson and I would have that someday.

Across the highway from Pat's was a staircase that led down to the beach. I disposed of all my trash, left my car where it was parked and made my way across the road and down the stairs. I took off my tennis shoes and rolled up my pants before I began walking along the sand and marveled at the beauty of the beach and ocean.

I was going to miss the clear water and soft sand under my feet. The beach that's close to Lake Shores has seaweed covering the sand and the water was browner, dirtier. My parents told us growing up that it's because it opens up into the Gulf of Mexico.

At least it's a beach, I thought to myself. *And that dirty beach is where Jaxson is, so it's okay.*

As the sun moved past the midday point in the sky and began to slowly make its descent west, I made my way back to my car and headed home to finish labeling everything I had packed that morning. There were only two bags going with me on the airplane, aside from my carry-on.

All my other stuff was being picked up by a small moving truck at eight in the morning and they'd be driving it down to Texas for me. I wanted to make sure the boxes were properly labeled and set out where the movers could easily get to them.

I was still trying to think of a way to surprise Jax with my impending change of address while I pushed the boxes to a corner of the entry way by the front door and wrote the name of the contents on the tops flaps. When the idea finally hit me as I pushing the last box into place, I eagerly called my Mom because the only way it'd work is if I had her help me execute it.

"Hey sweetie! How's LA?" she said when she answered.

"It's good, thanks. Listen, Mom, I need your help."

February 14, 2014

I was so impatient to get home this morning that the alarm clock didn't even have the chance to wake me up. I was out of bed and moving before the sun came up. Finishing getting the house ready for my departure didn't take too long since all the bags and boxes had been lined up and settled last night.

Just adjusting the thermostat so it wouldn't run all the time, making sure every door and window were locked and all the lights were off.

A town car service was going to pick me up at nine since my car would be staying here. I didn't want to drive it across country plus, Jax told me he had an older truck I could use anytime I needed it. Little did he know that it'd be used a lot more often than he probably thought. Leaving my Mercedes in California just seemed smart. That way we'd always have a car available when we made it here.

By the time I finished everything, the movers had arrived.

The two men were typical California guys; light hair, tanned skin, blue eyes. After directing them to the boxes to be loaded, they told me that my belongings would be in Lake Shores in about five days. When the last box was gone I went to get myself ready.

I took my time in the shower, shampooing and conditioning my hair as well as shaving my legs. I applied a light coat of makeup–just a touch of mascara and blush–and blow dried my hair, pulling it up into a low ponytail with my natural waves resting against my back. I wanted to look nice for Jaxson when I got home but comfort on an airplane was my primary concern. Jeans and a long-sleeved white blouse would have to do.

After a glance at the clock I saw that the car should be arriving any minute, so I took the opportunity to make one last walk around the house that had been my home for some years now.

So many memories. Thank you, Annie, for all of them.

The car honked out front, drawing me back into the present. I carried the bags to the front porch and the driver came to help me load them. I grabbed my purse off the entry hall table, looked up and around the house one last time, then locked the door of my past behind me. An hour and a half later, I was on a plane headed home to my future.

Momma had picked me up at the airport and it was just after five in the evening when we pulled into town. I had Jaxson's Valentine's Day present–that my Mom helped me with–sitting in my lap. I was so excited about it that it felt like it was going to burn a hole through my pants.

I noticed out of the corner of my eye that my Mom kept looking at me anxiously. It was starting to make me a little paranoid, like maybe I had some kind of growth coming out of my forehead.

"Mom, are you okay? Why do you keep looking at me like I have a third eye or something?" I finally asked her when I couldn't stand the stares anymore.

"No, no. I'm fine." She tried to laugh but it was a little too high pitched and similar to a cackle to be thought of as genuine. "I was just thinking you should let your hair down. You look so pretty when your red ringlets curve around your face and shoulders. I think Jaxson would appreciate it since he hasn't seen you in two days."

"Oh-Kay," I drug out my response. Eyeing her suspiciously, I opted to oblige and gently tugged my hair tie out, letting my long hair flow all across my back.

I bent over to put the tie in my purse right as we pulled onto the gravel driveway of the Burnt Aggie Ranch. I got out of the car with my purse on my shoulder and the present in my hand. I grabbed my small carry-on suitcase from the back seat and was getting ready to grab my other two bags from the trunk when I stopped.

"If it's okay with you, Mom, I'm only going to take my carry-on and the present with me tonight. I'll bring Jax with me tomorrow to get my other bags. I'm just too tired to get everything tonight and besides, it'll be a good excuse to get him out of the house." I said through the open passenger window.

"Sure sweetie, that's fine." She paused and I knew there was more she wanted to say. "Make sure… don't jump to… have a nice night, dear." she finally stuttered out and put the car in reverse, driving off before I had a chance to respond to her ramblings.

What is with her? I thought to myself as I walked up the front porch steps and opened the door. I set down my bag on the floor in the foyer and my purse on the table by the door. Gripping Jaxson's present tight against my chest, I set out to find him.

"Jax? Babe, are you in here?" I called out and rounded the corner to the living room. And froze dead in my tracks like a deer caught in headlights.

Jaxson was standing on the other side of the large room in the same place the Christmas tree had been just six weeks ago. He was wearing a black suit, white shirt–unbuttoned at the top and revealing a small, teasing amount of tanned skin–and the black caiman boots he only wore on special occasions.

He was holding a bouquet of at least two dozen yellow roses with white baby's breath mixed in to add some contrast. There were more yellow and white roses throughout the living room. I counted at least fifteen vases resting on top of the coffee table, end tables and mantle. Loose petals were spread over the floor making it look like a field dotted in the heavily perfumed blooms.

Adding to the rosy fragrance were white candles. They were in all different sizes from tall cylinders to short squares and set in groups of five on every hard surface. The smell of fresh linen, my favorite, wafted toward my nose as well.

Frank Sinatra was crooning quietly in the background about the way someone looked.

My eyes roamed over the entire scene before coming back to rest on Jaxson. It was then that I noticed that his wheelchair, as well as his crutches and leg brace, were nowhere to be seen.

"Hey baby." He broke the hushed stillness. "Did you have a nice flight?"

"Umm, I did. Why aren't you in your chair? Or at least using your crutches. Do you want to tell me what's going on?" I asked as he started to walk methodically toward me. Stunned by the setting laid out in front of me, I hadn't realized I was counting his steps until the word twelve popped up in my mind.

I started to rush over to him, wanting to be ready in case he fell. But Jax held up his right hand to stop me, slowly shaking his head no like he might do to correct a child. That one gesture brought me up short and for some reason my feet stopped. Satisfied that I wouldn't move again, he resumed his walking.

Seventeen steps now.

"Do you know how much I missed you?" he asked me, still walking, twenty-two steps. "Do you know how lonely this house gets when you aren't around to fill it with your love?"

He was like a predator, methodically closing in on his kill; twenty-nine steps.

"Do you have any idea how much you mean to me?" Thirty-two steps and he was finally in front of me.

I let out a sigh as he came to a stop.

"You've been holding out on me." I quietly reprimanded him.

He cocked his head to the side and raised an eyebrow as if to say 'whatever do you mean'. He handed me the flowers he'd been holding in his left hand. I moved to hold his present under one arm and took them graciously. I brought them to my face and inhaled deeply as he ran the knuckles of his right hand gently down my cheek, wiping away the lone tear that had escaped.

He slowly bent down so that he was resting on his left knee. Placing his hands on either side of my waist, he raised his head to look into my eyes and spoke again, at last.

"I may have already been blessed by you're saying yes to my proposal. But this never would have felt right to me unless I did it properly. And I've told you countless times that I want *us* to be done right." He paused, gauging my reaction.

"I love you Brinley. More than what should be humanly possible. I thank God every day for bringing you into my life. I know things might be difficult for us at first, at least until we get our living situation worked out. But we will work it out. Just like we'll tackle any other problems that may arise in our future. I will spend the rest of my days honoring and devoting myself to you. And I will spend every waking moment showing you with my words and actions what a blessing you are to me.

"Will you marry me, my love?"

I was so taken back by this entire scene that my voice had long since left me. I slowly knelt down in front of Jaxson until I was staring into his eyes; dark, chocolate brown and full of passion. I set the flowers and his present both down on floor, took his face in my hands and kissed him forcefully, hungry for his touch and his taste. He curled his fingers around mine, squeezing them tightly before pulling to look into my eyes.

"Is that a yes?" he asked, smirking at me.

I quickly nodded my head yes, tears falling onto the floor with the movement, and kissed him again.

Before I knew it, he was guiding me backwards until we were lying on the floor together; legs intertwined, hands roaming shamelessly over the other's body. He felt so powerful; the corded muscles in his arms and back rippling against my palms as I tried to find a way to get closer. No one would have ever been able to tell he was in a wheelchair less than a month ago.

His rough, blue collar hands were softly stroking my sides and hair, calluses tingling my skin in a delicious way that sent my butterflies soaring. His tongue was delicately caressing the tip of my own, tempting me but never quite giving enough. He deftly rolled me over so that I was lying on my back and he was directly on top of me, holding his weight up by his hands on either side of my head. I ran my hands up his forearms, relishing the power I could feel in those parts of his body.

Jax tore his mouth away from mine and kissed my cheek. Moving to my ear, he nibbled on my lobe and the sensitive spot right below before making his way down my neck. The sweet torture continued as he moved across my collar bone–taking a moment to plant a wet kiss in the hollow of my throat–and made his way up the other side.

Instead of attacking my lips again like I desperately wanted him to, he kissed the top of my nose and leaned back to look me in the eyes–his brown to my green. There was so much love and desire in his gaze; I couldn't take my eyes off of him. We laid there staring at each other for I don't know how long. It could have been minutes. It could have been hours.

The sun had set and it was dark out; the only light coming from some of the candles that hadn't already burned out. There was a sharp pain in my backside from lying on the hard floor but I didn't care. There was no place else I wanted to be on this Valentine's Day than here, with Jaxson.

And that reminded me; I still have his surprise.

"I have a present for you." I whispered in the growing darkness.

"Really. Well, let's have it."

He sat up into a sitting position on the floor next to me, legs straight out in front and leaning back on his elbows for support. I quickly sat up too, thankfully relieving the pressure, and reached around him to grab the gift. I brushed right by his chest and closed my eyes, savoring his sweet smell of sunshine and the feel of his lips as he brushed them across my still damp neck.

Don't get distracted!

I sat back on my heels and nervously handed it to him. It was a large rectangle package wrapped in red paper with a big white bow.

He shook it like a little kid with a gleam in his eyes, trying to figure out what it was but only looked more puzzled when no rattling or other noise sounded. Eyeing me curiously, he finally tore the wrapping off to reveal the present underneath and stared.

Resting in his hands was a dark mahogany wooden sign with three names engraved into it. *'Mathews'* was carved in the middle, taking precedence over the space. Just above it in smaller engravings were our names, side by side.

"What is this?" he looked quizzically at me.

"It's a sign. For our front door. For after the wedding. I thought maybe people should know that this was my home too. If that's okay with you."

I watched for his reaction as he looked back down at his gift. Trying to tell if he was happy, disappointed or maybe even indifferent. He only slowly shook his head; like he was confused.

"Does this mean–" I cut him off before he could finish his question and he stared at me as I spoke.

"It means that this is my home. Not LA; but here, with you. Always. Happy Valentine's D–" His forceful kiss broke off my words.

My body and my mind became his to control as he laid me back down on the floor, following the movement with his own. My train of thought and any objections I might have had went out the window when Jaxson plunged his tongue back into my mouth; possessing the only part of me we were willing to give each other yet.

And once again, we were a tangled mess on the floor, oblivious to anything except for one another.

Chapter 22

"Therefore shall a man leave his father and his mother, and shall cleave unto his wife: and they shall be one flesh." Genesis 2:24

April 23, 2014

On a beautiful spring day with the sky looking like a pale blue water-colored picture and the trees budding new life with flowers, Jaxson and I drove through town to our church for the rehearsal for our wedding.

The two months following Valentine's Day went by in a rush, thank God. It was getting harder to be around Jaxson without wanting to take our relationship to the next level. It's not that either of us still had our 'virtue'. We might not want to run around shouting it from the roof tops but the fact was that neither of us were a virgin. But I was in full agreement with him when he said he wanted our relationship to be without mistakes. As much as was in our power anyways.

This was sending both of our hormones into lethal limits though.

So, to make it a little easier to keep up with our promise to each other, I'd been sleeping in one of the spare bedrooms. It's helped with our abstinence but I definitely miss going to sleep and waking up in Jaxson's arms.

I often laughed to myself when I thought about our decision and arrangement and what Annie would say in regards to it.

I could hear her good-natured scolding toward the situation, and me, even now.

Brin, you have to take the car for a test drive before you buy it! What if this said car doesn't... you know... get good gas mileage?

With Jaxson, I had a gut feeling that some things would be worth the wait. Just thinking about what lay ahead for us tomorrow made my heart swell and my insides tremble with anticipation.

All of the wedding plans had come together nicely. Even though we were more than capable of hiring a wedding coordinator, I had wanted to do the planning and decorating myself, with the help of my family. It was something Annie and I would talk about for hours when we were growing up, planning our own weddings and doing everything ourselves to make those dreams come to fruition.

That was the way it'd been in all aspects of our lives. From getting the date we wanted for senior prom to making a name for ourselves in Hollywood.

This wedding would be no different. Because of the support we had for each other, I was trying to make sure Annie was brought out in as much of the wedding as possible. From the bouquets to the reception centerpieces to the music play list.

It was going to be perfect.

As long as we could make it through the rehearsal dinner tonight. I was meeting the rest of his family and the fear that they might not approve had me on pins and needles.

We arrived at the church at precisely five in the evening. Walking hand in hand into the narthex of St. Timothy's, I couldn't help but feel that this was where our relationship had really taken off. Had it not been for my soulful confession to the Lord and His subsequent message, there's no telling what would have become of us. I grinned up at him as we walked into the chapel and were bombarded by family.

Jaxson's two brothers, their wives and his five nieces and nephews were there along with his sister and mother, who were sitting in the front pew on the left aisle of the church.

He squeezed my hand reassuringly as Alise and Lori, his sisters-in-law, and his sister Rachel caged me in and walked me towards Beth. Some of my nervousness faded as these women, who'd been a part of the Mathews family for years, brought me into their fold like old time friends. Fighting back a pang of sadness at the fact that my best old time friend wouldn't be here, I gave Beth a hug before turning to the other side of the aisle.

My parents were there as well as both of my brothers and my sister-in-law. Mom and Daddy each gave me a kiss on the cheek before turning me over into the hands of my brothers. Aaron pulled my in tight, telling me he was so happy for me and his best friend.

"My best friend becomes my brother-in-law." He shook his head a little at the craziness of it. "At least I won't ever have to worry about you being taken care of. Jaxson is a good man, Brin. I'm happy for you." Jess held on tight to Aaron's side and nodded her agreement.

"Thanks Aaron. It means a lot to know that you're okay with this. With us."

I felt another pair of arms come around my shoulders and immediately knew Alex had come to take his turn. He enfolded me in a bear hug and squeezed. Alex and I had always been so close and it meant the world that he'd been able to come home for my wedding.

"Thank you, Alex." I whispered, not really sure what I was thanking him for but knowing that I needed to. He tilted my face up to look at him and smiled.

"I should be thanking you." At my confused look he explained. "I've seen how far you've come these last seven months, Brinley. You did a lot of work yourself but with Jaxson by your side you've shown me that you can conquer anything. Easily. And that family really is the way to happiness. It's made me realize that my time in the Navy is up. I'm ready to move forward and focus on the next chapter in my life. So, come August when my duty is up for renewal, I'll be retiring and moving back here."

The thought of being so close to Alex again made my smile grow in unfettered joy. I hugged him tightly around his neck until a deep clearing throat brought me back to the situation at hand.

I spun around and found Jax standing a couple feet away with his arm out, waiting for me to take it.

"The minister is ready to start, baby. We all need to get into place."

I nodded and took his offered arm, walking to stand right in front of Reverend Pierce with our attendants on either side of us. Neither Jax nor I had wanted to have a large wedding party–especially me, since my best friend would only be here in spirit–so Jessica was my matron of honor.

And Jaxson's oldest brother, Thomas–who was married to Ali–was his best man. When I had asked why he chose Thomas, Jax said it was because both he and Brent had already served as best man before. Apparently they had a rotation of sorts. I didn't really get it but never pushed for details. They knew what they were doing.

But only having two attendants helped the rehearsal to go smoothly and quickly since we didn't have extra opinions being thrown around. I decided smaller wedding parties were very much the way to go to minimize drama.

We chose to go with a traditional and simple Episcopalian service only without communion. Our decision would end up making our nuptials around thirty minutes. *Perfect.* After going over the highlights of the service and doing two quick run-throughs, we were leaving the church less than an hour after we got there and were all headed to Dido's Seafood Restaurant.

Dido's is a house turned restaurant that sits right on the San Bernard River and has been frequented by my family for years. White clapboard shutters lay open to let the evening sun filter through the windows. Old ceiling fans squeaked overhead in their efforts to spin and cool the large dining room.

The owners, Paul and Suz, greeted us as we walked in the front door, congratulating Jax and I. They direct us to a corner of the room that has been set up with tables pushed together to hold our families and point to the far wall where a long buffet has been set out for us. By half past six, all our family members were stuffing their bellies with fried and grilled shrimp, fried fish, green beans, homemade coleslaw, hush puppies and Dido's famous shrimp dip.

The Lamberts and the Mathews seemed to get along really well. Everyone was walking around, chatting with each other. Jax's nieces and nephews were running around in circles, playing a game of tag amongst the other diners. No one appeared to mind and watching them made me eager for the day we would start our own family.

As desserts of banana pudding and some kind of coconut cake were being served, Jax and I stood up at the front of the room to give our thanks.

"Listen," Jaxson began with his deep voice that got everyone's attention, "Brinley and I want to extend our sincere appreciation to all of you. We know this may seem like a bit of a whirlwind romance to some, but…" he stopped to glance at me and I got lost momentarily in his gaze. His piercing brown eyes made me hold my breath before he continued.

"When God brings your one love into your life, like He's done with us, who are we to argue that? Bottom line, we love you all and thank you for being here with us during the beginning of the rest of our lives."

He lifted his glass–filled with his favorite Jack Daniels and Coke–and I raised my wine glass half full of chardonnay. Our glasses gave a soft clink when we brought them together and toasted with our intimate sized crowd.

There was a chorus of 'cheers' going up all around us as they all raised their own glasses and drank. Jaxson set his glass on the table and leaned down to give me a chaste kiss on the forehead, his lips cool and wet against my skin from his drink.

By nine everyone was saying their goodbyes and heading home for the night. My parents waited patiently for me in Daddy's truck, giving me a minute to say bye to Jax since I was staying with them tonight. Some traditions just couldn't be broken and for me, the whole 'can't see the bride before the wedding' thing was a no-brainer.

I was leaning against his chest; the muscles there hard beneath my cheek. Lightning bugs began to make their appearance, blinking in tune with the steady beat of Jax's heart. Idly playing with the pearl snaps of his blue plaid shirt, he reached around and locked his hands together behind me.

"You gonna make it tonight?" he asked and kissed the top of my head.

"No problem. Tonight I'll be fine. I'm just ready for tomorrow. More specifically, ready for tomorrow night." I grinned up at him and he laughed loudly at my honesty.

"Ah, baby. Me too. More than you know. Go home and get some sleep. I'll see you tomorrow."

"Okay. I'll meet you at the altar, say, around five o'clock. Sound good?"

I stared into his beautiful eyes and saw a mischievous twinkle that had me wondering what was going on his head. He brought his left hand up and cupped my cheek tenderly–his right still firmly held against my lower back–and pulled my lips to his. A kiss full of yearning and a hint of the desperation I felt, too. When Jax pulled away and kissed below my ear with his open mouth, his softly whispered words sent shivers down my spine.

"Sleep sweet tonight baby… you'll need it."

April 24, 2014

It's funny how a person's internal alarm clock will work at the strangest time. I don't know if it was from sheer exhaustion because of not sleeping well at Jaxson's the last two months or if it was the two glasses of wine I'd had at dinner.

Either way, I woke up this morning feeling rested and excited.

Glancing at the clock on the nightstand in my childhood bedroom, the time said seven-thirty in the morning. I wasn't due to get up for another half hour but apparently my mind knew today was a big day.

Lying on my pillow, I watched the sunlight streaming through the window and revealing the dust bunnies swirling in the air. It made me think about tonight and how our friends and family would be swirling around a dance floor at our wedding reception. Right as a stupid grin curled up on my face, my mother came bursting into my room at just after eight and all but skipped to my bed.

"Happy Wedding Day!"

Judging by the way she all but threw herself on my bed, she might have been more thrilled than me. I smiled at her and sat up in bed, eagerness taking over thoughts about what lay ahead for me today.

"Thanks Momma." I said and leaned in to give her a bear hug. "For everything. I know it might not have shown but I really appreciate you never giving up on me after Annie died. I don't know what I would have done without you."

She smiled at me and wiped tears from her eyes with the back of her hand, sniffling loudly and immodestly like only a mother can. Then she took a deep breath and visibly shook off that tearful expression.

"Come on; don't start on all that mushy stuff now. We've got a long day ahead of us. Let's get this show on the road, shall we?"

An hour later, we were at the salon. I had a full makeover coming at me today–hair, toes, nails, makeup–so I was ushered straight to the foot bath as soon as we walked through the door.

Soaking my feet in the warm water, I drank a bloody mary and chatted with Tiny, the pedicurist, as she worked on my toes. Once they were painted a deep red–the color chosen because Ann always, always wore red toenail polish–I was handed over to Patti who went to work on my hair. She had cut my hair from the time I was five until I moved away. She was also responsible for my hair when we went to all those formal dances in high school.

Patti was the only option for me when it came to wedding hair-styling.

Sipping another bloody mary, I laughed with her as she relayed the story of the first time she ever cut my hair.

"...needless to say, your Momma was a mess! I mean, who wouldn't be? Your three year old brother had just cut off half your hair up to your ears! Oh, I tell you, I've never seen a mom so upset about her daughter's little curls being gone." I had to set my drink down to keep from spilling it, I was laughing so hard. I'd forgotten all about the time Alex had cut off eight inches of my hair.

"At least it grew back. And just as beautiful as ever." She kept right on talking until all of my locks had been pinned up with what I thought had to be a whole package of bobby pins.

Leaving the tiara and veil for last, I made my way over to the make-up station. Keeping my eyes closed while Isa—who I'd flown in yesterday for this very job–worked on my face, Tiny came over to start on my manicure. The whole process of turning me into a bride took about five hours but the time flew by with the help of those bloody maries and a glass of champagne.

The place was filled with music from an oldies country station and laughing women. There were no nerves, no doubts. Just joy. Stories were being told by both the Lambert women as well as the Mathews women of previous weddings, honeymoons and such.

Everyone was happy go lucky and everything was perfect.

Until the sudden pang of sadness hit in my gut as I watched the two sides of my family entertain themselves. My future mother-in-law took notice of my quiet demeanor first.

"Brinley, are you okay?" she asked, sitting down in the chair next to me and laying her hand on my knee. "You're not having second thoughts about any of this, are you?"

"Oh no! No, no, no. I just… I can't help but feel emotional because Annie isn't here with me. I didn't realize how much I would miss her today, you know?"

"I think that's only natural." Beth said. "She was your best friend for years. You two dreamt about this day together. But you know she's here in spirit, watching over you. From what your mother has told me, Annie wouldn't be okay with you sitting here like this, sulking and wallowing over her absence. This is a happy day. I get a new daughter-in-law."

She kissed my cheek and I took a deep, cleansing breath. She was right; Ann would be pissed at me right now.

"And I get to marry the man of my dreams. So thank you for that."

By three o'clock we had left the salon and driven the four blocks over to the church. Right after we walked into the backdoors and made our way to the Guild Room–the place where brides had been getting ready for years at St. Timothy's–the heavens opened up and the rain came down. Sheets as thick as ice pounded down on the grass and cars in the parking lot. I couldn't help but smile and laugh, thinking this might have been Annie's way of saying she was around.

"Well." I said, turning to the women in the room. "I always heard it was good luck for it to rain on your wedding day."

Laughing filled the room as everyone started to get dressed. My matron of honor was helping me get into my wedding dress, clasping the hooks together in the back.

I'd wanted elegant and simple. It was strapless with a straight neck line and crystal beads sown all around the bodice. There was a pleat down the front of the a-line skirt with matching beadwork in the middle. The train was only about two feet long but my skirt pillowed widely out around me from my petticoat.

My tiara was small and sat straight across the top of my head, like a headband turned on its side. It nestled perfectly in front of my pinned up hair. My veil had two layers, one hanging down to the base of my back and the other just brushing my elbows, with tiny white pearls decorating the tulle in random places.

And my shoes. My shoes were perfect.

Four inch white satin stilettos with small cubic zirconias covering the front that fit like a pair of flip flops in between my toes and up the top of my feet. The strap that wound around my ankle was covered in the diamond-like jewels too with five two inch stands hanging down from each strap. They were right out of a fairytale. My own Cinderella shoes.

The photographer we hired to put or wedding and reception into memories of the four by six glossy variety came in and started giving directions of poses to make.

I looked expectantly out of a window, waiting for my groom to appear. My mother fastened my great-grandmother's diamond necklace around my throat. Jess and I signed the church registry. By the time she was satisfied with her pre-wedding shots, it was time to head to the alter.

When the organist began tapping out the opening chords to *Canon in D* by Johann Pachelbel, my stomach clenched in a sudden wave of tense nausea.

I closed my eyes and could hear Ann's voice in my head.

'You've got the man of your dreams waiting for you. You're doing great. Take a deep breath and get down that aisle.'

Opening my eyes, I glanced over at Daddy and he winked at me once. I gave a small nod and he began to escort me down the aisle. Once my gaze found Jaxson everyone else in the church turned hazy around me. It was like looking through a tunnel and he was the light at the end of it.

Jax looked absolutely gorgeous in his black tuxedo, white bow tie and cummerbund. His broad shoulders stood out from the jacket, making him look more imposing than normal. He held his hands clasped together in front of his hips. His dark chocolate eyes burned a hole through my dress, straight to my heart. Even from the distance, I could see his breathing speed up as he slowly licked his lower lip.

We finally made it to the front and after Daddy stated that he and my Mom gave me over to be married, he kissed my cheek and graciously passed me off to Jaxson.

Everything after that passed in a blur. As he repeated his vows to me and slipped a white gold wedding band on my finger, I saw the glossiness in his eyes and it took all of my will power to keep from crying too. My hands were shaking so badly when it was my turn that I struggled to put his ring on.

I only remember four words from the entire service.

"I do," I blushed.

"I do," He declared.

Before I knew it, the Reverend was reciting *The Peace* and giving permission for the bride and groom to greet each other.

When Jaxson kissed me it was sweet, tender. But the light touch from the tip of his tongue to mine gave a hint of the passion that was waiting for us at the end of the night.

We rushed through the pictures after the ceremony as quickly as possible, eager to get to the party. We made our way to the doors of the church, ready to run through the rain to the limo that would drive us to the ranch. Right before we made our first leap, the rain stopped as suddenly as it began.

Smiling at each other, Jax and I hurried over and hopped in the back seat.

We were dropped off at the barn opening surrounded by cars and trucks that were covered in mud from the rain soaked dirt driveway. The sky turned from an overcast gray to a deep blue, preparing for the coming dusk. All our guests were waiting in the open area to greet 'Mr. and Mrs. Jaxson Mathews.'

Pride swelled in my chest at my new name when we made our way inside.

All the tables were covered with white linens. The centerpieces consisted of round, twelve inch in diameter mirrors with a set of five goblets of different heights sitting on top. Each goblet was adorned with crystal beads strung up around the stems and had white tea light candles inside. The glow from all the candles shimmering off the mirrors made the barn a truly romantic hideaway. Spread around the guest tables were white organza bags full of pastel colored dinner mints and chocolates.

We made our way to the head table where there was a large vase in the middle to hold my bouquet, made up of white and yellow calla lilies and roses.

To the right of us was the cake table which had a large backdrop of white tulle hanging down to the ground in sheets with white lights wrapped up inside.

The entire place was just as I had imagined it when Ann and I would talk about *my* day all those years ago. Soon everyone was swept up in the party that was our reception. There was eating, dancing, drinking, laughing. Everyone appeared to be enjoying themselves and our two families were blending well together.

When Jax and I walked out to the temporary wooden floor for our first dance to Kenny Chesney's *Me and You,* our mothers held hands and cried.

The single ladies squealed like crazy, their voices blending in with Cyndi Lauper singing *Girls Just Wanna Have Fun,* when I threw my toss bouquet and it broke in mid-air into seven smaller bouquets, all miniature versions of my own. When Melanie caught the largest of them, I ran over and hugged her tight, ignoring her comments about never getting married.

The single men catcalled and hollered as I sat on Thomas' knee and Jax slowly peeled off my garter as ZZ Top sang about legs and tossed it to the waiting hounds. I laughed as my brother Alex caught it and yelled to him, "You're next!" The uncertain look of something akin to panic made Jax and I laugh even more.

We stood with a knife poised in our linked hands for more pictures before cutting into our cake. Four tiers stood beautifully with white and yellow roses separating each of the layers. The cake was strawberry filled and covered with white frosting.

We promised each other not to smash the sweets in the other's face. And I'm not ashamed to admit that I was skeptical until the moment when he gently placed the cake square inside my open mouth.

By the end of the night, exhaustion was beginning to set in from all the drinking, dancing and socializing.

I was sitting at the head table resting my feet and looked across the room to where Alex and Mel were talking by the drink table. Alex's dress whites stood out in stark contrast to Mel's little black dress and black stilettos. A tingle of hope ran through me when she placed her hand on his forearm and laughed at something he said. They looked great together and I thought that maybe, just maybe, it might be the beginning of something special.

The DJ got our attention and I stood up to go meet Jaxson in the middle of the dance floor for our last dance. It was still hard to believe as I walked to meet him that not so long ago he and I had stood in this same spot, dancing, and I was fighting back my feelings. Now we were here as man and wife.

Thank you, thank you, thank you Lord!

Jaxson took my right hand in his left and pulled me close with his arm around my lower back right as the first notes of the song started.

Cliché as it might be, we danced to *I've Had the Time of My Life.*

As he whirled me around the floor, he leaned down and kissed my nose, slinking his mouth around to the side of my neck with a smile playing on his lips.

"My life is just beginning." he whispered in my ear, "And I'd like for it to start right now."

When he brought his head back and looked into my eyes they were full of love, promise, desire. And hunger.

We left before the song ended.

April 25, 2014

I was dreaming; images flitting through my mind in vivid pictures. My gown dropping to the floor of the hotel suite bathroom. My white silk and lace wedding night lingerie slowly being peeled down and off my shoulders, slithering down my body to pool at my feet. My skin tingling under his soft, wet kisses. My insides clutching in response to the anticipation. Dark eyes staring into mine from above. Unhurried, sliding movements sending my body into a quaking overload of sensations. Panting breaths, desperately trying to regulate with pounding hearts.

Pure kisses and whispers of 'I love you'.

I slowly opened my eyes–feeling satisfied and yet still longing for more–with Jaxson's arms wrapped protectively around me and my head lying perfectly in the nook of his shoulder. The dawn of a new day was just beginning outside, the hustle of a waking Houston breaking through the stillness of our room.

I turned my head up to look at Jaxson. He looked so peaceful and relaxed that at first I didn't want to wake him. He might have even been as content as I was.

Doubtful.

His long eyelashes fanned out, looking like little crescent moons; his cheeks had a hint of color that you'd expect to see after a wedding night; his lips–*oh, his lips*–were slightly parted as he breathed shallowly, in and out. He was beautiful when he slept but I didn't want to wait any longer.

I lifted his left hand to my mouth and softly kissed his ring, now firmly in place saying that he was mine forever. He stirred only a little, making a small grumbling noise and tightening his hold on me.

Hmm, so it's gonna take more to wake you up. I turned my face inward and placed my lips on the side of his ribs, just below his pectoral muscles.

I kissed there once. Twice. Three times when he finally gave in.

Jaxson's arms gripped me firmly and rolled me over so that I was lying directly on top of him.

"Good morning, Mrs. Mathews."

"And to you, Mr. Mathews." I kissed his nose. "Did you sleep well?" I asked.

"Very. Who knew a wedding could be so tiring. Although I don't know what wore me out more. The wedding party or… *our party*." He didn't try to hide the wicked looking grin on his face that brought a sparkle of amusement–maybe even challenge–to his eye.

"Well then I vote we get our party started again. You know, in case you need a refres–"

He attacked my mouth before I had a chance to finish my ploy to make love. Deftly rolling me over again so that I was on my back, Jax hovered over me, holding himself up on his elbows and gazing intimately into my eyes.

"I love you so much baby." he said as he ran the tips of his fingers lightly down my torso.

I quivered under his touch. He kissed down my neck, giving a small lick to my rapidly beating pulse. He made his way across my chest and belly, down to my hips where he nipped at my hip bones. Further still until I was lost in a world where he ruled over my body.

Definitely good gas mileage, was my last thought before I closed my eyes and gave myself over to his sensual care.

Two hours later, after we showered together and packed up our toiletries, we were headed to the airport for our flight to Cozumel for our honeymoon. While he maneuvered his truck into a parking spot in the garage, sandwiched between another truck and minivan, I marveled at how absolutely fulfilled I felt.

"Well, Mrs. Mathews, did you enjoy yesterday?" Jax questioned as he grabbed our suitcase from the back seat and took my hand in his free one.

"I did. I don't imagine anyone could have had a better wedding day than we did. Or night for that matter. Good call on not wanting to make mistakes. I do believe that made the night all the more better," I teased as I leaned up to kiss his neck.

"I think we should 'not make mistakes' much more often."

He dropped the handle on the luggage, stopped walking and yanked me into his arms, lifting me off the ground so that my face was even with his. I threw my arms around his shoulders, still amazed at the power that radiated from him.

After kissing me more fiercely than should be allowed in an airport parking garage, he slowly set me back down, keeping his arms locked around my waist. Gently nipping at my lips with his teeth then taking the sting away with a light stroke of his tongue, he stood up straight and looked down at me, the heady combination of love and lust evident in his molten chocolate eyes.

"Thank God the flight is only two hours." he murmured and he grabbed my hand once more, pulling me straight toward what I knew would be a week filled with ecstasy.

Chapter 23

"And they were both naked, the man and his wife, and were not ashamed." Genesis 2:25

We arrived at the Melía Cozumel around two o'clock in the afternoon. The weather was beautiful; warm but not humid with a bright azure sky laid out above us.

It was a little surreal when the concierge, a short Hispanic man with dark hair and equally dark eyes, greeted us at the welcome desk by name, already expecting our arrival.

"Buénos Tárdes, Mr. and Mrs. Mathews. Welcome to the Melía. Your room is not quite ready yet but we'd like for you to enjoy the grounds while you wait. If you want, we'll take care of your luggage for you. Here are your wristbands."

He strapped two bands each around mine and Jax's left wrists.

"Please keep them on during the entirety of your stay. The blue one is for your food. The pink one is for your drinks. Por favór, feel free to walk around and get a feel for the property and any amenities you are in the mood for. We will find you when your suite is ready."

We thanked the man and set off to the nearest bar for a couple of 'fruity drinks', as Jax called them. He carried my piña colada and some blue concoction he ordered towards the beach where we relaxed in some padded loungers on the sand.

The water in front of us looked like glass, still and reflecting the sun high overhead. He reached over and linked his fingers with mine, swaying them back and forth between our chairs. Content to enjoy the beauty and quiet, we never spoke.

About an hour after we sat down a bellboy came and told us they had our suite ready. We dropped off our glasses at the bar and followed him to the elevator. Stepping inside, the young bellboy pushed the button and we made our way up to the fourth floor. Our room, 402, was right across the hallway from the elevators and the young man unlocked the door then stood aside to allow us to walk into our room.

Stepping over the threshold, I gasped in awe of the sight before us.

There were red roses in blue vases everywhere as well as loose petals on the bed. There were candles lit, resting on the windowsill and the dresser in front of the television, and sending the sweet smell of lavender around the room. They had even made two swans out of bath towels and set them at the foot of the king sized bed with their necks wrapped around each other.

All of the hard surfaces were made of a dark brown marble and there was a fifty inch flat screen T.V. mounted on the wall opposite of the bed. The large balcony overlooked the ocean and the open sliding glass door allowed the sea breeze to come barreling in, blowing a set of sheer white curtains toward us.

On a bistro table set by the balcony door was a bottle of champagne resting in a bucket of ice. I walked over to open it while Jax graciously tipped the bellboy.

I heard the soft click of the door closing and the lock sliding into place. Once again we were alone.

He casually walked to where I was standing by the open balcony door. Taking the bottle from me, he set it back in the bucket and turned to walk me backwards to the bed. Running the back of his left hand down the side of my cheek, he pulled me into him with his right.

"Víva lá México." he said quietly, urging me to lie back on the white comforter.

I closed my eyes and sighed in pleasure when he followed me down and took my mouth possessively, bringing me to a transcontinental passion-filled trance.

April 26, 2014

It was only seven in the morning when we woke up. But out of sheer excitement at being in Cozumel on our honeymoon, we couldn't go back to sleep. I lay wrapped up in Jax's warm embrace while his hands lightly drew circles on my belly. Not wanting to get out of bed just yet, I watched the sun rise over the water and a cruise ship sail past slowly, making its way to the port. He chuckled in my ear.

"What's so funny?" I asked, turning to face him and his hands took the opportunity to continue their lazy drawing on my backside.

"I was thinking about what my brothers used to always tell me about their wives and marriages. They said they knew the honeymoon was over when they got home because their wives went from being sultry and insatiable to restrained and a little cold." He laughed again.

"Why is that funny? What am I missing?"

"Just because I don't see that being a problem for us, that's all." He kissed me on the lips, promising with his mouth that the sultry would be coming out again before changing the topic. "Well, Mrs. Mathews, what would you like to do today?"

"I don't know. Snorkeling maybe?"

"That sounds good to me. Do you want to get up and go now?"

"No." I pulled him closer, "I think we need to do something about your obvious pleasure in waking up with me this morning."

I let my eyes roam down, indicating the pressing insistence I felt.

"Oh. Well then, baby, let's take care of that shall we?" he said as he dragged me over on top of him.

He sat up easily, maneuvering me so that I was straddling his lap and tugged my black satin nightgown off, throwing it onto the floor. Wrapping his arms tightly around me, he pulled my body flush against his and my mouth down to his lips. He kissed me hungrily and I was desperate for more until he broke free and let his mouth roam over my body. Starting at my neck, he licked his way to my throat and paused in the center of my chest.

In a rapid move, he had me flipped onto my back and was towering over me, settling into the place I wanted him most. He stared at me with a look of wonder in his eyes while holding his weight off of me with his arms, his biceps rippling with veined muscle and standing out in powerful lines.

"You are so beautiful. Let me love you."

"Always," I whispered, and his mouth came down on mine, slowly mimicking to my lips what he was doing to my body. Loving me tenderly and showering me with his worshiping movements.

I sighed in absolute surrender as he took possession of my heart and my body again and again.

Snorkeling in Cozumel is something many enthusiasts seek out to do; or so I've heard.

When we finally made it downstairs, the concierge directed us to an activity table where we could rent our gear. Walking down the beach, about fifty yards from our hotel, we found a spot right next to a small reef that looked perfect.

Jax took off his t-shirt, leaving him in only a pair of white and red swim trunks. The scars on his belly were so small I could hardly see them. The two longer ones on his leg were still a dark pink but barely peeked out from underneath his shorts. I still couldn't believe how quickly he'd bounced back from his accident. Shaking off any depressing thoughts, I pulled off my dark blue cover-up, revealing my sky blue bikini underneath. Slinking away from Jax's wandering hands, I dove into the ocean before he could pull me back to the hotel.

Once we were under water, I understood why so many people sought this out. The clear, cerulean blue water allowed us to see the many colors of coral that lay under the surface.

Whites, pinks, pale oranges, several shades of green all came together in an oceanic bouquet that most people never see. It was an underwater garden and it was breathtaking.

Schools of fish swam all around us, not minding that we were in their territory. Queen triggerfish made their way to the teal coral. Stoplight parrot fish stayed in the open, their iridescent color helping them blend in. I watched about a dozen mullet swim back behind us before turning back to face the open sea.

That's when I spotted a larger, lone fish about fifteen yards in front of us. I tugged on Jax's arm, hoping he would know what it was because I couldn't tell.

Before I knew what its intent was, the long, dark silver fish swam like a bullet straight to our direction. I panicked, screamed through my snorkel and surfaced quickly, swimming back to the shore. Jaxson was not far behind.

"What's wrong baby?" he asked when we were safely on the beach, tossing his goggles and snorkel aside to kneel in front of me.

"What was that?"

"What was what?"

"That long fish. The one that looked like it was about to take our heads off!"

"It was just a barracuda." He was trying, unsuccessfully, to hide his amusement.

"Well that barracuda scared the hell out of me. And why are you laughing? He was coming right for us! It's not funny!" I was rambling on in a panic, still trying to catch my breath and he fell to his side next to me, rolling over and laughing so hard it bordered on hysteria.

"It wasn't coming for *us*. It was going for the school of mullet. You saw them swim behind us. Barracudas aren't exactly known for going after humans. Unless maybe they're in a group and trying to protect their territory."

I scowled at him and he finally got himself under control.

"I'm sorry for laughing, really. Your reaction just caught me off guard. One minute I was holding your hand, watching those parrot fish. The next thing I knew, you were jerking away from me and nowhere to be found. I take it you don't want to go back in the water?"

"No." I frowned, thinking for a fleeting moment that maybe I should give it another chance. "No, I'm done. I think I'd rather go relax and drink at the hotel pool bar. At least I won't have to worry about any barracudas chasing me around."

"Okay. Whatever you want baby," he replied and stood up, taking my hands to pull me up next to him.

Giving me a quick peck on the lips, he reached down for our gear and we started to walk hand in hand back towards the Melía. The midday sun was drying us as we strolled and the white sand felt as smooth as satin under my feet.

We returned out supplies to the activity table and made our way to the bar that sat inside the pool. Jax leaned over and whispered in my ear as we took our seats on top of a couple of stools in the pool.

"Although I wouldn't count out being chased by an animal just yet."

I couldn't help but to lean in and kiss his half grin that was full of cockiness, more than willing for him to chase me to bed.

April 28, 2014

After the barracuda 'incident' I decided there was no way on God's green earth Jaxson was going to get me to go snorkeling again. So we spent the rest of that first day drinking Dos XX and Moppitt shots– compliments of our bartender, Júlio–at the pool.

Every time he would set one of his pink creations in front of Jax, he'd slam it up and down once yelling 'Moppitt, moppitt!' until Jax threw it back. The other patrons quickly joined in and I sat back to watch, enjoying seeing him have so much fun.

Yesterday we'd gone into town to a place known locally as *The Square*. There were shops of every kind–souvenir and trinket stores, Cuban cigar shops, clothing and handbag boutiques–and we used up the day by spending a lot of money. Despite Jaxson's constant bargaining. With the sky being overcast, emitting a dark gray tint, the weather had stayed cool and kept us from overheating in the late Mexican spring.

The Square was also where the port for the cruise ships was. So while we ate beef and bean burritos from a little taco stand, we watched all the people coming and going from the different cruise lines.

"People watching could possibly be my favorite pastime." Jaxson had said.

When the sky turned to a midnight blue and the stars began to twinkle awake, the last ship sailed off and we headed back to the hotel. Because we were so exhausted by the time we made it back to the room last night, we decided to forego dinner and drinks at one of the restaurants and went to bed early.

Just not to sleep.

This morning we woke up well rested and ready to go have a fun filled day.

We went back to the pool bar.

Some people would probably think it's boring, sitting in a pool all day instead of swimming in the ocean or going to one of the old Mayan ruins. But in all honesty, there was something to be said about sitting in the warm water, the shade from the bar's cabana keeping the sun at bay and never having to get up to get a drink. They even had a grill set up on the opposite side of the pool so we ate our lunch of cheeseburgers and fries right there, too. We just found it hard to stay away.

To make up for being borderline sloths all day, I told Jax I wanted to hit the town this evening. So tonight we planned to go to the local chain of Carlos N Charlie's. We didn't have to leave the hotel at all; they had five restaurants and three bars. But we needed a change of atmosphere. At least one story apart from those at the Melía to have when we went home.

At six o'clock, I walked out of the bathroom wearing a white linen skirt that sat just below my knees, a pale pink fitted halter top and pink high heels to match. I had straightened my hair so that it hung down to the middle of my back. My make-up was done to tie in with my clothes, a light rose eye shadow and blush with clear pink lip gloss.

I walked over and did a little spin for Jaxson who was standing on the balcony with his elbows propped up on the railing behind him. His eyes grew wider as I turned.

"Do we have to go out?" he asked, stalking over to me and placing his lips on that oh-so-sensitive spot right below my ear. "Or can we just stay here and I'll have you for dinner?"

His carnal invitation sent my heart racing as his mouth lingered over my neck; his warm breath making my knees weak and sending my insides into a trembling chaos.

"I guess we could stay. But then I'd still be hungry." I leaned my head to the side, giving him better access to my throat. "Besides, you have to wait for at least a little while before you can see what's underneath this skirt."

I pulled away, took his face in my hands and kissed him intensely. After a quick nibble on his lower lip, I turned and grabbed my white clutch purse off the bed, walking out the door.

I heard him groan before he followed me to the elevator.

Walking into the restaurant reminded me of the time Jax and I had gone to Las Paísas back in December, except this place was two stories with the dining on the main floor and a sunken lower level where dancing took place.

Bright colors dominated the décor. Orange and blue vinyl covered chairs surrounded tables with lacquered finishes. Soft mariachi music played from a jukebox set up in the corner. Votive candles burned in purple holders on the tables.

When the waitress brought us each a margaríta and took our orders, we sat back to enjoy the atmosphere while we waited on our food. I looked up from my drink to find Jax staring at me and knew he was thinking about my little confession before we'd left the hotel. The thought brought a teasing smile to my lips.

The heated looks passing between us were ready to reach a boiling point when she finally brought our plates to the table.

We filled up on a Tex-Mex style meal of beef enchiládas, rice, beans and qúeso. One margaríta apiece turned into two, loosening our inhibitions.

After our food had settled, Jax stood and took my hand, pulling me up from the table to head downstairs to the dance floor. There was no soft, mood music playing here. The loud techno beat made me want to swing my hips as we made our way to the middle of the black and white checkered tile floor.

Couples of all ages and nationalities surrounded us, dancing in different styles from salsa to country two-stepping. My body moved seductively, catching the rhythm of the bass pumping from the speakers.

I've always loved to dance but the feel of Jaxson's hands around my waist and his hard chest flush against my back took the experience to a different level. He guided my movements with a roll of his hips and his face pressed against the side of my tilted neck.

That, mixed with the pulsing beat and the white strobe lights pounding in front of my eyes, made our dancing feel much more intimate, more sensual. He really was a good dancer; strong, independent and confident in his actions. It made it easy for me to get lost in the touch of his hands roaming up my sides.

When his warm breath touched my ear as he kissed my neck, I couldn't take it anymore. I turned to face him–linking my hands together behind his neck to play with his sweaty hair–and leaned my mouth close to his ear, making sure he could hear me.

"Do you want to know what's under my skirt now?" My husky voice left no room for doubt as to what my mind was on.

He jerked his head back in surprise then nodded excitedly, like a kid in a candy store.

I pulled him back down and gave him a little wet kiss on the neck, loving the saltiness of his fiery skin, and whispered in his ear, "Nothing."

I don't know if it was my breathy admission or the action itself that made him go so still, completely shell shocked. But as soon as he regained his composure, I heard a low growl from his throat before being pulled off the dance floor and up the stairs to the exit.

The cool night air kissed my body when we stepped outside, causing goose bumps to pop out of my heated skin. There were taxis lined up all along the street, the lights on the tops of their roofs lit up and ready to take tourists just like us back to their hotels. He practically shoved me into the first cab we saw.

Luckily for us it was a van so we crawled into the back while the driver took off toward the Melía.

He kissed me almost violently but it felt wonderful. It was full of passion, desire, raw need and, of course, love.

I had to slap Jax's hand away several times to keep him from feeling his way up to the emptiness underneath my skirt.

No need to give the driver more than what we pay for.

He wasn't so modest when I ran my hand across his chest, heading down toward his flat belly, never taking my lips from his open mouth.

A clearing throat brought Jax's lips from mine and he mumbled a half-hearted apology. I buried my face into his shoulder, trying to hide my embarrassment and laughter at the same time.

After ten agonizing minutes, we were at our hotel and running up the stairs to our room, deciding that the elevator took too long.

He fumbled with the key card three times while I stroked his chest and kissed his neck, tracing the corded muscles softly with my tongue.

"We're never going to make it inside if you don't give me a second," he said between clenched teeth, holding the card so tightly it's a wonder it didn't snap in half.

So I held up my hands in surrender and took a small step back, giving him the space he needed to unlock our room.

As soon as the door swung open Jaxson bent down and picked me up around my thighs, throwing me over his shoulder and carrying me to the bed. He tossed me down in a way that was surprisingly gentle considering the caveman aura emanating from him right now.

He tore his clothes off with no thought of where they landed and I stared unabashedly, loving to look at the flex of his muscles when he moved. It was like watching a jungle cat, power radiating in his calculating moves, preparing to strike.

I tried to sit up to take off my top and skirt too, ready to follow his lead. But evidently it was his turn to slap my hand away.

"Oh no you don't love. Just leave that where it is. My turn to give back the sweet torture you just put me through," he said as he crawled on top of me.

Tonight was frenzied. A throbbing experience with each of us taking the other to levels of intimacy yet to be explored.

When we collapsed onto the bed, both sweaty and exhausted, I decided to make it a point to go salsa dancing more often.

April 30, 2014

On our last day and night here in Cozumel, we decided to take the more personal route and bring out the natural romance surrounding us. We lay on the beach all day, side by side, in two lounge chairs. The big floppy white hat on my head allowed me to sneak peeks at Jax from the corner of my eye, admiring the beauty that was his tanned body.

Occasionally we would walk out to the water to cool off.

But with his hands roaming over me and playfully trying to untie the string of my black bikini, the water tended to heat up just as rapidly as lying in the sun. So we would usually come back to the sand just as quickly and take turns lathering each other up with sunscreen.

Every hour or so a waitress would come and replenish our drinks. We mostly drank water so we didn't get dehydrated but did have a few beers with our lunch of grilled chicken sandwiches and onion rings.

We took silly pictures of each other, making faces as the sun beat down like a blazing ball of fire. And one with me lying on my back against Jax's chest. He extended his arms in front of us and snapped the photo while kissing me sweetly on the neck.

That's the one I'll blow up and frame. Fun, tender, loving. Everything this honeymoon has been.

For dinner we went to the restaurant with a balcony for dining. It was more formal than the other places here at the hotel so Jax had to wear slacks and a long-sleeved button up shirt, his brown boots polished to a shine. I'd chosen a white tea length halter dress with pink and green Hawaiian flowers covering it and a pair of brown stilettos.

As we sat on the balcony overlooking the ocean, the breeze from the water sent a salty tang to mingle with our dinners. I had grilled salmon with a vegetable medley. Jax had the seafood platter. We split an obscenely expensive bottle of chardonnay that brought out the flavors of our respective meals wonderfully, crisp with a hint of a fruity aftertaste. We were both stuffed and refused the waiter's offer for dessert. Jax laid a generous tip on the table and took me by the hand to help me up when it was time to leave.

We walked along the beach, heading toward the direction of the reef we'd swam at a few days ago, for what seemed like hours. I'd taken off my heels and carried them by a finger in my left hand, my right wrapped snugly around Jax's hip.

He had his arm around my shoulders and would squeeze tight whenever a strong gust of wind blew over. The moon was full and the stars twinkling above were all bright; enough so that I could clearly see his face, happiness etched at the corners of his mouth as he stared out at the water.

It reminded me of our first walk together at his ranch. His eyes were dark and sexy; his jaw was toned and sculpted, with a hint of a beard coming through even though he'd shaved right before dinner. And his mouth was full and tender, curved in a way that just begged to be kissed. Manly or not, he was beautiful.

When we got to the pier running the length of the reef we turned and made our way back toward our hotel property. Standing right in front of the stairs leading to the pool bar we'd spent so much time at, Jaxson stopped and pulled me into his embrace. We stood facing each other and I rested my cheek against his strong chest, the power there making me antsy to get back to our room.

While the waves started crashing in towards us with the tide, the sound just like putting your ear to a seashell, he murmured softly into my ear. His warm breath mixed with his words and made my heart pulsate with love, sending my butterflies free.

I pray I always feel this with him, Lord.

"I love you Brinley. I don't know what I did to be so blessed and marry you. But I promise, as God is my witness, that you will always be loved, cherished and desired."

He leaned back and held my face in his hands, the seriousness in his chocolate eyes and the rough pads of his fingers keeping me still. I leaned my face into the hold he had with his left hand and placed my right hand over his while I listened.

"You are my life. You are my happiness. You… you are my reason."

My breath hitched at the tenderness in his words right before he kissed me. He kept his lips locked onto mine, taking control of my mouth as he lifted me up and carried me the rest of the way back to our room.

May 1, 2014

I woke when the sun came shining through the balcony windows. The bright yellow lit the room through the curtains and cast a caressing glow over the man beside me. It was only half past seven but our flight home left at noon, so I knew we needed to get up and get moving.

Jax's arm was draped tightly around my waist, snuggled up tight against my back. I gave his hand a light squeeze and lifted it to my lips for a brief kiss.

He played right into my plan and leaned in, his overnight beard scratching sensitive skin as he nuzzled my neck and splayed his strong fingers open over my bare belly.

He lifted his hand from my body and moved his head back momentarily when I turned to face him. But quickly lowered it again when it looked like I was settling in for more amorous action. He began methodically stroking my lower back, right where I loved it.

"Mmm. Morning baby. Our last sunrise. Should we make it memorable?" he asked sleepily but making his intent clear by pulling me between his legs.

I hummed a little in his ear and kissed his cheek before leaning back and patting the side of his face in loving mockery.

"Sorry babe. Honeymoon's over!" I giggled and hopped out of bed, running to the other side of the room before he could try to prove me wrong.

But he was too busy holding his belly and laughing so hard–a booming laugh that made the bed shake underneath him–that he didn't notice I'd gotten up.

I cherished watching how happy I could make him and feeling how happy he made me.

"I love you, Jaxson."

My soul felt like it glowed with my devotion to him.

Hearing my quiet voice he stopped laughing and rose, walking slowly to where I stood, never taking his eyes off of mine. When he reached me and took my hands in his he kissed both of my palms and folded them up warmly in his own, pressing them against his heart so that we were connected.

"I love you baby. Let's go home. Forever."

When he kissed me he poured so much love and passion from his lips to mine that I almost pushed him back into the bed.

Almost.

"I'll be forever home with you."

Chapter 24

"I thank my God always on your behalf, for the grace of God which is given you by Jesus Christ." I Corinthians 1:4

Journal Entry Thirteen – May 24, 2014

"Dear Annie, It's a gorgeous late spring day here in Lake Shores. I'm leaning up against your headstone while I write to you. The sun is desperately trying to find a break in the trees overhead to get to me but it's no use. I'm surrounded by oaks and dogwood. The birds are chirping a beautiful song that reminds me of you.

I'll always think of you when the songbirds come out and that will never change.

Oh, Annie. There's no easy way to say this. Actually, I'm sorry. Maybe that was the case once upon a time but it's not anymore. The truth is that this is easy.

And maybe I should feel bad about that but I don't and I think you're okay with it.

This will be my last journal entry to you.

I know you've seen everything that has happened since I last wrote you back in December. What a crazy and amazing ride this has been. But I wouldn't change it for anything in the world.

Yes, I wish you had been there for my wedding but I brought you out in so much of the reception that I know you were present. I felt you. And even that isn't something I would change.

Once, yes. But not now. I guess that's what true healing does to a person. No regrets.

Married life is pretty damn amazing, I gotta tell ya. We finally got settled into the house, unpacking all my stuff from California and making it our home instead of just Jaxson's.

The sign I got him for Valentine's is hanging up on the front door. The look of pride on his face when he placed it on the nail was priceless. And hot. Who would have thought that having a sweet, strong, totally devoted man call me 'wife' would be so sexy? I never in a million years would have believed it could be like this.

Every morning we get up with the sun. Sometimes we make love, others we settle for a cup of coffee before he saddles up and rides out with the guys. I've turned into quite the homemaker when he's gone. Making sure the house is clean and the laundry is done.

And I finally, finally got to cook for him. We were so exhausted after he got out of the hospital that mostly we had take-out or Mom cooked for us. But a few days after we got back from Mexico he got his first home cooked meal by me. I made Momma's fried chicken with my own little secret ingredient and you know how amazing it is; not to toot my own horn.

He said something along the lines of 'If nothing else, we'll stay married just so I can eat more of this.' I tried to act offended but it turned into him kissing away my fake pout. Which turned into a lot of kitchen time fun!

Anyway, some people might think this housewife stuff is nuts but I'm really enjoying it. After so many years of walking and never having anything steady in my life, except for you, this just feels right.

He feels right. In every way.

You know what is kind of crazy though, Ann? And even I'll admit this one. We're thinking about trying to have a baby. I don't know why but *that* just feels right too, you know? That feeling you get in the pit of your stomach right before an audition that tells you to go for it? To just lay it all out on the line? That's what I feel every time we've discussed starting a family. Lord knows I'm not getting any younger so why not if it feels right?

So I came off of the birth control I'd been using to regulate myself the day after we got back. We're praying it happens soon.

Momma and Daddy are ecstatic about the thought of becoming grandparents. Aaron and Jess are still trucking along happily. They said they aren't ready to have any children yet and we all respect that but Jax and I decided that we wanted nothing more than to bring our love for one another out in the form of a tiny bundle of joy.

Oh, and you'll never believe who hit it off at the wedding! Alex and Melanie have been emailing and texting all the time. At least, that's what Mom tells me. I think it's pretty wonderful and funny because I had a feeling that the two of them would have something. We'll see.

I put some fresh flowers in the stone vase by your grave today. Beautiful red roses with these huge blooms as big as my hand. The smell is drifting around me now and I know it's from you.

Ah, Annie. I thank God every day for bringing you to my side when we were kids. And for the amazing friendship we had. I thank Him for giving you and me what we both needed. He gave you an eternal home. He gave me Jaxson. Thank you for giving me that kick in the butt I needed. That dream was the catalyst to everything that has happened since and I'll be forever grateful for it. For you.

But it's time for me to let you go now. You'll always have a special place in my heart and in my prayers. And I know you'll always keep a watchful eye over me.

Until we meet again. I love you, Annie. Always.

Epilogue

"Lo, children are an heritage of the Lord: and the fruit of the womb is his reward." Psalms 127:3

May 31, 2014

How has it only been thirty seconds? Why does it have to take this long? I thought to myself, glancing down at my watch for about the hundredth time.

There are only so many places to pace around a house but I can't stand to stay in the bathroom. It's like waiting and watching for water to boil. One minute down.

That's it? Ugh!

Who knew I would be this wound up right now? It's not like I never thought this would happen. Okay. I never thought this would happen up until a few months ago so I really shouldn't be letting my nerves get the best of me, turning me into a panicked mess on the verge of tearing out my hair. But I am. Who cares? No one's here to see it. I glance at my watch again. Two minutes down.

Please, Lord, help us with this. We've had too much strife to deal with anything less than a blessing right now.

A part of me hates being here alone for this but I really don't think I'd be able to contain my craziness in the slightest if he was here with me. He's probably more nervous, and excited, about this than I am. But then again, he's had a lot more time to get used to this notion of extension. Honestly, I didn't really think it would happen this fast. It's only been a few weeks!

My wrist has been turned towards my face so many times by now that it's almost instinctual to raise it. Two and a half minutes down.

My arms feel like they're being rubbed raw from the anxious stroking I keep doing. Up, down. Up, down.

Maybe I'm not ready for this. Is that why I can't stand still and keep my emotions in check?

I'm crying big fat tears that roll unchecked down my cheeks. Which would be just fine except that there's a scowl on my face, too. And the laughing! Really, why I can't quit giggling is beyond me. The entire mix of emotions has me questioning my sanity and how completely foolish is that? Even my mind can't decide whether to be happy, sad or angry.

I glanced at my watch one last time and froze.

Three minutes.

I painstakingly walk back to the bathroom and pick up that little stick that will determine our future. I had to look twice just to be sure that my crying wasn't blurring the lines.

Thank you God... It's positive.

I sat down on the toilet for just a minute, taking a deep breath and laughing at the stupid grin on my face. Knowing Jax would be home in a couple of hours, I shook myself into gear and immediately set to work getting things ready for dinner. I had hoped and prayed this would happen but didn't want to jinx it by starting my plans early. Now I was booking it.

After getting dinner in the oven I went and took a nice, long bubble bath to try to calm my nerves. Reclining back in the stainless claw foot tub I idly played with the bubbles floating over my belly, marveling at the fact that there was a little Mathews inside there.

Listening to Emmylou Harris sing *Save the Last Dance for Me* and letting the lavender scent of my candles lined up on the windowsill wash over me, I was finally able to release some of the pent up energy I had inside.

When my fingers started to wrinkle, I got out of the tub and wrapped a towel around my hair. Standing at the pedestal sink, I took extra care putting on my makeup.

I'd decided to wear the white skirt and pink halter top from our honeymoon because I knew how much Jaxson liked that outfit. So I applied some deep rose eye shadow to match the top and bring out the green in my eyes, a pale pink blush, a little eyeliner on my bottom lids to make my eyes pop and my go-to soft pink hued lip gloss.

I dried my hair and curled all the ends under so they lay around my shoulders and down my back in soft waves. As I was finishing putting on a pair of pink strappy sandals, ready to head to the other side of the house, I heard Jax walking in the back door.

"Hey, babe. Great timing, dinner is almost ready." I said to him as I walked into the kitchen, doing my best to act like nothing was out of the ordinary.

He looked up from going through a stack of mail at the bar and froze when he saw me. He got that look in his eyes that said he would rather skip the food.

"Isn't that the skirt you were wearing when we went dancing in Mexico?" He laid the mail back on the counter and began slowly walking over to me. I put my hand on his chest when he stood inches away to stop his progress. There was no way I was going to let that sexy, seductive smile of his lure me away from my purpose for the evening.

"Yes, it is. And sorry to disappoint you, but just so we're clear, tonight there *is* something underneath my skirt." Watching his face fall just a little had me biting back a smile.

I could've told him there wasn't much material to what I was wearing. But I was having too much fun keeping him off balance.

"And you smell like cows. Go shower while I set the table. I'll have dinner ready when you get back."

He leaned in and kissed me anyways, a hard and passionate kiss filled with promises of retribution for making him wait.

I felt his smile against my lips when I sighed into his mouth. *He's trying to weaken me*, I thought to myself.

Not going to happen.

"You sure you don't want to join me?" he stepped back and pulled my hand, looking me up and down and trying to pull me in the direction of our room. "Because you look so good right now, I think I'd rather go straight to dessert."

"As tempting as that sounds, I'm hungry. Now go, and hurry up."

Grudgingly he let go of my hand and walked away. As soon as he was out of sight, I pulled the large roasting pan out of the oven and placed it on the table. I set out some of our new Lennox china and crystal, lit some tall dinner candles and placed a special card I got for Jax on the top of his place setting.

When he came out of the bedroom twenty minutes later, I shamelessly stared at him. He looked so good in a pair of new jeans, a crisp white western shirt unbuttoned at the neck with the sleeves rolled up to show the flex of his forearms and his good caiman boots shined. I almost passed on dinner just as he'd been hinting at earlier.

Again, almost.

Obviously a clean and spiffed up Jaxson was just as hard for me to pass over as I was for him. I was waiting at my chair at our dining room table when he walked over to me, taking in the china, crystal and candles.

"Something smells wonderful. Did I miss a special occasion?"

He pulled out my chair then seated himself to my left at the head of the table. I loved that he was a gentleman even when it was just the two of us.

I could see him looking over all of the food in the roaster with a curious eye before he looked at me with a question in his expression. What we were eating was normally something he'd put on the bar-b-que pit and his confusion at why I would cook it inside showed.

"Roasted baby back ribs on a bed of baby carrots and baby new potatoes." I answered in unasked inquiry.

Jaxson furrowed his brow, looking at me like I might be a little crazy. But when his eyes got wide with realization, I prodded him to open the card I had laid on his plate. He did so, skimming over the printed words about an everlasting love, then opened it completely.

On the inside of the tri-fold card was the positive pregnancy test I had taken earlier in the day.

"You're going to be a Daddy, Jaxson." I said softly, waiting for him to respond while he sat there staring at the test.

He stood up so fast that the chair fell backwards. When he came to pull me into his arms, I went willingly and wrapped my arms around his broad shoulders. He crushed his mouth to mine and kissed me with all the love I knew we felt for one another, the card with the test clutched tightly in his left hand.

"And you, Mrs. Mathews, are going to be the Momma of my children." Emotion was thick in his voice and I felt my own throat get tight.

"I cannot thank God enough for bringing you to me. And I'll never stop showing you how grateful I am to you. That you chose me."

I looked into those beautiful chocolate brown eyes that I have loved since our beginning. Placing my hands on either side of his face, I brought my mouth within an inch of his.

"There was never any choice, Jax. It was always meant to be you. It was always meant to be us."

Be on the lookout for the next story in the Lake Shores Series… Coming early 2015

About the Author

Aimee Martin, an International Best Seller, brings her first novel, Forever Home, into print with digital copies sold in more than a dozen countries including Spain, Japan, France, Australia and many throughout the United Kingdom.

Aimee, from the Texas Hill Country, is a stay at home mother and a nurse. She lives with her husband, three children and many animals. When she's not living the life of a wife and mother, she can be found reading and writing. Forever Home is her first novel, the beginning of a four part series of stand-alone novels. Connect with her via her Facebook page, http://www.facebook.com/AimeeMartinAuthor

www.ingramcontent.com/pod-product-compliance
Lightning Source LLC
Chambersburg PA
CBHW050904250626
47155CB00001B/104
9780996306317